MORE PRAISE FOR
A *SLOW FIRE BURNING*

'Gripping and intriguing, I loved every moment of
A *Slow Fire Burning*. Hawkins goes from strength to strength.'
S. J. WATSON

'Paula Hawkins' plotting is meticulous. *A Slow Fire Burning*
is a clever onion of a book, expertly peeled.'
BELINDA BAUER

'An unflinching look at the damage sparked by grief, loss and
betrayal – and the revenge and retribution that ensue. Compelling
and intricately plotted, it was its flawed and utterly credible women,
and the warmth and wit of their irreverent voices, that I loved the most.'
SARAH VAUGHAN

'With a beautifully wrought cast of characters who are real
and likeable even when they are complicated and flawed,
this is a high-class read. Paula Hawkins is a genius.'
LISA JEWELL

'Dark and disturbing, this twisted story with its cast of
damaged characters builds to a brilliant conclusion.
This one will stay with you for a long time.'
SHARI LAPENA

www.penguin.co.uk

A
SLOW
FIRE
BURNING

PAULA
HAWKINS

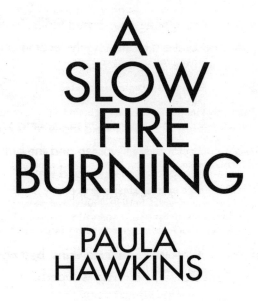

doubleday

TRANSWORLD PUBLISHERS

Penguin Random House, One Embassy Gardens,
8 Viaduct Gardens, London SW11 7BW
www.penguin.co.uk

Transworld is part of the Penguin Random House group of companies
whose addresses can be found at global.penguinrandomhouse.com

First published in Great Britain in 2021 by Doubleday
an imprint of Transworld Publishers

A CIP catalogue record for this book
is available from the British Library.

ISBNs 9780857524447 (hb)
9780857524454 (tpb)

Typeset in 11/15.75pt ITC Giovanni Std by Jouve (UK), Milton Keynes.
Printed and bound in Great Britain by Clays Ltd, Elcograf S.p.A.

The authorized representative in the EEA is Penguin Random House Ireland,
Morrison Chambers, 32 Nassau Street, Dublin D02 YH68.

Penguin Random House is committed to a sustainable
future for our business, our readers and our planet. This book
is made from Forest Stewardship Council® certified paper.

This book is dedicated to the memory of Liz Hohenadel Scott,
whose radiance made the world a warmer place.
She will be forever missed.

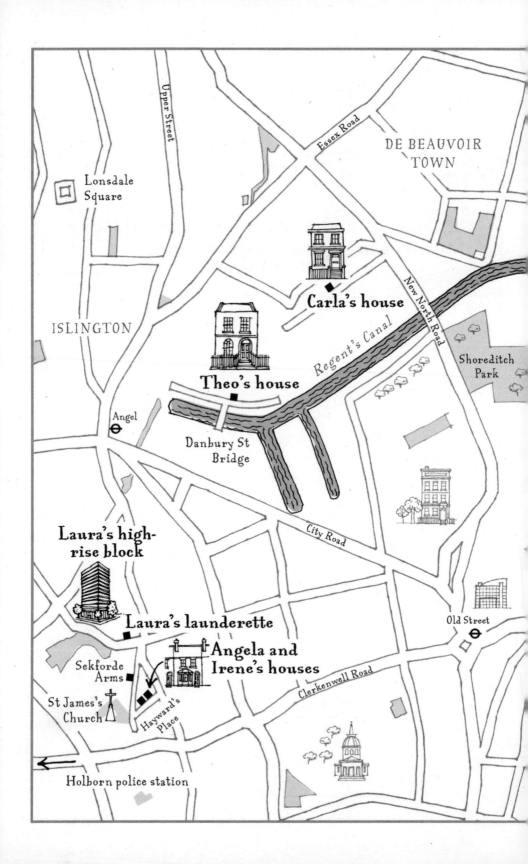

Upper Street

Essex Road

DE BEAUVOIR TOWN

Lonsdale Square

Carla's house

ISLINGTON

New North Road

Regent's Canal

Theo's house

Shoreditch Park

Angel

Danbury St Bridge

City Road

Laura's high-rise block

Old Street

Laura's launderette

Angela and Irene's houses

Sekforde Arms

Clerkenwell Road

St James's Church

Hayward's Place

Holborn police station

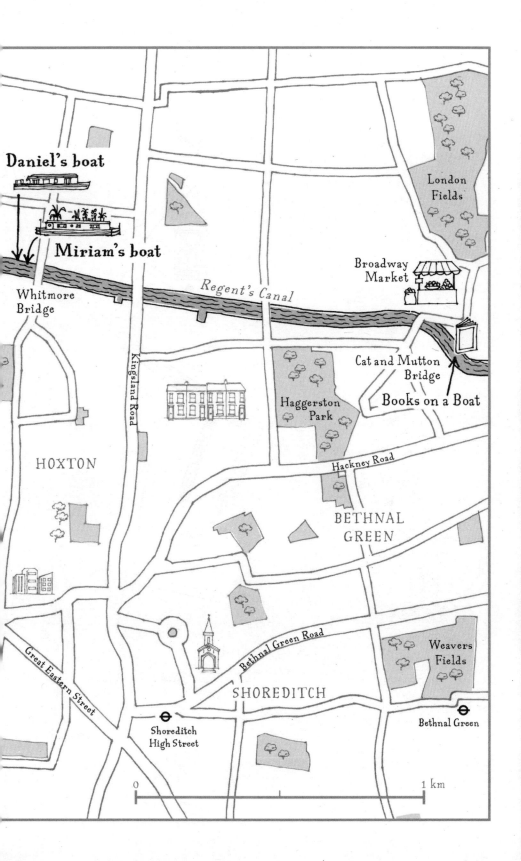

'some of us are made to be carrion birds,

& some of us are made to be circled.'

Emily Skaja, 'My History As'

Blood-sodden, the girl staggers into the black. Her clothes are dishevelled, hanging off her young body, revealing expanses of pale flesh. Shoe lost, foot bleeding. She is in agony, but the pain has become inconsequential, eclipsed by other sufferings.

Her face is a mask of terror, her heart is a drum, her breath is the stricken pant of a fox gone to ground.

The night's silence is broken by a low hum. A plane? Wiping blood from her eyes, the girl looks up at the sky and sees nothing but stars.

The hum is louder, lower. A car changing gear? Has she reached the main road? Her heart lifts, and from somewhere deep in her gut she summons the energy to run.

She feels rather than sees the light behind her. She feels her shape illuminated in the black and knows that the car is coming from behind her. It's coming from the farm. She turns.

She knows, before she sees, that he has found her. She knows, before she sees, that it will be his face behind the wheel. She freezes. For a second she hesitates, and then she leaves the road, takes off running, into a ditch, over a wooden fence. She scrambles into the adjacent field and runs blind, falling, picking herself up, making no sound. What good would screaming do?

When he catches her, he takes handfuls of her hair, pulls her down. She can smell his breath. She knows what he is going to do to her. She knows what is coming because she has already seen him do it, she saw him do it to her friend, how savagely he—

'Oh, for God's sake,' Irene muttered out loud, snapping the book shut and slinging it on to the charity-shop pile. 'What utter drivel.'

1

I nside Laura's head, Deidre spoke. *The trouble with you, Laura,* she said, *is that you make bad choices.*

Too fucking right, Deidre. Not something Laura expected to say or even think, but standing there in her bathroom, shaking uncontrollably, blood pulsing hot and steady from the cut to her arm, she had to admit that imaginary Deidre was bang on the money. She leaned forward, her forehead resting against the mirror so that she wouldn't have to look herself in the eye, only looking down was worse, because that way she could watch the blood ooze out of her, and it made her woozy, made her feel like she might throw up. So much blood. The cut was deeper than she'd thought, she ought to go to A&E. There was no way she was going to A&E.

Bad choices.

When at last the flow of blood seemed to slow, Laura took off her T-shirt and dropped it on the floor, she slipped out of her jeans, dropped her knickers, wriggled out of her bra, inhaling sharply through her teeth as the metal catch scraped against the cut, hissing, 'Fuck fuck mother of fuck.'

She dropped the bra on the floor too, clambered into the bathtub and turned on the shower, stood shivering under the paltry trickle of scalding water (her shower offered a choice of very hot or very cold, nothing in between). She ran the tips of her wrinkled fingers back and forth over her bone-white, beautiful scars: hip, thigh, shoulder, back of skull. *Here I am*, she said quietly to herself. *Here I am.*

Afterwards, her forearm wrapped ineffectually in reams of toilet paper, the rest of her wrapped in a threadbare towel, sitting on the ugly grey pleather sofa in her living room, Laura rang her mother. It went to voicemail, and she hung up. No point wasting credit. She rang her father next. 'You all right, chicken?' She could hear noises in the background, the radio, 5 Live.

'Dad.' She felt a lump rise to her throat and she swallowed it.

'What's up?'

'Dad, could you come round? I . . . I had a bad night, I was wondering if you could just come over for a bit. I know it's a bit of a drive, but I—'

'*No, Philip.*' Deidre, in the background, hissing through clenched teeth. '*We've got bridge.*'

'Dad? Could you take me off speaker?'

'Sweetheart, I—'

'Seriously, could you take me off speaker? I don't want to hear her voice, it makes me want to set fire to things . . .'

'Now, come on, Laura . . .'

'Just forget it, Dad, it doesn't matter.'

'Are you sure?'

No I'm not no I'm not no I'm fucking not. 'Yeah, sure. I'm fine. I'll be fine.'

On her way to the bedroom, she stepped on her jacket, which she'd dropped in the hallway in her rush to get to the bathroom. She bent down and picked it up. The sleeve was torn, Daniel's watch still in the pocket. She took the watch out, turned it over, slipped it on to her wrist. The toilet paper around her forearm bloomed scarlet, her limb throbbing gently as the blood pulsed out of her. Her head swam. In the bathroom, she dropped the watch into the sink, tore off the paper, dropped the towel on the floor. Climbed back under the shower.

Using a pair of scissors to scrape beneath her fingernails, she watched the water running rosy at her feet. She closed her eyes. She listened to Daniel's voice asking, *What is wrong with you?* and Deidre's voice saying, *No, Philip, we've got bridge,* and to her own. *Set fire to things. Set fire. Set fire set fire set fire.*

2

Every second Sunday, Miriam cleaned out the toilet. She had to lift the (always surprisingly, unpleasantly heavy) cassette out of the little toilet at the back of the boat, carry it through the cabin and out on to the towpath, and from there a full hundred yards to the loo block, where the waste had to be tipped out into the main toilet and flushed away, the cassette rinsed out to clear whatever remained. One of the less idyllic parts of narrowboat living and a task she liked to carry out early, when there was no one else around. So undignified, to ferry one's shit about among strangers, dog-walkers, joggers.

She was out on the back deck, checking she had a clear run – that there weren't any obstacles on the path, bicycles or bottles (people could be extremely anti-social, particularly late on Saturday nights). It was a bright morning, cold for March, though white buds on glossy new branches of plane and birch hinted at spring.

Cold for March, and yet she noticed that the cabin doors of the neighbouring narrowboat were open, just as they had been the night before. So, that was odd. And the thing was, she'd been meaning to talk to the occupant of that boat, the young man, about overstaying. He'd been in that mooring sixteen days, two full days longer than he was entitled to be, and she'd intended to have a word with him about moving along, even though it wasn't really her job, not her responsibility, but she – unlike most – was a permanent fixture around here and that imbued her with a particular sense of public-spiritedness.

That was what Miriam told DI Barker, in any case, when he asked her, later on, *What was it made you look?* The detective was sitting opposite her, his knees almost touching her own, his shoulders hunched and back rounded. A narrowboat is not a comfortable environment for a tall man, and this was a very tall man, with a head like a cue ball and a perturbed expression, as though he'd been expecting to do something else today, something fun, like taking his kids to the park, and now he was here with her, and he wasn't happy about it.

'Did you touch anything?' he asked.

Had she? Touched anything? Miriam closed her eyes. She pictured herself, rapping smartly on the window of the blue and white boat. Waiting for a response: a voice, or a twitch of a curtain. Bending down, when no such response came, her attempt to peer into the cabin thwarted by the net curtain coupled with what looked like a decade's worth of city and river grime. Knocking once more and then, after a few moments, climbing up on to the back deck. Calling out, *Hello? Anyone at home?*

She saw herself, pulling on the cabin door very gently, catching as she did a whiff of something, the smell of iron, meaty, hunger-inducing. *Hello?* Pulling the door open all the way, climbing down the couple of steps to the cabin, her last *hello* catching in her throat as she took it all in: the boy – not a boy, a young man, really – lying on the floor, blood everywhere, a wide smile carved into his throat.

She saw herself sway on her feet, hand over mouth, pitching

forward for a long, dizzying moment, reaching out, grabbing the counter with her hand. *Oh, God.*

'I touched the counter,' she told the detective. 'I think I might have held on to the counter, just there, on the left-hand side when you come into the cabin. I saw him, and I thought . . . well, I felt . . . I felt sick.' Her face coloured. 'I wasn't sick though, not then. Outside . . . I'm sorry, I . . .'

'Don't worry about it,' Barker said, his eyes holding hers. 'You don't need to worry about that. What did you do then? You saw the body, you leaned against the counter . . . ?'

She was struck by the smell. Underneath the blood, all that blood, there was something else, something older, sweet and rank, like lilies left too long in the vase. The smell and the look of him, impossible to resist, his beautiful dead face, glassy eyes framed by long lashes, plump lips drawn back from even, white teeth. His torso, his hands and arms were a mess of blood, his fingertips curled to the floor. As though he was hanging on. As she turned to leave, her eye snagged on something on the floor, something out of place – a glint of silver mired in sticky, blackening blood.

She stumbled up the steps and out of the cabin, gulping mouthfuls of air, gagging. She threw up on the towpath, wiped her mouth, cried out, 'Help! Somebody call the police!' But it was barely seven thirty on a Sunday morning, and there was no one around. The towpath was still, the roads up above quiet too, no sounds save for the throb of a generator, the squabble of moorhens ghosting gently past. Looking up at the bridge above the canal, she thought she might have seen someone, just for a moment, but then they were gone, and she was alone, gripped by paralysing fear.

'I left,' Miriam told the detective. 'I came straight back out of the boat and . . . I called the police. I vomited, and then I ran to the boat and called the police.'

'OK, OK.'

When she looked up at him, he was gazing around the room, taking in the tiny, neat cabin, the books above the sink (*One Pot Cooking, A New Way with Vegetables*), the herbs on the sill, the basil and coriander in their plastic tubs, the rosemary going woody in a blue-glazed pot. He glanced at the bookcase filled with paperbacks, at the dusty peace lily sitting on top of it, at the framed photograph of a homely couple flanking their big-boned child. 'You live here alone?' he asked, but it wasn't really a question. She could tell what he was thinking: fat old spinster, tree-hugger, knit-your-own-yoghurt curtain-twitcher. Poking her nose into everyone else's business. Miriam knew how people saw her.

'Do you . . . do you get to know your . . . neighbours? Are they neighbours? Don't suppose they really can be if they're only here for a couple of weeks?'

Miriam shrugged. 'Some people come and go regularly, they have a patch, a stretch of the water they like to cover, so you get to know some of them. If you want to. You can keep yourself to yourself if you like, which is what I do.'

The detective said nothing, just looked at her blankly. She realized he was trying to figure her out, that he wasn't taking her at her word, that he didn't necessarily believe what she was telling him.

'What about him? The man you found this morning?'

Miriam shook her head. 'I didn't know him. I'd seen him a few times, exchanged . . . well, not even pleasantries really. I said hello or good morning or something like that, and he responded. That was it.'

(Not *quite* it: it was true that she'd seen him a couple of times since he'd moored up, and that she'd clocked him right away for an amateur. The barge was a mess – paint peeling, lintels rusted, chimney all askew – while he himself looked much too clean for canal life. Clean clothes, white teeth, no piercings, no tattoos. None visible, in any case. A striking young man, quite tall, dark-haired, dark-eyed, his face all planes and angles. The first time she saw him, she'd said good morning and he'd looked up at her and smiled and all the hair had stood up on the back of her neck.)

She noted this, at the time. Not that she was about to tell the detective that. *When I first saw him, I got this strange feeling . . .* He'd think she was a nutcase. In any event, she realized now what it was, what she'd felt. It wasn't premonition, or anything ridiculous like that, it was *recognition*.

There was an opportunity here. She'd had that thought when she first realized who the boy was, but she'd not known how best to take advantage. Now that he was dead, however, it felt as though this was all meant to be. Serendipity.

'Mrs Lewis?' Detective Barker was asking her a question.

'Ms,' Miriam said.

He closed his eyes for a moment. 'Ms Lewis. Do you remember seeing him with anyone? Talking to anyone?'

She hesitated, then nodded. 'He had a visitor. A couple of times, perhaps? It's possible he might have had more than one visitor, but I only saw the one. A woman, older than he was, closer to my age, maybe in her fifties? Silver-grey hair, cut very short. A thin woman, quite tall I think, perhaps five eight or nine, angular features . . .'

Barker raised an eyebrow. 'You got a good look at her, then?'

Miriam shrugged again. 'Well, yes. I'm quite observant. I like to keep an eye on things.' May as well play up to his prejudices. 'But she was the sort of woman you'd notice even if you didn't, she was quite striking. Her haircut, her clothes . . . she looked *expensive.*'

The detective was nodding again, noting all this down, and Miriam felt sure it wouldn't take him long to figure out exactly who she was talking about.

Once the detective had gone, officers cordoned off the towpath between De Beauvoir and Shepperton, moving along all the boats save his, the crime scene, and hers. At first, they'd tried to persuade her to leave, but she made it clear she'd nowhere else to go. Where were they going to house her? The uniformed officer she spoke to, young, squeaky-voiced and spotty, looked perturbed by this shifting of responsibility from her shoulders to his. He looked up at the sky and down at the water, up and down the canal and back to her, this small, fat, harmless middle-aged woman, and relented. He spoke to someone on a radio and then came back to tell her she could stay. 'You can go back and forth to your own . . . uh . . . *residence*,' he said, 'but no further than that.'

That afternoon, Miriam sat out on the back deck of her boat in the pallid sunshine, taking advantage of the unusual quiet of the closed-off canal. With a blanket pulled around her shoulders and a cup of tea at her elbow, she watched the policemen and the scene-of-crime officers scurrying back and forth, bringing dogs, bringing boats, searching the towpath and its borders, poking around in the murky water.

She felt oddly peaceful, given the day she'd had, optimistic almost, at the thought of new avenues opening up before her. In the pocket of her cardigan she fingered the little key on its keyring, still sticky with blood, the one she'd picked up off the floor of the boat, the one whose existence she'd withheld from the detective without even really thinking about why she was doing it.

Instinct.

She'd seen it, glinting there next to that boy's body – a key. Attached to a little wooden keyring in the form of a bird. She recognized it straight away, she'd seen it clipped to the waistband of the jeans worn by Laura from the launderette. Mad Laura, they called her. Miriam had always found her quite friendly, and not mad at all. Laura, whom Miriam had witnessed arriving – tipsy, Miriam suspected – at that shabby little boat on that beautiful boy's arm, two nights ago? Three? She'd have it in her notebook – interesting comings and goings, they were the sort of thing she wrote down.

Around dusk, Miriam watched them carry the body out, up the steps and on to the street where an ambulance was waiting to take him away. She stood as they walked past her; out of respect, she bent her head and said a quiet and unbelieving *Go with God*.

She whispered a thank-you, too. For by mooring his boat up next to hers and then getting himself brutally murdered, Daniel Sutherland had presented Miriam with an opportunity she simply could not allow to slide by: an opportunity to avenge the wrong that had been done to her.

Alone now and, despite herself, a little afraid in the darkness and strange quietude, she took herself into her boat, bolting and padlocking the door behind her. She took Laura's key from her pocket and placed it in the wooden trinket box she kept on the top bookshelf. Thursday was laundry day. She might give it back to Laura then.

Or then again, she might not.

You never knew what was going to turn out to be useful, did you?

3

'**M**rs Myerson? Do you need to sit down? There you go. Just breathe. Would you like us to call anyone, Mrs Myerson?'

Carla sank down on to her sofa. She folded in half, pressing her face to her knees. She was whimpering, she realized, like a dog. 'Theo,' she managed to say. 'Call Theo, please. My husband. My ex-husband. He's in my phone.' She looked up, scanning the room, she couldn't see the phone. 'I don't know where it is, I don't know where I—'

'In your hand, Mrs Myerson,' the woman detective said gently. 'You're holding your phone in your hand.'

Carla looked down and saw that so she was, gripping her mobile tightly in her violently trembling hand. She shook her head, handing the phone to the policewoman. 'I'm going mad,' she said.

The woman pressed her lips into a small smile, placing a hand on Carla's shoulder for just a moment. She took the phone outside to make the telephone call.

The other detective, DI Barker, cleared his throat. 'I understand that Daniel's mother is deceased, is that right?'

Carla nodded. 'Six . . . no, eight weeks ago,' she said and

watched the detective's eyebrows shoot up to where his hairline might once have been. 'My sister fell,' Carla said, 'at home. It wasn't . . . it was an accident.'

'And do you have contact details for Daniel's father?'

Carla shook her head. 'I don't think so. He lives in America, he has done for a long time. He's not involved, he's never been involved in Daniel's life. It's just . . .' Carla's voice cracked, she took a deep breath, exhaled slowly. 'It was just Angela and Daniel. And me.'

Barker nodded. He fell silent, standing ramrod straight in front of the fireplace, waiting for Carla to compose herself. 'You've not lived here very long?' he asked, after what Carla imagined he thought to be a respectful pause. She looked up at him, bemused. He indicated with one long forefinger the boxes on the dining-room floor, the paintings leaning against the wall.

Carla blew her nose loudly. 'I've been meaning to hang those paintings for the best part of six years,' she said. 'One day I'll get round to getting picture hooks. The boxes are from my sister's house. Letters, you know, photographs. Things I didn't want to get rid of.'

Barker nodded. He folded his arms, shifting his weight from one foot to the other, and opened his mouth to say something but was cut off by the front door slamming shut. Carla jumped. The woman detective, DC Chalmers, scuttled into the room, ducking her head apologetically. 'Mr Myerson's on his way. He's said he won't be long.'

'He lives five minutes away,' Carla said. 'Noel Road. Do you know it? Joe Orton lived there in the Sixties. The playwright? It's where he was killed, bludgeoned to death, I think, or was it stabbed?' The detectives looked at her blankly. 'It's not . . . *relevant*,' Carla said. She thought for a horrible moment she might laugh. Why had she said that anyway? Why was she talking about Joe

Orton, about people being bludgeoned? She *was* going mad. The detectives seemed not to notice, or not to mind. Perhaps everyone behaved like a lunatic when they received news of a family member murdered.

'When did you last see your nephew, Mrs Myerson?' Barker asked her.

Carla's mind was completely blank. 'I . . . *Christ*, I saw him . . . at Angela's house. My sister's house. It's not far, about twenty minutes' walk, over the other side of the canal, on Hayward's Place. I've been sorting out her things, and Daniel came to pick some stuff up. He'd not lived there for ages but there were still some of his things in his old bedroom, sketchbooks, mostly. He was quite a talented artist. He drew comics, you know. Graphic novels.' She gave an involuntary shudder. 'So that was, a week ago? Two weeks? Jesus, I can't remember, my head is just *wrecked*, I . . .' She scraped her nails over her scalp, pushing her fingers through the short crop of her hair.

'It's perfectly all right, Mrs Myerson,' Chalmers said. 'We can get the details later.'

'So, how long had he been living there down on the canal?' Barker asked her. 'Do you happen to know when—'

The door knocker clacked loudly and Carla jumped again. 'Theo,' she breathed, already on her feet. 'Thank *God*.'

Chalmers got to the door before Carla could, and ushered Theo, red-faced, perspiring, into the hall.

'Christ, Cee,' he said, grabbing hold of Carla, pulling her tightly against him. 'What in God's name happened?'

The police went over it all again: how Carla's nephew, Daniel Sutherland, had been found dead that morning on a houseboat moored near De Beauvoir Road on Regent's Canal. How he'd been stabbed multiple times. How he'd likely been killed between twenty-four and thirty-six hours before he'd been found; how they'd be able to narrow that down in due course. They asked questions about Daniel's work and friends, and did they know of any money troubles and did he take drugs?

They didn't know.

'You weren't close?' Chalmers offered.

'I hardly knew him,' Theo said. He was sitting at Carla's side, rubbing the top of his head with his forefinger, the way he did when he was anxious about something.

'Mrs Myerson?'

'Not close, no. Not . . . well. My sister and I didn't see each other very often, you see . . .'

'Despite the fact she lived just over the canal?' Chalmers piped up.

'No.' Carla shook her head. 'We . . . I hadn't spent time with Daniel for a very long time. Not really. Not since he was a boy. When my sister died I saw him again, as I said. He'd been living abroad for a while. Spain, I think.'

'When did he move to the boat?' Barker asked.

Carla pressed her lips together, shaking her head. 'I don't know,' she said. 'I honestly don't.'

'We had no idea he was living there,' Theo said.

Barker gave him a sharp look. 'He must be fairly close to your home, though. Noel Road, wasn't it? That's what? About a mile from where the boat was?'

Theo shrugged, and rubbed his forehead harder, the skin turning quite pink up near his hairline. He looked as though he'd been in the sun. 'That may well be, but I'd no idea he was there.'

The detectives exchanged a look. 'Mrs Myerson?' Barker looked at her.

Carla shook her head. 'No idea,' she said quietly.

The detectives fell silent then, for quite a long time. They were waiting for Carla to say something, she imagined, for her or for Theo to speak.

Theo obliged. 'You said . . . twenty-four hours, is that right? Twenty-four to thirty-six hours?'

Chalmers nodded. 'We're estimating time of death some time between eight p.m. Friday night and eight a.m. Saturday morning.'

'Oh.' Theo was rubbing his head again, staring out of the window.

'Have you thought of something, Mr Myerson?'

'I saw a girl,' Theo said. 'Saturday morning. It was early – six, maybe? Out on the towpath, going past my house. I was standing in my study and I saw her, I remember her because she had blood on her. On her face. On her clothing, I think. She wasn't drenched in it or anything, but . . . but it was there.'

Carla gawped at him, incredulous. 'What are you talking about? Why didn't you tell me?'

'You were sleeping,' Theo said. 'I got up, I was going to make coffee, and I went to get my cigarettes from the study. I saw her out of the window. She was young, probably not much more than twenty, and she was coming along the towpath. Limping. Or swaying, maybe? I thought she was drunk. I didn't . . . really think much of it, because London is awash with strange, drunk people, isn't it? That time of day, you often see people on their way home . . .'

'With blood on them?' Barker asked.

'Well, perhaps not. Perhaps not the blood. That's why I remembered her. I thought she'd fallen, or been in a fight. I thought—'

'But why didn't you say anything?' Carla said.

'You were *asleep*, Cee, I didn't think—'

'Mrs Myerson was asleep at *your* home,' Chalmers interrupted, frowning. 'Is that right? You stayed the night with Mr Myerson?'

Carla nodded slowly, her expression one of utter bewilderment. 'We'd had dinner on Friday, I stayed over . . .'

'Although we're separated, we still have a relationship, you see, we often—'

'They don't *care* about that, Theo,' Carla said sharply, and Theo flinched. Carla pressed a Kleenex to her nose. 'Sorry. I'm *sorry*. But it's not important, is it?'

'We never know what's going to be important,' Barker said enigmatically, and started moving towards the hall. He handed out business cards, said something to Theo about formal identification, about family liaison, about staying in touch. Theo nodded, slipping the business card into his trouser pocket, and shook the detective's hand.

'How did you know?' Carla asked suddenly. 'I mean, who was it who reported . . . who found him?'

Chalmers looked at her boss, then back at Carla. 'A woman found him,' she said.

'A woman?' Theo asked. 'A girlfriend? Was she young? Slim? I'm just thinking of the person I saw, the one with the blood. Perhaps she . . .'

Chalmers shook her head. 'No, this was someone living on another of the narrowboats, not a young woman, middle-aged, I'd say. She noticed that the boat hadn't moved in some time and went to check up on him.'

'She didn't see anything, then?' Theo asked.

'She was very helpful, actually,' Barker said. 'Very observant.'

'Good,' Theo said, rubbing the top of his head, 'very good.'

'A Mrs Lewis,' Barker added, and Chalmers corrected him: '*Ms.*'

'That's right,' he said. Carla watched the colour drain from Theo's face as Barker went on, 'Ms Miriam Lewis.'

4

'He started it, all right? Before you say anything. He started it.'
They were waiting for her when she got home. Must
have been, because they banged on the front door literally thirty
seconds after she'd got in from Iceland. She'd not even got her
breath back – she was on the seventh floor and the lifts were out
again – and there they were, and it just made her angry, and nervous too. So, like a fucking idiot, she started talking right away,
which she knew full well you shouldn't do. It's not like this was
her first time in trouble.

Granted, usually it was a different sort of trouble. Public
intoxication, petty theft, trespass, vandalism, disorderly conduct. She'd been found not guilty of simple assault on one
occasion. One ABH charge pending.

But *this* wasn't *that*. And she realized that almost right away,
because as she stood there huffing and puffing and running her
mouth off, she thought, Hang on, these are *detectives*. They'd
said their names and ranks and all that, which she'd forgotten
right away, but still: they were standing in front of her in plain
clothes, and that was a whole different order of trouble.

'Would you mind if we came in, Miss Kilbride?' the bloke
said, politely enough. He was tall, rangy, bald as an egg. 'It might

be better to talk about this inside.' He cast a beady eye at the kitchen window, which she'd boarded up, badly.

Laura was already shaking her head. 'I don't think so, no. I don't think so. I need an appropriate adult, you see, you can't question me . . . What's this about, anyway? Is this the guy in the bar? Because that's already, you know, in the system. I've got a court summons, it's stuck to my fridge with a magnet. You can see for yourself if you want . . . No, no, no, hang on. Hang on. That wasn't an invitation to come in, it's a figure of speech . . .'

'Why would you need an appropriate adult, Miss Kilbride?' The other one – about a foot shorter than her colleague, wiry dark hair, small features all crowded together in the middle of her big moon face – raised her monobrow. 'You're not a minor, are you?'

'I'm twenty-five, as well you know,' Laura snapped.

She couldn't stop them – Egg was already halfway down the hallway, Eyebrow pushing past, saying, 'How on earth would we know that?'

'Who started what, Miss Kilbride?' Egg called out. She followed his voice into her kitchen, where he was bent over, hands clasped behind his back, peering at the summons.

Laura huffed loudly, and shuffled over to the sink to get some water. She needed to compose herself. Think. When she turned back to face him, he was looking first at her, and then over her shoulder, at the window. 'Had some trouble?' He raised his eyebrows, innocent-like.

'Not exactly.'

The other one appeared, beetling her brow. 'Have you hurt yourself, Laura?' she asked.

Laura drank her water too quickly, coughed, scowled at the woman. 'What happened to *Miss Kilbride*, eh? We're mates now, are we? BFFs?'

'Your leg, Laura.' He was at it too. 'How did you hurt it?'

'I was hit by a car when I was a kid. Compound break to the femur. Got a wicked scar,' she said, moving her fingers to the fly of her jeans. She held his eye. 'You wanna see it?'

'Not particularly,' he said mildly. 'What about your arm?' He indicated with a finger the bandage wrapped around her right wrist. 'That didn't happen when you were a kid.'

Laura bit her lip. 'Lost my key, didn't I? Friday night. Had to break in when I got back.' She jerked her head backwards, indicating the kitchen window, which gave out on to the exterior walkway running the length of the apartment block. 'Didn't do a very good job.'

'Stitches?'

Laura shook her head. 'Wasn't that bad.'

'Did you find it?' He turned away from her, wandering through the alcove connecting the kitchen to the living room, casting about like he was considering making an offer on the place. Not likely, the flat was a tip. She knew she ought to be ashamed of it, of the cheap furniture and the blank walls and the ashtray on the floor which someone had kicked over, so now there was ash in the carpet and fuck knows how long that had been there because she didn't even smoke and she couldn't remember the last time she'd had someone over, but she couldn't bring herself to care enough.

'Well? Did you?' Eyebrow wrinkled her nose as she took Laura in, head to toe and back again, her baggy jeans, stained T-shirt, chipped nail polish, greasy hair. Sometimes Laura forgot to shower, sometimes for days, sometimes the water was scalding and sometimes it wasn't hot at all, like now, because the boiler had a mind of its own, sometimes it worked and sometimes it didn't and she didn't have the money to pay the call-out fee for a plumber and no matter how many times she called the council they still did fuck-all.

'Did I what?'

'Find your key,' Eyebrow said, a hint of a smile on her lips like she'd caught her out, caught her in a lie. 'Did you find your key?'

Laura took a last gulp of water, swallowed, sucked her teeth. Chose to ignore the question. 'Do you mind?' she called out, elbowing her way past Eyebrow in order to follow Egg.

'Not a bit,' he replied. He was standing in the middle of her living room now, looking at the room's sole adornment, a framed photograph of a family: parents and a young girl. Someone had gone to the trouble of defacing it, drawing horns on the father's head and a forked tongue emerging from the mother's mouth, they'd put Xs over the child's eyes, coloured her lips blood red, before framing it and hanging it. Egg raised his eyebrows and turned to look at her. 'Family portrait?' he asked. Laura shrugged. 'Dad's a devil, is he?'

She shook her head, looked him dead in the eye. 'Cuckold,' she said.

Egg pursed his lips, nodding slowly, and turned to look back at the picture. 'Well,' he said, 'well.'

'I'm a vulnerable adult,' Laura said once more and the detective sighed.

'No, you're not,' he said wearily. He turned away from the photograph and lowered himself heavily on to her sofa. 'You live alone, you have a part-time job at the Sunshine Launderette on Spencer Street and we know for a fact that you have been interviewed by the police on a number of occasions without an appropriate adult present, so let's just leave that one, shall we?'

There was an edge to his voice, his clothes were crumpled and he looked very tired, as though he'd had a long journey, or a short night's sleep. 'Why don't you sit down? Tell me about Daniel Sutherland.'

Laura sat down at the little table in the corner of the room, the one where she ate her dinner while she watched TV. For a moment she felt relieved. She shrugged her shoulders up against her ears. 'What about him?' she asked.

'You know him, then?'

'Obviously I do. Obviously he's complained to you about me. Which is bullshit, can I just say, because nothing happened and, in any case, he started it.'

Egg smiled. He had a surprisingly warm smile. 'Nothing happened, but he started it?' he repeated.

'That's right.'

'And when did this nothing happen,' Eyebrow said, wandering into the room from the kitchen, 'that he started?' She sat down next to her colleague on the ugly pleather two-seater sofa. Side by side, they looked ridiculous – little and large, him long and lean, Lurch to her fat little Fester. Laura smirked.

Eyebrow didn't like that, her face darkened as she snapped, 'Is something funny? Do you think there's something amusing about this situation, Laura?'

Laura shook her head. 'Fester,' she said, smiling. 'You're like Uncle Fester, but with hair. Has anyone ever told you that?'

The woman opened her mouth to speak, but Egg, deadpan, cut her off. 'Daniel Sutherland,' he said again, louder this time, 'didn't tell us anything about you. We came to speak to you because we lifted two sets of fingerprints from a glass which we found in Daniel's boat, and the set that wasn't his was yours.'

Laura suddenly felt cold. She rubbed her clavicle with her fingers, clearing her throat. 'You lifted . . . what? You lifted *fingerprints*? What's going on?'

'Can you tell us about your relationship with Mr Sutherland, Laura?' Eyebrow said.

'Relationship?' Laura laughed, despite herself. 'That's a bit strong. I fucked him twice, Friday night. Wouldn't really call it a *relationship*.'

Eyebrow shook her head in disapproval, or disbelief. 'And how did you meet him?'

Laura swallowed hard. 'I met him because, you know, sometimes I help out this lady, Irene, she lives on Hayward's Place, you know, just over by the church there, on the way to the little Tesco. I met her a few months back and, like I say, I help her out from time to time, because she's old and a bit arthritic and forgetful and she had a bit of a fall a while back, twisted her ankle or something, she can't always get to the shops. I don't do it for money or anything, although she does tend to bung me a fiver every now and again, just for my time, you know, she's nice like that . . . Anyway. Yeah, Dan – Daniel Sutherland – he used to live next door to Irene, he hasn't done for ages but his mother still lived there, at least until she died, which was when we met.'

'You met him when his mother died?'

'After,' Laura said. 'I wasn't actually in the room when she croaked.'

Eyebrow glanced at her colleague, but he wasn't looking at her, he was looking at the family portrait again, a sad expression on his face.

'OK,' Eyebrow said, 'OK. You were with Mr Sutherland on Friday, is that right?'

Laura nodded. 'We went on a *date*,' she said, 'which for him meant two drinks in a bar in Shoreditch and then back to his crappy boat for a shag.'

'And . . . and he hurt you? Or . . . pressured you into something? What did he *start*?' Egg asked, leaning forward, his attention fully focused on Laura now. 'You said he started something. What was that?'

Laura blinked hard. She had a memory, startlingly clear, of the look of surprise on his face as she went for him. 'Everything was fine,' she said. 'We had a nice time. I thought we had a good time.' Out of nowhere, she blushed, she felt an intense burst of heat spreading from her chest to her neck and up to her cheeks. 'And then he's suddenly all, like, cold or whatever, like he doesn't even want me there. He was . . . offensive.' She looked down at her bum leg, sighed. 'I have a condition. I'm a vulnerable adult. I know you said I wasn't, but I am. Vulnerable.'

'So you argued with him?' Eyebrow asked.

Laura nodded. She was looking at her feet. 'Yeah, you could say that.'

'Did you fight? Was it physical?'

There was a stain on her trainer, right above the little toe of her left foot. A dark brown stain. She hooked her left foot behind her right ankle. 'No, not . . . Well. Not *seriously*.'

'So, there was violence, but not what you would term serious violence?'

Laura moved her left foot against the back of her right calf. 'It was nothing,' she said. 'It was just . . . handbags.'

She looked up at Egg, who was rubbing his forefinger over his thin lips; he in turn looked over at Eyebrow and she back at him, and something passed between them, wordless. An agreement.

'Miss Kilbride, Daniel Sutherland's body was discovered in his boat on Sunday morning. Can you tell us exactly when you saw him last?'

Laura's mouth was suddenly painfully dry, she couldn't swallow, she heard a roaring in her ears, she squeezed her eyes tight shut. 'Hang on . . .' She got to her feet, steadying herself on the table, she felt the world tip. She sat down again. 'Hang on,' she said again, 'his *body*? Are you saying . . . ?'

'That Mr Sutherland is dead,' Egg said, his voice quiet and even.

'But . . . he's not, is he?' Laura heard her own voice crack. Egg nodded slowly. 'Sunday morning? You said Sunday morning?'

'That's right,' Egg replied. 'Mr Sutherland was discovered on Sunday morning.'

'But . . .' Laura could feel her pulse in her throat, 'but I saw him on Friday night, I left Saturday morning. I left on Saturday morning. Seven, maybe, maybe even earlier than that. *Saturday morning*,' she repeated, one last time, for emphasis.

Eyebrow started to say something, her voice light and musical as though she was telling a funny story and was just about to get to the punchline. 'Mr Sutherland died of massive blood loss, he had knife wounds to the chest and neck. His time of death is yet to be formally established, but our science officer felt it likely to be around twenty-four to thirty-six hours before he was discovered. Now you say you were with Mr Sutherland on Friday night, is that right?'

Laura's face burned, her eyes stung. Idiot. She was an idiot. 'Yes,' she said quietly. 'I was with him on Friday night.'

'On Friday night. And you went back to his houseboat with him, yes? You had sex with him, you said? Twice, wasn't it? And what time exactly on Saturday morning did you leave Mr Sutherland?'

A trap. It was a trap, and she'd walked straight into it. Idiot. She scraped her teeth over her lower lip, bit down hard. *Don't say anything*, she imagined a solicitor would say to her. *Don't talk to anyone.* She shook her head, a small sound coming from the back of her throat, seemingly without her volition.

'What was that? Laura? Did you say something, Laura?'

'I'm sorry he's dead and everything,' she said, ignoring the advice coming from within her own head, 'but I didn't do anything. You hear me? I didn't do anything. I didn't stab anyone. Anyone who says I did is a liar. He was . . . I don't know, he said stuff to me, stuff I didn't like. I didn't *do* anything. Maybe I hit him, maybe . . .' She could taste blood in her mouth, she swallowed hard. 'Don't . . . just don't try to say that I did this, because I had nothing to do with it. Maybe there was some pushing and shoving, but that was it, you know, and then he was gone, so that was that, you know. That was that. It's not my fault, you see, it's not my fault, even . . . the fight or what-ever, it's not my fault.'

Laura could hear her own voice going on and on and on, ris-ing higher and higher, she could tell what she sounded like, like a mad person ranting, like one of those crazy people who stands at a street corner and shouts at nothing, she knew that was what she sounded like and she couldn't stop herself.

'*Gone?*' Eyebrow said. 'You said, "then he was gone". What did you mean by that, Laura?'

'I mean he was gone. He left, walked out, what d'you think? After we fought – not really fought, but you know – after that, he just put on his jeans and he walked out and just left me there.'

'In his house . . . on his boat, alone?'

'That's right. I suppose he was the trusting sort,' she said, and she laughed, which she knew was completely inappropriate and yet still she couldn't stop herself, because it was funny, the thought that he was trusting, wasn't it? Under the circumstances? Not funny ha ha, maybe, but still. Once she'd started laughing, she found that she couldn't stop; she felt herself going red in the face, as though she were choking.

The detectives looked at each other.

Eyebrow shrugged. 'I'll just go and get her a glass of water,' she said at last.

A moment later, Laura heard the detective call out, not from the kitchen, but from the bathroom. 'Sir, do you want to come through here a minute?'

The bald one got up, and as he did, Laura felt a wave of panic rise, chasing the laughter clean out of her chest. She said, 'Hang on a minute, I didn't say you could go through there,' but it was too late. She followed them to the threshold of the bathroom, where Eyebrow stood, pointing, first at the sink, where Laura had left the watch (the one belonging, unmistakably, to Daniel Sutherland, his initials engraved on the back) and then to Laura's blood-stained T-shirt, scrunched in a ball in the corner of the room.

'I cut myself,' Laura said, her face burning red. 'I told you that. I cut myself when I climbed through the window.'

'You did tell us that,' Egg said. 'Do you want to tell us about the watch, too?'

'I took it,' Laura said sullenly, *'obviously*. I took it. But it's not what you think. I just did it to piss him off. I was going to . . . I don't know, throw it in the canal, tell him to go fetch. But then I . . . I don't know, I thought it might mean something, you know, when I saw the engraving on the back and I thought, like, what if his mother had given it to him before she died or whatever and it was irreplaceable? I was going to give it back to him.'

Egg looked at her sadly, as though he had some very bad news, which in a way he did. 'What's going to happen now,' he said, 'is that we're going to take you over to the police station to answer some more questions. You'll be answering questions under caution, you understand what that means? And we're also going to take some samples from you, for comparison with what was found at the scene.'

'Samples? What does that mean?'

'An officer at the station will scrape under your fingernails, comb your hair for fibres, that sort of thing, it's nothing invasive, nothing to worry about . . .'

'What if I don't want to?' Laura's voice quavered, she wanted someone to help her and she couldn't think who. 'Can I say no?'

'It's all right, Laura.' Eyebrow's voice turned soothing. 'It's all very simple and easy, there's nothing to be frightened of.'

'That's a lie,' Laura said. 'You know that's a lie.'

'The other thing we're going to do,' Egg said, 'is apply for a warrant to search your home, and I'm sure you realize that under the circumstances we're not going to have any trouble getting one, so if there's anything else you think we need to know about, it'd be a good idea to tell us now, OK?'

Laura considered the question, she tried to think whether there was anything she should tell them, but her mind was a blank. Eyebrow was talking to her, touching her arm, and she flinched. 'Your clothes, Laura? Can you show us what you were wearing on Friday night?'

Laura plucked random items of clothing from the floor in her room, she handed them a pair of jeans which she may or may not have been wearing, she flung a bra in their general direction. She went to the loo, leaving the two of them in the hallway, Egg's head bent down to listen to whatever it was Eyebrow was saying. Laura paused at the bathroom door, heard the woman mutter something about *engraved* and *odd* and *not really all there, is she?*

Sitting on the loo, her knickers around her ankles, Laura smiled ruefully to herself. She'd been called worse. Not all there? *Not all there* was nothing, *not all there* was pretty much a compliment in comparison to all the other things she'd been called over the years: *mong, freak, spaz, cabbage, retard, nutter.*

Fucking psycho was what Daniel Sutherland called her, when she'd gone for him, properly gone for him, kicking, punching, clawing at him. He grabbed her, digging his thumbs into the flesh of her upper arms. 'You fucking psycho, you . . . crazy *bitch*.' It all turned so fast. One moment she was lying there on his bed smoking a cigarette, and the next she was on the towpath with blood on her face and his watch in her pocket.

As the detectives escorted her down the stairs, Laura wondered how she could tell them the truth of the thing: that she'd taken the watch out of spite, yes, but strangely out of hope, too. She'd wanted to punish him, but she'd also wanted to give herself an excuse to return, to see him again.

No chance of that now though, was there?

5

At the police station, a police officer – a young woman, with a kind smile – scraped beneath Laura's fingernails, she took a swab from the inside of her cheek, she combed her hair, slowly and gently, a sensation Laura found so soothing and so deeply reminiscent of childhood it brought tears to her eyes.

In Laura's head, Deidre spoke again. *You've no self-worth, that's your problem, Laura.* Deidre, the scrawny, hard-faced woman in whose arms her broken-hearted father had sought solace after Laura's mother left, could, if pressed, come up with a whole litany of Laura's problems. Low self-worth was a particular favourite. *You don't value yourself enough, Laura. Fundamentally, that's your problem. If you valued yourself a little more, you wouldn't just go with whoever paid you any attention.*

A few days after Laura turned thirteen, she went to a party at a friend's house. Her father caught her sneaking back into the house at six in the morning. He grabbed hold of her shoulders, shaking her like a doll. 'Where were you? I was going out of my mind, I thought something had happened! You can't do that to me, chicken. Please don't do that to me.' He hugged her close to him, she rested her head on his broad chest and felt as though

31

she were a child again, normal again. 'I'm sorry, Dad,' she said quietly. 'I'm really sorry.'

'She's not in the slightest bit sorry,' Deidre said an hour or so later, when they were sitting at the breakfast table. 'Look at her. Just look at her, Philip. Like the cat that got the cream.' Laura grinned at her over her bowl of cereal. 'You've got that look,' Deidre said, her mouth pursed in disgust. 'Hasn't she got that look? Who were you with last night?'

Later, she heard her father and her stepmother arguing. 'She's got no self-respect,' Deidre was saying. 'That's her problem. I'm telling you, Phil, she's going to end up pregnant before she's fifteen. You've got to do something. You've got to do something about her.'

Her father's voice, supplicating: 'But it's not her fault, Deidre, you know that. It's not her fault.'

'Oh, it's not her fault. That's right. Nothing's *ever* Laura's fault.'

Later still, when Deidre came upstairs to Laura's room to call her for dinner, she asked, 'Did you use protection, at least? Please tell me you weren't stupid enough to do it without a condom?'

Laura was lying on her bed, staring up at the ceiling. Without looking, she picked up a hairbrush from her bedside table and hurled it in her stepmother's general direction. 'Please just fuck off, Deidre,' she said.

'Oh yes, that's charming, isn't it? I'll bet your filthy mouth is not your fault either.' She turned to leave, but thought better of it. 'You know, Laura, you know what your problem is? You don't value yourself enough.'

Low self-worth was indeed one of Laura's problems, but it wasn't the only one. She had a whole host of others to keep it company, including but not limited to: hypersexuality, poor impulse control, inappropriate social behaviour, aggressive outbursts, short-term memory lapses and quite a pronounced limp.

'There now,' the policewoman said, once she was done. 'You're all set.' She saw that Laura was crying and squeezed her hand. 'You'll be all right, love.'

'I want to phone my mum,' Laura said. 'Is it all right if I phone my mum?'

Her mum wasn't answering her phone.

'Do I get another call?' Laura asked. The officer at her side shook her head but, seeing Laura's dismay, she glanced this way and that along the hall and then nodded. 'Go on then,' she said. 'Quickly.'

Laura rang her father next. She listened to the phone ring a few times, her hopes soaring as the call connected, only to be immediately dashed as she heard Deidre's voice. 'Hello? Hello? Who is this?' Laura hung up, meeting the officer's inquisitive look with a shrug. 'Wrong number,' she said.

The police officer took Laura to a tiny, stuffy room with a table at its centre. The police officer gave her a glass of water and said someone would bring some tea in a minute, but the tea never materialized. The room was over-heated and smelled of something strange and chemical; her skin itched, her mind felt muddied with exhaustion. She folded her arms and laid her head down upon them and tried to sleep, but in the white noise she heard voices – her mother's, Deidre's, Daniel's; when she swallowed she thought she could taste metal, and rot.

'What are we waiting for?' she asked the police officer eventually and the woman ducked her head and shrugged.

'Duty solicitor, I think. Sometimes it takes a while.'

Laura thought about her groceries, the frozen pizzas and the ready-meal curries she'd spent her last tenner on, sitting on the counter in her kitchen at home, gently defrosting.

*

After what felt like hours but was probably ten minutes, the detectives turned up, solicitor-less.

'How long do you think this is going to take?' Laura asked. 'I've got a long shift tomorrow, and I'm fucking knackered.'

Egg looked at her long and hard, and sighed, as though he were disappointed in her. 'It could be a while, Laura,' he said. 'It's . . . Well, it's not looking great, is it? And, you see, the thing is, you've got form on this score, haven't you?'

'I bloody have not. Form? What are you talking about? I don't go around stabbing people, I—'

'You stabbed Warren Lacey,' Eyebrow chipped in.

'With a *fork*. In the *hand*. Fuck's sake, it's not the same thing at all,' Laura said, and she started laughing, because, honestly, this was ridiculous, this was apples and oranges, the one thing was not like the other in any way, but she didn't really feel like laughing at all, she felt like crying.

'It's interesting,' Eyebrow said, 'I think it's interesting, in any case, that you seem to find this so amusing, Laura. Because most people – in your situation, I mean – I don't think most people would find this all that funny . . .'

'I don't. I don't think it's *funny*, I don't . . .' Laura sighed in frustration. 'Sometimes I struggle,' she said, 'to match my outward behaviour to my emotional state. I don't think it's funny,' she said again, but still she couldn't stop smiling, and Eyebrow smiled back at her, horribly. She was about to say something else, but they were at last interrupted by the long-awaited duty solicitor, a harassed-looking, grey-faced man with coffee breath who failed to inspire much confidence.

Once everyone was settled, introductions made, formalities out of the way, Eyebrow continued. 'We were talking a moment ago,' she said, 'about how you struggle to match your outward behaviour to your emotional state. That is what you said, isn't it?' Laura nodded. 'You have to speak up, Laura, for the tape.' Laura muttered her assent. 'So, it's fair to say that you cannot always control yourself? You have emotional outbursts which are beyond your control?' Laura said they were. 'And this is because of the accident you had when you were a child? Is that correct?' Laura answered in the affirmative again. 'Can you talk a bit more about the accident, Laura?' Eyebrow asked, her voice reassuring, coaxing. Laura jammed her hands underneath her thighs to keep herself from slapping the woman across the face. 'Could you talk about the accident's effect on you – physically, I mean?'

Laura glanced at the solicitor, trying to communicate a silent *Do I have to?*, but he seemed incapable of reading her, so, sighing heavily, she reeled monotonously through her injuries: 'Fractured skull, broken pelvis, compound fracture of the distal femur. Cuts, bruises. Twelve days in a coma. Three months in hospital.'

'You suffered a traumatic brain injury, didn't you, Laura? Could you tell us a bit about that?'

Laura puffed out her cheeks, rolled her eyes. 'Could you not just fucking google it? *Jesus*. I mean, is this really what we're here to talk about? Something that happened to me when I was ten years old? I think I should just go home now because, frankly, you've got fuck all, haven't you? You've got nothing on me.'

The detectives watched her, impassive, unimpressed with her outburst. 'Could you just tell us about the nature of your head injury?' Egg asked, his tone polite, infuriating.

Laura sighed again. 'I suffered a brain injury. It affected my speech temporarily, as well as my recall . . .'

'Your memory?' Eyebrow asked.

'Yes, my memory.'

Eyebrow paused – for effect, it seemed to Laura. 'There are

some emotional and behavioural consequences to this sort of injury, too, aren't there?'

Laura bit her lip, hard. 'I had some anger-management issues when I was younger,' she said, looking the woman dead in the eye, daring her to call her a liar. 'Depression. I have disinhibition, which means sometimes I say inappropriate or hurtful things, like for example that time I called you ugly.'

Eyebrow smiled, rose above it, pressed on. 'You have impulse-control problems, don't you, Laura? You can't help yourself, you lash out at people, you try to hurt them. That's what you're saying, isn't it?'

'Well, I . . .'

'And so, on the boat on Friday night, when Mr Sutherland rejected you – when he was, as you put it, cold and offensive – you lost your temper, didn't you? You attacked him, didn't you? Earlier you said you hit him. You really wanted to hurt him, didn't you?'

'I wanted to rip his fucking throat out,' Laura heard herself say. Next to her, she felt the solicitor flinch. And there it was: the police didn't, as she'd said, have *fuck all*, because of course they had *her*. They had Laura. They didn't need a weapon, did they? They didn't need a smoking gun. They had motive and they had opportunity and they had Laura, who they knew could be counted on, sooner or later, to say something really stupid.

6

In the armchair in her front room, her favoured reading spot, Irene waited for Laura, who was late. The armchair, once part of a pair although its partner had long since been consigned to the dump, was pushed right up against the window of the front room. It was the spot which trapped the sun for most of the morning and well into the afternoon, too; the spot from which Irene could watch the world go by and the world could, in turn, watch her, fulfilling its expectations of the aged: sitting in a chair in a room alone, musing on the past, on former glory, on missed opportunities, on the way things used to be. On dead people.

Which Irene wasn't doing at all. Well, not exclusively, in any case. Mostly, she was waiting for Laura to turn up to fetch her weekly groceries, and in the meantime she was sorting through one of the three boxes of musty-smelling books that Carla Myerson had left for her. The books had belonged to a dead person – Angela. Carla's sister and Irene's neighbour; also Irene's dearest friend.

'They're not worth anything,' Carla had told Irene when she dropped them off some time last week. 'Just paperbacks. I was going to take them to the charity shop, but then I thought . . .' She'd given Irene's living room a quick once-over, a wrinkle appearing at the bridge of her nose as she said, 'I thought they might be to your taste.'

A veiled insult, Irene supposed. Not that she cared, particularly. Carla was the sort of woman who knew the price of everything and the value of nothing. Not worth anything? Showed what she knew.

It was true that when Irene opened up some of the more ancient Penguins, their bright orange covers tattered and worn, the pages began to crumble beneath her fingertips. Succumbing already to slow fire, the acidification of the paper eating away at the pages, making them brittle and breakable, destroying them from within. It was terribly sad, when you thought about it, all those words, all those stories slowly disappearing. Those books, in any case, she'd have to throw out. But as for the rest of them, they were very much to her taste – so much so that she'd already read quite a few of them. She and Angela used to swap books all the time, they shared a predilection for the best sort of crime novels (not the bloody ones, but the clever ones, like Barbara Vine or P. D. James) and the sort of book-club fiction at which the likes of Carla Myerson no doubt turned up their nose.

The fact that Irene had read most of them was beside the point. The important thing – the thing that Carla probably didn't know, even though this was her *own sister* they were talking about – was that Angela was a vandal when it came to books – a cracker of spines, a dog-earer of pages, a scribbler in margins. So, when you leafed through Angela Sutherland's copy of *The Haunting of Hill House*, for example, you might notice that she'd underscored certain lines (*the poor girl was hated to death; she hanged herself, by the way*); when you turned the pages of Angela's well-thumbed *A Dark-Adapted Eye*, you discovered how strongly she sympathized with Vera's feelings towards her sister: *Exactly this!* she had scrawled in the margin next to the line that told us,

Nothing kills like contempt and contempt for her came upon me in a hot flood. Every now and again, you might even come across some little scrap of Angela's past – a bookmark, say, or a train ticket, or a scrap of paper with a shopping list on it: *cigarettes, milk, pasta.* In *No Country for Old Men*, there was a postcard purchased at the V&A, a photograph of a house with a white picket fence; in *In the Woods*, there was a scrap of paper with a drawing on it, two children holding hands. In *The Cement Garden*, she found a birthday card, blue and white with a picture of a boat on it, the paper creased, worn thin with handling. *To darling Daniel,* the message read, *with all my love on your tenth birthday. Kisses, Auntie Carla.*

Not worth anything? Showed what Carla knew. The truth was that when you read a book that had previously been owned and read by Angela Sutherland, you became part of a conversation. And since, tragically, there were never to be any more actual conversations with Angela, that, to Irene, was valuable. That was *invaluable.*

If it weren't for the nagging worry of the whereabouts of Laura, Irene might have been quite contented, basking like a lizard in the morning sunlight, sorting through the books, watching the office workers and the mums with their children hurrying past in the lane outside.

Irene's little two-up, two-down house sat on one side of Hayward's Place, a narrow lane in the heart of the city. Not much more than a footpath cutting between two larger roads, Hayward's Place was flanked on one side by five small, identical houses (Irene's was number two), and on the other by the site of the Red Bull Theatre (which may or may not have burned down in the Great Fire of London and which had now been developed into an uninspiring office space). It offered a convenient short-cut and was, on weekdays at least, busy day and night.

Where *was* Laura? They had said Tuesday, hadn't they? She usually came on a Tuesday, because on Tuesdays she had a later start at the launderette. Was today Tuesday? Irene thought that it was, but she was starting to doubt herself. She pulled herself up out of her chair, gingerly – she'd not long ago twisted an ankle, which was one of the reasons she needed help with the shopping in the first place – and with effort circumvented the little piles of books on the floor, the read and unread, the favoured and the destined-for-the-Oxfam-shop, and pottered across her living room, furnished simply with her chair and a small sofa, a dresser on which sat an unfashionably small and rarely watched television set, and a bookcase atop which perched her radio. She turned the radio on.

At ten o'clock, the newsreader confirmed that it was indeed a Tuesday: Tuesday the thirteenth of March, to be precise. The newsreader went on to say that Prime Minister Theresa May had given the Russian premier until midnight to explain how a former spy was poisoned in Salisbury; he said that a Labour MP had denied slapping a female constituent on the buttocks; he said that a young woman was being questioned in connection with the murder of Daniel Sutherland, the twenty-three-year-old man found dead on a narrowboat on the Regent's Canal on Sunday. The newsreader went on to say a number of other things, too, but Irene couldn't hear him over the sound of blood rushing in her ears.

She was imagining things. She *must* be. Daniel Sutherland? It couldn't be. Her hands trembling, Irene turned the radio off and then back on again, but the newsreader had moved on now, he was talking about something else, about the weather, about a cold front moving in.

Perhaps it was a different Daniel Sutherland? How many Daniel Sutherlands were there? She hadn't bought the newspaper that morning, she hardly ever did these days, so she couldn't check that. She'd heard it was possible to find anything on a mobile phone, but she wasn't entirely sure how, and in any case she couldn't remember where she'd seen the phone last. Upstairs somewhere, probably. Battery dead as a dodo, probably.

No, she'd just have to do things the old-fashioned way, she'd have to go around to the newsagent's to get the paper. She needed milk and bread, in any case, if Laura wasn't coming. In the hallway, she shrugged on her coat and picked up her bag and house key, noticing just as she was about to open the front door, just in time, that she was still wearing her slippers. She went back into the living room to change her shoes.

She was forgetful, that was all. Funny, though, how nervous she felt when she left the house these days – she used to be out and about all the time, shopping, going to the library, volunteering at the Red Cross shop on the high street, but you fell out of the habit quickly, after a period of being housebound. She needed to watch that. She didn't want to end up being one of *those* old people, too frightened to walk out of their own front door.

She was, she had to admit, happy to avoid the supermarket – so full of the impatient, unthinking, distracted young. Not that she didn't like young people. She didn't want to become one of *those sorts* of elderly either – the bitter sort, closed-off and self-satisfied in their beige senior-citizen sandals ordered from the back pages of the Sunday supplements. Irene wore blue and orange New Balance trainers with a Velcro strap. They were a Christmas present from Angela. Irene had nothing against the young, she'd even been young herself once. Only young people made assumptions, didn't they? *Some* young people. They assumed you were deaf, blind, weak. Some of these things might be true (and some not – Irene had the hearing of a bat. She often wished, in fact, given the paper-thin walls of her house, that her hearing wasn't so acute). Nevertheless, it was the *assumption* that rankled.

Back home from the shops, she found nothing in the newspaper about Daniel Sutherland (and not only that, but she realized she'd forgotten to buy marmalade to have on her toast, so the trip was a bust). She did eventually locate her phone (in the bathroom), but its battery was (as she'd predicted) flat, and she couldn't for the life of her remember where she'd put the charger.

Infuriating.

But she wasn't losing her marbles. It wasn't dementia. That was the conclusion people jumped to when you were old and forgot things, as though the young didn't also misplace their keys or forget the odd thing off their shopping list. Irene was certain it wasn't dementia. She did not, after all, say 'toaster' when she meant 'tablecloth', she didn't get lost on the way home from the supermarket. She didn't (often) lose the thread of a conversation, she didn't put the remote control in the fridge.

She did have turns. But it *definitely* wasn't dementia, her doctor had told her so. It was just that if she let herself get run down, if she forgot to drink enough water and eat regularly, she became tired, and then she became confused, and before she knew it she'd quite lost herself. 'Your resources are depleted, Mrs Barnes,' the doctor told her the last time this had happened. '*Severely depleted.* You have to take better care of yourself, you have to eat well, you have to stay hydrated. If you don't, of course you will find yourself confused and dizzy! And you might have another fall. And we don't want that, do we?'

How to explain to him, this kind (if ever so slightly condescending) young man with his soft voice and his watery blue eyes, that sometimes she *wanted* to lose herself in confusion? How on earth to make clear to him that while it was frightening, the feeling could also be, on occasion, *thrilling*? That she allowed herself, from time to time, to skip meals, hoping it would come back to her, that feeling that someone was missing and that if she waited patiently they'd come back?

Because in those moments she'd forget that William, the man she had loved, whose bed she'd shared for more than forty years, was dead. She could forget that he'd been gone for six years and she could lose herself in the fantasy that he'd just gone out to work, or to meet a friend at the pub. And eventually she'd hear his familiar whistle out in the lane, and she'd straighten her dress and pat her hair down, and in a minute, just a minute, she'd hear his key in the door.

Irene had been waiting for William the first time she met Laura. The day they found Angela's body.

It had been terribly cold. Irene had been worried, because she'd woken up and William wasn't there, and she couldn't understand where he'd got to. Why hadn't he come home? She took herself downstairs and put on her dressing gown, she went outside and oh, it was *freezing*, and there was no sign of him. No sign of anyone out in the lane. Where *was* everyone? Irene turned to go back inside, only to find that the door had swung shut, but that was all right because she knew better than to go out without a key in her pocket, she wouldn't make that mistake again, not after last time. But then – and this was the ridiculous thing – she just couldn't get the key into the lock. Her hands were frozen into claws, and she just *could not* do it, she kept dropping the key, and it was so silly, but she found herself in tears. It was so cold, and she was alone, and she'd no idea where William was. She cried out, but nobody came, and then she remembered Angie! Angela would be next door, wouldn't she? And if she knocked softly, she wouldn't wake the boy up.

So she did. She opened the gate next to hers and knocked softly on the front door, calling out, 'Angela! It's me. It's Irene. I can't get back in. I can't open my door. Could you help me?'

There was no reply, so she knocked again, but still no reply. She fumbled for her key again, but how her fingers ached! Her breath was white in front of her face, and her feet were numb, and as she turned she stumbled against the gate, banging her hip and crying out, tears coursing down her cheeks.

'Are you all right? God, you're not all right, course you're not. Here, here, it's OK, let me help you.' There was a girl there. A strange girl wearing strange clothes, trousers with a flowery pattern, a bulky silver jacket. She was small and thin, with white-blonde hair and a sprinkling of freckles over the bridge of her nose. She had the most enormous blue eyes, her pupils like black holes. 'Fucking hell, mate, you're *freezing* . . .' She had both of Irene's hands in her own and was rubbing them gently. 'Oh, you're so cold, aren't you? Is this your place? Have you locked yourself out?' Irene could smell alcohol on the girl's breath – she wasn't sure she looked old enough to drink, but you never knew these days. 'Is there someone in? Oi!' she yelled, walking up the path and banging on Angela's door. 'Oi! Let us in!'

'Oh, not too loud,' Irene said. 'It's ever so late, I wouldn't want to wake the little boy.'

The girl gave her an odd look. 'It's six thirty in the morning,' she said. 'If they've got kids, they should be awake by now.'

'Oh . . . *no*,' Irene said. That couldn't be right. It couldn't be six thirty in the morning. That would mean William hadn't come home at all, that he'd been out all night. 'Oh,' she said, her freezing fingers raised to her mouth. 'Where is he? Where is William?'

The girl looked stricken. 'I'm sorry, darling, I don't know,' she said. She took a crumpled Kleenex from her pocket and dabbed at Irene's face. 'We'll sort it out, all right? We will. But first I've got to get you inside. You're ice-cold, you are.'

The girl let go of Irene's hands, turned back towards Angela's front door and banged hard with the side of her fist, then she crouched down, picked up a pebble and hurled it against the window.

'Oh dear,' Irene said.

The girl ignored her. She was kneeling now, pressing her fingers against the flap of the letter box, pushing it open. 'Oi!' she yelled, and then all of a sudden she jumped backwards, flailing in the air for a second before landing heavily on the flagstones on her bony bottom. 'Oh, fucking hell,' she said, looking up at Irene, her eyes impossibly wide. 'Jesus Christ, is this your house? How long . . . *Jesus Christ*. Who is that?' She was scrabbling to her feet, grabbing Irene's hands again, roughly this time. '*Who is that in there?*'

'It's not my house, it's Angela's,' Irene said, quite perturbed by the girl's odd behaviour.

'Where do you live?'

'Well, *obviously* I live next door,' Irene said, and she held out the key.

'Why the fuck would that be obvious?' the girl said, but she took the key anyway, put her arm around Irene's shoulder and guided her back to her own house. She unlocked the door without a problem. 'Come on then, you go in, I'll get you a cup of tea in a minute. Wrap yourself up in a blanket or something, yeah? You need to warm up.'

Irene went into the living room, sat down in her usual chair and waited for the girl to bring her a cup of tea, like she said she would, but it didn't come. Instead, she could hear sounds from the hall: the girl was making a call from her phone in the hallway.

'Are you calling William?' Irene asked her.

'I'm calling the police,' the girl said.

Irene heard the girl saying, 'Yeah, there's someone in there,' and 'No, no, no chance, it's way beyond that, definitely, one hundred per cent. You can smell it.'

Then she ran off. Not right away – first, she brought Irene a cup of tea with a couple of sugars in it, then she knelt at Irene's feet, took Irene's hands in her own and told her to sit tight until the police came. 'When they get here, tell them to go next door, all right? Don't you go yourself. OK? And then they can help you find William, all right? Just . . . don't go outside again, OK, you promise me?' She scrambled back to her feet. 'I've gotta scarper, I'm sorry, but I'll come back.' She crouched back down again. 'My name's Laura. I'll come see you later. OK? You stay golden, yeah?'

By the time the police arrived – two young women in uniforms – Irene had forgotten the girl's name. It didn't seem to matter terribly, because the police weren't interested in her, all they were interested in was whatever was going on next door. Irene watched from her own doorway as they crouched down, peering through the letter box as the girl had done, and then starting back, just as she had done. They spoke into their little radios, they coaxed Irene back into her living room, one of them put the kettle on, fetched a blanket from upstairs. A while later, a young man appeared, wearing a brightly coloured jacket, he took her temperature and gently pinched her skin, he asked her lots of questions, like when she'd last eaten and what day it was and who was prime minister.

She knew the last one. 'Oh, that awful May woman,' she said tartly. 'I'm not a fan. You're not a fan either, are you?' The man smiled, shaking his head. 'No, I'd imagine not, what with you being from India.'

'I'm from Woking,' the young man said.

'Ah, well.' Irene wasn't sure what to say to that. She was feeling a bit flustered, and very confused, and it didn't help that the young man was handsome, very handsome, with dark eyes and the longest lashes, and his hands were soft, and so gentle, and when he touched her wrist, she could feel herself blush. He had a beautiful smile and a kind manner, even when he admonished her gently for not taking care of herself, telling her she was very dehydrated and that she needed to drink lots of water with electrolytes in it, which was exactly what her GP had said.

The handsome man left, and Irene did as she was told, she ate a piece of toast with some honey on it and drank two large glasses of water without electrolytes because she didn't have any of those, and was at last starting to feel a little more like herself when she heard the most terrible crash from outside, a terrifying sound, and, heart racing, hurried to the window in the living room. There were men out there, men in uniforms using a sort of metal battering ram to smash Angie's door down. 'Oh dear,' Irene said out loud, thinking – stupidly – that Angela wasn't going to be pleased about that at all.

Somehow, still, the penny had not dropped, that Angela would never be pleased by anything ever again, and it wasn't until another police officer, a different woman, not in uniform, came round and sat her down and explained that Angela was dead, that she'd fallen down the stairs and broken her neck, that Irene finally understood.

When the policewoman told Irene that Angela might have been lying there for days, for as much as a whole *week*, Irene could barely speak for the shame. Poor Angela, lying alone, just on the other side of that wall, while she, Irene – having one of her *turns*, letting herself slip away into confusion – had not even missed her.

'She didn't cry out,' Irene said, when at last she found her voice. 'I would have heard her. These walls are paper thin.' The policewoman was kind, she told Irene it was likely that Angela was killed instantly when she fell. 'But surely you can *tell* when it was that she died?' Irene knew a little about forensics, from her reading. But the woman said that the heating had been on, turned up very high, and that Angela's body had been lying right up against the radiator at the bottom of the stairs, which made it impossible to ascertain her time of death with any accuracy.

No one would ever know, not really, what happened. The police said it was an accident, and Irene accepted that, though the whole thing felt wrong to her, too hastily concluded. There had been conflict in Angela's life, plenty of it: she'd argued with her sister, she'd argued with her son – or rather, it seemed to Irene that one or other of them had come by to harangue her, leaving her upset, setting her off on a binge. Irene mentioned the arguments – over money, over Daniel – to the police, but they didn't seem interested. Angela was an alcoholic. She drank too much, she fell, she broke her neck. 'It happens more often than you'd think,' the kind policewoman said. 'But if you think of anything else, anything that might be relevant,' she said, handing Irene a card with a telephone number on it, 'feel free to give me a call.'

'I saw her with a man,' Irene said suddenly, just as the policewoman was leaving.

'OK,' the officer said carefully. 'And when was this?'

Irene couldn't say. She couldn't remember. Her mind was a blank. No, not a blank, it was *fogged*. There were things in there – memories, important ones – only everything was shifting about hazily, she couldn't fix on anything. 'Two weeks ago, perhaps?' she ventured hopefully.

The officer pursed her lips. 'OK. Can you remember anything else about this man? Could you describe him, or . . .'

'They were talking out there, in the lane,' Irene said. 'Something was wrong. Angela was crying.'

'She was crying?'

'She was. Although,' Irene paused, caught between a resistance to disloyalty and an urge to tell the truth. 'She's quite often tearful when she has a little too much to drink, she gets . . . melancholic.'

'Right.' The officer nodded, smiled, she was ready for the off. 'You don't remember what this man looked like, do you? Tall, short, fat, thin . . . ?'

Irene shook her head. He was just . . . normal, he was *average*. 'He had a dog!' she said at last. 'A little dog. Black and tan. An Airedale, perhaps? No, an Airedale's bigger, isn't it? Maybe a fox terrier?'

That was eight weeks ago. First Angela had died, and now her son, too. Irene had no idea whether the police had ever enquired about the man she'd seen outside with Angela; if they did, it came to nothing, because her death was recorded as accidental. Accidents do happen, and they especially happen to drunks. But mother and son, eight weeks apart?

In fiction, that would never stand.

7

Theo's bedroom window overlooked a small walled garden, and beyond the wall, the canal. On a spring day like this one, the view was a palette of greens: bright new growth on the plane and oaks, the muted olive of weeping willows on the towpath, electric-lime duckweed spreading across the surface of the water.

Carla sat on the window seat with her knees pulled up under her chin, Theo's bathrobe, pilfered from the Belles Rives Hotel in Juan-les-Pins a lifetime ago, gathered loosely around her. It was almost six years since she'd moved out of this house, and yet this was the place she felt most herself. More than the much grander house she'd grown up in on Lonsdale Square, certainly more than her drab little maisonette down the road, this house, Theo's house, was the one that felt like home.

Theo was lying in bed, the covers thrown back, reading his phone and smoking.

'I thought you said you were cutting down,' Carla said, glancing over at him, her teeth grazing lightly over her lower lip.

'I am,' he said, without looking up. 'I now smoke only post-coitally, post-prandially, and with my coffee. So that's an absolute maximum of five cigarettes a day, assuming I get a shag, which, I regret to say, is no longer by any means a foregone conclusion.'

Carla smiled, despite herself. 'You need to start looking after yourself,' she said. 'Seriously.'

He looked across at her, a lazy grin on his face. 'What,' he said, flicking a hand downwards over his torso, 'you think I'm out of shape?'

Carla rolled her eyes. 'You *are* out of shape,' she said, jutting her chin out, indicating his gut. 'It's not a matter of opinion. You should get another dog, Theo. You do far more exercise when you have a dog, it gets you out of the house, you know it does, otherwise you just sit around, eating and smoking and listening to music . . .'

Theo turned back to his phone. 'Dixon might turn up,' he said quietly.

'Theo.' Carla got to her feet and clambered back on to the bed, the dressing gown slipping open as she knelt in front of him. 'He went missing six weeks ago. I'm sorry, but the poor chap isn't coming home.'

Theo looked up at her dolefully. 'You don't know that,' he said and reached for her, placing his hand gently on her waist.

It was warm enough to eat breakfast outside on the patio. Coffee and toast. Theo smoked another cigarette and complained about his editor. 'He's a philistine,' he said. 'About sixteen years old, too. Knows nothing of the world. Wants me to take out all the political stuff, which is, when you think about it, the very heart of the novel. No, no, it's not the heart, that's wrong. It's at the root. It *is* the root. He wants it *deracinated*. Deracinated and cast into a sea of sentimentality! Did I tell you? He thinks Siobhan needs a romance, to *humanize* her. She is human! She's the most fully realized human I've ever written . . .'

Carla tipped her chair back, resting her bare feet on the chair in front of her, her eyes closed, only half listening to him. She'd heard this speech, or some variant thereof, before. She'd learned that there wasn't a great deal of point putting forward her view, because in the end he'd do whatever he wanted anyway. After a while, he stopped talking, and they sat together in companionable silence, listening to the neighbourhood sounds: children shouting in the street, the ding ding ding of bicycle bells on the towpath, the occasional waterfowl quack. The buzz of a phone on the table. Carla's. She picked it up, looked at it and, sighing, put it down again.

Theo raised an eyebrow. 'Unwelcome suitor?'

She shook her head. 'Police.'

Theo looked at her for a long moment. 'You're not taking their calls?'

'I will. Later.' She bit her lip. 'I will, I just . . . I don't want to keep going over it, to keep seeing it. To keep imagining it.'

Theo placed his hand on top of hers. 'It's all right. You don't have to talk to them if you don't want to.'

Carla smiled. 'I think I probably do.' She swung her feet off the chair, slipping them into the too-large slippers she'd borrowed from Theo. She leaned forward and poured herself a half-cup of coffee, took a sip and found that it was cold. She got to her feet, clearing away the breakfast things, placing the silver coffee pot and their mugs on to the tray, carrying them up the stone steps towards the kitchen. She reemerged a moment later, an old Daunt Books tote bag slung over her shoulder. 'I'm going to go and get changed,' she said. 'I need to get back across to Hayward's Place.' She bent down, brushing her lips momentarily against his.

'Aren't you done there yet?' he asked, his hand closing over her wrist, eyes searching her face.

'Almost,' she said, lowering her lids, turning away from him, disentangling herself. 'I'm almost done.'

'Are you going to do it, then?' she called back over her shoulder, as she headed up into the house. 'Are you going to *humanize* Siobhan? You could always give her a dog, I suppose, if you don't want to give her a lover. A little Staffie, maybe, some pitiful rescue mutt.' Theo laughed. 'It's true, though, isn't it? You're supposed to give your character something to care about.'

'She has plenty of things to care about. She has her work, her art . . .'

'Ah, but that's not enough, is it? A woman without a man or a child or a puppy to love, she's cold, isn't she? Cold and tragic, in some way dysfunctional . . .'

'You're not,' Theo said.

Carla was standing in the kitchen doorway. She turned to face him, a sad smile on her lips. 'You don't think so, Theo? You don't think my life is tragic?'

He got to his feet, crossed the lawn and climbed up to meet her, taking her hands in his. 'I don't think that's *all* your life is.'

Three years after they married, Theo published a book, a tragicomedy set in a Sicilian town during the Second World War. It was prize-nominated (although it didn't actually win anything), a huge bestseller. A below-par movie adaptation followed. Theo made a great deal of money.

At the time, Carla wondered whether the book might spell the end of their marriage. Theo was away all the time, touring, going to festivals accompanied by pretty young publicists, mingling with ambitious twenty-somethings promoting much-praised debuts, rubbing shoulders at parties with impossibly glamorous Hollywood development executives. Carla worked in the City at the time for a fund manager, in sales. At dinner parties, people's eyes glazed over when she told them what she did; at cocktail parties, they glanced over her shoulder in search of more stimulating conversational partners.

She needn't have worried about Theo's head being turned. He tired quickly of touring life, of the punishing enthusiasm of bright young things. All he really wanted to do was to stay at home, with her, and to write – he was planning a prequel to his successful novel, chronicling his protagonist's mother's experiences in the First World War. After Carla fell pregnant, he was even less minded to travel, and once the baby was born, less so still.

Theo had missed two deadlines and was on course to miss a third when, just after his son's third birthday, Carla announced that she had to go to Birmingham for a sales conference. She'd only recently gone back to work and it was vital, she said, that she make trips like this one if she wasn't going to be sidelined, shunted on to the Mommy track.

'Maybe I could come with you?' Theo suggested. 'You, me and Ben – we could make a weekend of it?'

Carla's heart sank a little – she'd been fantasizing about the hours she might spend alone, soaking in the bath undisturbed, putting on a face mask, fixing herself a long drink from the minibar. 'That *would* be lovely,' she said carefully, 'only I'm not sure how that would be perceived. You know, me turning up with my husband and toddler in tow? Oh, don't look like that, Theo! You've *no idea* what it's like. If you showed up to a work do with Ben, they'd give you a medal for Father of the Year. If I do it, they'll say she can't cope, her mind's not on the job, there's no way she can handle any more than she already does.'

Instead of yielding, instead of just saying, *Oh, all right then, darling, I'll stay in London with Ben, you go ahead*, Theo suggested they should leave Ben with his parents.

'In Northumberland? How am I supposed to get him all the way to Alnmouth before Friday?'

'They could probably come and pick him up. They'd love it, Cee, you know how Mum adores him . . .'

'Oh, for *God's sake*. If you really insist on coming, he'll have to go to my sister's. And don't make that face, Angie adores him too, and she's five minutes away and I don't have time to organize something else.'

'But . . .'

'Let Angie have him this time, then next time he can go to your Mum's.'

There never was a next time.

On the Sunday morning, they received a phone call in their hotel room. They were packing, getting ready to return to London, quarrelling about the best route to take. The man on the phone asked them to come down to the reception desk, then he seemed to change his mind, he spoke to someone else and then said that in fact they should wait in their room, that someone would come to them.

'What on earth is this about?' Carla asked, but she received no reply.

'I bet some fucker's broken into the car,' Theo said.

There were two police officers, a man and a woman. There had been an accident, they said, at Carla's sister's home. Ben had fallen from the balcony on the first floor of the house on to the garden steps below.

'But she keeps the study door shut,' Carla said dumbly. 'The railings on the balcony are broken, so the door is always shut.'

The door hadn't been shut, though, and little Ben had toddled out and slipped through the railings, falling on to the stone steps twenty feet below. His eight-year-old cousin, playing in the garden, found him; he'd called an ambulance right away.

'Is he going to be all right? Is he going to be all right?' Carla kept asking the same question over and over, but Theo was already on his knees, howling like an animal. The police officer, the woman, had tears in her eyes and her hands were shaking. She shook her head and said that she was very sorry, the paramedics had arrived within minutes but there was nothing they could do to save him. 'But is he going to be all right?' Carla asked again.

After Carla and Angela's mother died, too young, of breast cancer, their father stayed on in the rambling three-storey family home on Lonsdale Square, although it was obvious it was too much for him, the climb from his study on the first floor to the bedrooms on the second taking longer and longer, becoming more and more precarious. The garden became wild and overgrown, the gutters went uncleared, the roof leaked, the window frames began to rot. And the wrought-iron railings on the little Juliet balcony leading off his study rusted all the way through.

Their father moved into a care home six months before he died, and since Carla was already living with Theo by this time, Angela took the old place over. She had grand plans for it, she foresaw years of painstaking renovation, she designed murals she planned to paint in the hallways and above the staircase. First off, however, were the essential repair jobs, the top priority being the roof. That, of course, took all the money there was to spare, so everything else had to be put on hold.

The rusted railings were barely thought of until Daniel was born. Once he was old enough to crawl, Angela locked the study door and left it that way. The rule was the study door stayed shut. At all times, the study door stayed shut.

'Where was Angela?' Carla and Theo were sitting in the back of a police car; neither were in a fit state to drive. 'Where was she?' Carla's voice was barely more than a whisper, her eyes squeezed tightly shut. 'I just . . . I don't understand. Where was Angela?'

'She was in her bedroom,' the policewoman told her. 'She was upstairs.'

'But . . . why did Daniel have to call the ambulance? What was my sister doing?'

'It seems she was sleeping when the accident happened,' the policewoman said.

'She wasn't sleeping,' Theo said, 'she was sleeping it *off*. Wasn't she?'

'We don't know that,' Carla said, reaching for his hand.

He snapped his hand from hers as though scalded. 'Don't we?'

The police drove them straight to Whittington Hospital. They were met by a family liaison officer, who tried to persuade them not to see the body. 'It would be far better,' she said, 'to remember your little boy at his happiest. Running around, or riding his bike . . .' They didn't listen to her. Neither of them could countenance never seeing him again, it was an absurd thing to ask.

In a cold and brightly lit room, they sat for more than an hour, passing their son between them. They kissed his chubby fingers, the soles of his feet. They warmed his cold flesh with their hands and their tears.

Afterwards, the police drove them back to their home on Noel Road, where Theo's parents were waiting for them. 'Where is she?' were Theo's first words to his mother.

She jerked her head towards the stairs. 'Up there,' she said, her face and voice tight as a drum. 'She's in the spare room.'

'Theo,' Carla said, 'please.'

She heard him shouting. 'You were fucking sleeping it off, weren't you? You were hungover, weren't you? You left him, you left him alone, you left the door open, you left him. You left him. You left him.' Angela was wailing, keening in agony, but

Theo would not relent. 'Get out of my house! Don't you ever come back here! I never want to see you again.'

Carla heard Daniel, who was crying too. 'Leave her alone! Uncle Theo! Please! Leave her alone!'

They came downstairs, Angela and Daniel, holding hands. Angela tried to embrace her sister, but Carla would not have it; she turned away, hunched her shoulders and crouched down, curling herself into a ball like an animal protecting itself from a predator.

When they were gone and the front door was closed, Theo's mother turned to Carla and said, 'Why didn't you let him come to me? I would have looked after him.'

Carla got to her feet, balled her hands into fists, walked through the kitchen into the back garden where her son's tricycle lay on its side in the middle of the lawn, and started to scream.

Carla and Theo blamed themselves and each other endlessly; every sentence began with an if.

If you hadn't gone to the conference . . .

If you hadn't insisted on coming . . .

If you hadn't been so worried about *perceptions* . . .

If we had taken him to my parents . . .

Their hearts were broken, shattered for ever, and no amount of love – no matter how deep, how fierce – could mend them.

8

Twenty-three hours after they'd picked her up, the police told Laura she could go home. It was Egg who delivered the news. 'We'll likely need to speak to you again, Laura,' he said, 'so don't go anywhere.'

'Oh yeah, no problem, I'll cancel that trip to Disney World I had planned, don't you worry,' Laura replied.

Egg nodded. 'You do that,' he said, and he smiled his sad smile at her, the one that told her something bad was coming.

It was after ten when she walked out of the station into a cold and steady drizzle. She caught the bus on Gray's Inn Road, collapsing exhausted on to the only spare seat on the downstairs deck. The woman next to her, broad-beamed and smartly dressed, wrinkled her nose, shifting closer to the window in an attempt to minimize contact with this damp and smelly new arrival. Laura tilted her head back against the seat, closing her eyes. The woman sucked her teeth. Laura ignored her, turning her face away. The woman sighed. Laura felt her jaw tense and her fists tighten. *Count to ten*, her father used to say, so she tried, *One two three one two three one two three* – she couldn't get past three, couldn't get anywhere at all, and the woman sighed again, shifting her fat arse around, and Laura wanted to scream at her, *It's not my fault it's not my fault it's not my fucking fault.*

She got to her feet. 'I know,' she snapped, eyeballing her neighbour, 'I *stink*. I know I do. I've been in a police station for twenty-four hours and before that I was doing my grocery shopping and before that I had an eight-hour shift at work, so I haven't had a shower in, like, two days. Not my fault. But you know what? In half an hour I'll be smelling of roses and you'll still be a stupid fat cow, won't you?'

Laura turned away and got off the bus three stops early. All the way home she couldn't stop seeing the woman's hurt expression, her face crimson with embarrassment, and she had to bite the inside of her cheek to stop herself from crying.

The lift was still out of order. She dragged herself up the seven flights of stairs, fighting tears all the way: tired, her leg aching, the cut on her arm throbbing, *starving*. She'd been given food at the station, but in her anxiety hadn't been able to swallow a mouthful. She was ravenous, her head light with hunger as she slipped her spare key into the lock, jiggled it about, coaxed the door open. The kitchen looked as though it had been ransacked – it *had* been ransacked, she supposed, by the police – the drawers and cupboards open, pots and plates strewn about. Among them lay the ruined food she'd bought from the supermarket with the last of her money.

She turned her back on it all. Turned off the lights and went to her room without showering or brushing her teeth. She crawled into bed, sobbing quietly, trying to soothe herself by stroking the nape of her neck, the way her father used to do to ease her to sleep when she was troubled, or in pain.

She'd had plenty of it, trouble and pain. Her early childhood, lived out in grimy south London, was uneventful. So uneventful she remembered almost nothing of it except for an oddly sepia-toned mental image of a terraced house on a narrow street, the sensation of dry, scratchy lawn beneath her feet in summer. Her memory seemed only to bloom into full colour from around the age of nine, which was when she and her parents moved to a little village in Sussex. Where all the trouble started.

Not that there was anything wrong with the village. Laura liked the village, it was quaint and pretty, with stone cottages and cricket on the village green, polite neighbours with blonde children and Labradoodles. Laura's mother, Janine, declared it *stultifying*, which was a bad thing, apparently. Laura liked it. She liked the village school, where there were only fifteen people in her class, where the teachers declared her a very advanced reader. She liked riding her bike, completely unsupervised, along narrow country lanes, in search of blackberries.

Laura's father, Philip, had secured a job in a nearby town. He'd given up on his dreams of a life in theatre stage design and was now working as an accountant, a fact that prompted Janine to roll her eyes whenever it was mentioned. 'An *accountant*,' she would hiss, drawing hard on her cigarette, plucking at the sleeves of her peasant top. 'Doesn't that sound like fun?'

'Life can't be about fun all the time, Janine. Sometimes one just has to be adult.'

'And God forbid adults should have any fun, right, Philip?'

Her parents hadn't always been like this, it seemed to Laura. She vaguely remembered her mother being happier. She remembered a time when her mother had not sat at the dinner table with her arms folded across her chest, barely picking at her food, replying in sullen tones to her father's every question. There was a time when her mother had laughed all the time. When she had sung!

'We could go back to London,' Laura would suggest, and her mother would smile for a moment and smooth her hair, and then look wistfully into the middle distance. But her father would reply – too brightly, with a little too much vim – 'We can't go back, chicken, I've got a job here now. And we've got such a nice house here, haven't we?'

At night, Laura heard them arguing.

'You've got a *job*,' her mother hissed in a horrible voice, 'in financial advice! Christ's sake, Philip, is that *really* what you want to do with your life? Count other people's money all day?'

And: 'Is that really the life we're going to live? An *ordinary* one? In the *countryside*? In *Sussex*? Because you know that's not what I signed up for.'

And: '*Signed up for*? This is a marriage, Janine, not a drama course.'

Laura, a hopeful child, pretended not to hear the arguments, convinced that if she worked very hard and behaved very well then whatever it was that was making her mother unhappy would blow over. Laura tried hard to please her, she was quick to pass on compliments from her teachers or to show her mother any drawings she'd done at school.

At home in the afternoons, Laura stayed by her mother's side. She helped out if there was cleaning to do, or sat beside her while she read, or followed her quietly from room to room as she moved restlessly around the house. She tried to read her mother's facial expressions, tried to imagine what it was she was thinking about, that made her sigh like that or blow the fringe out of her eyes in that way, tried to figure out what she could do to earn a smile, which sometimes she succeeded in doing, although sometimes her mother would yell, 'Christ's sake, Laura, give me a minute, would you? Just one minute to myself?'

In the autumn, Janine started taking art classes. And by the time the Christmas holidays came around, something had changed. A freezing wind blew in from the east, bringing with it achingly beautiful blue skies, a bitter chill and, as if from nowhere, a familial thaw. A truce seemed to have been declared. Laura had no idea why, but something had shifted, because the arguments stopped. Her father no longer looked hangdog, harassed. Her mum smiled while she did the washing up, she cuddled up close to Laura while they watched television in the evenings, instead of sitting apart, in the armchair, reading her book. They'd even been on outings to London, once to Hamleys and once to the zoo.

The New Year started in a glow of optimism, her mother waving her off to school in the morning with a smile on her lips. There was even a promise of a family sledding trip at the weekend, if it snowed.

It did snow, but they didn't go sledding.

That Friday, two and a half inches of snow fell in less than an hour, enough to cancel football practice. It was only just after three o'clock when Laura freewheeled down the hill towards home, riding out in the middle of the road where the snow had melted clean away due to the weight of traffic, but it was already getting dark, and she neither saw nor heard the car that swung out into the road. It seemed to come from nowhere.

She was thrown twelve feet, landing on her back on the road, the crack of her helmet on the tarmac audible to her mother, who was standing in the driveway in front of the house. Her skull was fractured, her leg and pelvis badly broken. The driver of the car that hit her did not stop.

Then came the trouble, and the pain. Six operations, months and months in hospital, hours upon hours of agonizing, exhausting physical therapy, speech therapy, trauma counselling. Everything healed, eventually. More or less. But a bad seed had been sown, and so although everything got better, Laura was left worse. She was slower, angrier, less lovable. Inside her a bitter darkness bloomed as she watched, with helpless desperation, her once limitless horizons narrow.

In the morning, Laura put all the defrosted food into the microwave and blitzed the lot. She ate as much of it as she could stomach, threw the rest in the bin and got dressed for work.

'What d'you think you're doing?' Maya, Laura's boss at the launderette, said when she came in from the back room to find Laura taking off her coat, hanging it on the peg behind the counter.

'It's my shift,' Laura said. 'It's Wednesday.'

'Yeah, and yesterday was Tuesday, and it was also your shift, only you didn't show up, did you?' Laura started to say something, but Maya held up the palm of her hand. 'Nah, I'm not interested. I'm sorry, but I'm not flipping interested, Laura. I don't care what your excuse is this time, I've absolutely had it . . .'

'Maya, I'm sorry . . .'

'Do you know what yesterday was? Do you? It was my grandson's fifth birthday and his mum was taking him on a special outing to the zoo and I was supposed to be there an' all, only I flipping wasn't, was I? Because I was *here*, covering for *you*, and you didn't even have the decency to call me.'

'I couldn't, Maya. I'm so sorry, I really am, I'm so sorry for letting you down . . .'

'You couldn't *call*? Why? Banged up, were you?' Laura hung her head. 'Oh, you've got to be bloody joking! Excuse my French, but you got arrested *again*?' Maya raised both hands in a gesture of surrender. 'I'm sorry, love, but I can't have this. I just can't. Enough's enough. I've put up with enough of your nonsense. And you've been warned, haven't you? Time and again. Late, unreliable, rude to the customers . . .'

'But, Maya, it wasn't . . .'

'I know! I know what you're going to say. It wasn't your fault.

It's never your fault. Maybe it isn't. Maybe it isn't your fault, but it's flipping well not mine, is it?'

Laura vomited on the pavement outside the launderette. Fish-fingers and pizza all over the place. 'I didn't do it on purpose!' she yelled through the window at Maya, who was watching her, open-mouthed, aghast. She didn't do it on purpose. It wasn't like she could throw up on demand – it was just that she'd stuck her card into the cash machine right next door to the launder-ette and confirmed that she had seven pounds and fifty-seven pence in her bank account, which, combined with the four pounds in change she had in her purse, was all she had in the world. And now she'd been sacked. It hit her then, like a straight punch to the solar plexus – getting sacked meant getting sanc-tioned. They could withhold her housing benefit, they'd done it to people she knew, sometimes for months. She'd be homeless, she thought, unless she went to prison for murder. That was when she threw up. She wiped her mouth and walked away, biting down on her bottom lip, trying to quell the feeling rising in her freshly emptied stomach of pure panic.

As soon as she got home, she rang her mother, because no matter how badly her mother disappointed her, how many times her mother let her down, Laura couldn't seem to stop herself from loving her, from believing that this time things might be different.

'Mum? Can you hear me?' There was a crackle on the line, noise in the background. 'Mum?'

'Laura! How are you, darling?'

'Mum . . . I'm not so good. Could you come and see me?' A long pause. 'Mum?'

'Sorry, sweetheart?'

'I said, would you be able to come for a visit?'

'We're in Spain at the moment, so that might be tricky!' She laughed, a low, throaty laugh that made Laura's heart ache. 'We'll be back in a few weeks, though, so maybe then.'

'Oh. A few weeks? I . . . where are you?'

'Seville. You know, like the oranges.'

'Yes, I've heard of Seville.' She swallowed hard. 'Listen, Mum, some shit's happened and I'm in a bit of trouble . . .'

'Oh, Laura! Not again.'

Laura bit her lip. 'Yes, *again*. Sorry. But . . . I was wondering, could you lend me some money, to tide me over? I've just had a bit of bad luck, it really wasn't my fault.'

'Laura . . .' There was another crackle on the line.

'I missed that, Mum.'

'I'm saying it's just not such a good time at the moment, things are very tight for us.'

'In Seville?'

'Yes, in Seville. Richard's got some pieces in an art fair here, but it's one of those deals where you have to pay the dealer for space, so . . .'

'He's not sold any, then?'

'Not yet.'

'OK.'

There was a long pause, another crackle. Laura heard her mother sigh, and in that moment something cracked. She felt her disappointment wrap like a fist around her heart.

'Laura, are you crying? Oh, Laura, don't. *Please*. Don't do this. You know I can't bear it when people try to emotionally manipulate me.'

'I'm not,' Laura said, but she was sobbing now. 'I'm not.'

'Listen to me,' her mother said, her tone brisk, business-like. 'You have a good cry, and then you ring me back, all right? I'll talk to Richard about the money, OK? Laura? You take care now.'

Laura cried for a little while, and when she was done, all emotion spent, she called her father, who didn't pick up. She left a message. 'Dad, hi. Yeah, so I got arrested yesterday, accused of murder, they've let me go without a charge, but I got fired 'cos I missed work due to being in police custody and all the food I bought went off and I've got fuck-all money left so could you give me a call back? Cheers. It's Laura, by the way.'

The One Who Got Away

When he wakes that morning, he can't imagine how the day is going to go, can't imagine how it's going to end up, all the highs and lows. Doesn't imagine, while he's shaving in the dirty mirror in the back bathroom, rusty water in the sink, stink of shit everywhere, doesn't imagine that he'll meet such a lovely girl.

How could he imagine how it'd go? How she'd tease him and flirt with him and hurt his feelings and then come running back, thumb stuck out, asking for help, asking for his company, for his hand on her lovely soft thigh in the front seat of the car.

When he wakes that morning, he can't imagine the rough and tumble later on, the excitement of it, the anticipation.

9

Four days a week, Miriam worked at Books on a Boat, a floating bookshop on the canal, just beyond Broadway Market. The shop, a mix of new and used books, had been circling the plug-hole of bankruptcy for years. Nicholas, its owner, had in recent times been forced to rely on – in his words – the kindness of hipsters (crowdfunding) to keep the place afloat. (This was literally true: they'd recently crowdfunded to repair damage to the boat's hull when it started to take on water.)

Miriam's function was, to a large degree, back-office – she did the accounts, kept on top of most of the admin, stacked shelves and kept the place tidy. She was no longer permitted to serve customers (too rude), nor was she allowed to write the shelf-talkers – the little blurbs where bookshop staff gave their views on the latest releases (too brutal). Plus, she was off-putting. Nicholas never said so, but he didn't need to. Miriam knew very well that she was not an appealing person to look at, that she did not draw people to her, that whatever the opposite of magnetism was, she had it in spades. She was conscious of these things and was prepared to face them. Why not, after all? What would be the alternative? There was little point in pretending that things were other than they were, that *she* was other than she was.

Wednesdays, Nicholas went to see his therapist, so Miriam opened up the shop. Always on time, never late, not by a minute, she couldn't afford to be. This morning, she ducked under the Cat and Mutton Bridge at exactly quarter to nine and so was surprised to see that there was a customer already standing outside the shop, hands cupped around his face, trying to peer through a window. A tourist, she thought, and then the man stepped back and looked her way and Miriam froze, adrenaline spiking. Theo Myerson.

Recovering, she reminded herself: this worm was turning. She took a deep breath, drew herself up to her full five feet two inches, and marched confidently towards him. 'Can I help you?' she called out.

His face darkening, he turned and came to meet her. 'You can, actually,' he said.

As luck would have it, there was a momentary lull in foot traffic and they found themselves alone on the towpath. The bridge behind her, the boat before her, Theo Myerson was in her way. 'We're not open yet,' she said, and she stepped out towards the water, trying to edge past him. 'We open at nine. You'll have to come back.'

Myerson shifted in the same direction, blocking her path once more. 'I'm not here to browse,' he said. 'I'm here to warn you to stay out of my business. To leave my family alone.'

Miriam shoved her trembling hands into her pockets. 'I haven't been anywhere near your family,' she said. 'Unless . . . do you mean your nephew?' She looked him dead in the eye. 'Horrible business.' Retrieving the bookshop key from her bag, she elbowed her way past him at last. 'I'm a witness, did they tell you that? The police came to see me, asked me a whole lot of questions, and I answered them.'

She turned to look at Theo, a tight smile on her face. 'Would you have had me do otherwise? I tell you what' – she reached into her handbag and took out her mobile phone – 'shall I give them a ring? I have the detective's number in my phone, he said I should call if I remembered anything, or if I noticed anything untoward. Shall I ring him now? Shall I tell him that you've come here to see me?' Miriam watched the consternation pass over his face like a shadow, and the rush of pleasure she felt was intense and quite unexpected. 'Mr Myerson?'

So this, Miriam thought to herself, is what power feels like.

When Miriam got home from work that evening, before she'd even made herself a cup of tea or washed her hands, she took her wooden box, the one in which she kept her trinkets, from the shelf above the wood burner and placed it on her kitchen table. She opened it up and sorted through its contents, a ritual she engaged in from time to time to soothe her anxiety, a way of calming herself, ordering her thoughts, focusing on what it really was that was important to her.

She was an odd fish and she knew it, she knew what she was and she knew how people saw her. People looked at Miriam and they saw a fat, middle-aged woman with no money and no hus-band and no power. They saw an outsider, living in a houseboat, clothes from the charity shop, cutting her own hair. Some people looked at her and dismissed her, some people looked at her and thought they could take whatever they liked, imagined she was powerless and couldn't do a thing about it.

From the box in front of her, Miriam took out a piece of paper, a sheet of A4, folded in half and then into quarters; she unfolded it, spread it out in front of her, ran the heel of her hand over the letterhead. She read the words again, words she had read so often she felt she might be able to recite them, or at least the most offensive parts of them, by heart.

Dear Mrs Lewis,

I write as in-house counsel for Harris Mackey, Theo Myerson's publishers, in response to your letter of February 4. I write on behalf of both the company and Mr Myerson, who has approved the contents of this letter. We wish to make it clear from the outset that Mr Myerson completely denies the allegations of copyright infringement made in your letter; your claim is entirely without merit.

Your claim that *The One Who Got Away*, the novel penned by Mr Myerson and published under the pseudonym Caroline MacFarlane, copies 'themes and significant portions of the plot' of your memoir is flawed for a number of reasons.

In order to establish a valid copyright infringement claim, there needs to be a causal connection between the claimant's work and the allegedly infringing work; you must demonstrate that your memoir was used by Mr Myerson in writing *The One Who Got Away*.

Mr Myerson acknowledges that you asked him to read your manuscript and, despite his extremely busy schedule and considerable demands on his time, he agreed to do so. As Mr Myerson explained to you when you went to his house on December 2, he placed the manuscript into his luggage when he flew to Cartagena for the Hay Festival; unfortunately, his luggage was lost by British Airways and was not recovered. Mr Myerson was therefore unable to read your manuscript.

The similarities you claim between *The One Who Got Away* and your own memoir are nothing more than generic themes and ideas . . .

> We consider it neither reasonable nor necessary to address every weak comparison you attempt to make . . .
>
> You have made serious and false allegations against Mr Myerson . . .
>
> Any legal action by you would be inappropriate and unreasonable and would be robustly defended by Mr Myerson; he would look to recover all legal costs from you, which, in the light of the above, we have no doubt the court would grant.

There it was, in black and white. For all the insults they hurled at her, for all the hurtful, unpleasant accusations, for all the dismissal of her claims as *entirely without merit, flawed, weak, false, inappropriate, unreasonable,* the substance of their argument, boiled down to its essence, could be found in that final sentence: we have all the money and therefore all the power. You have nothing.

Hands trembling, Miriam refolded the letter and tucked it back into the bottom of the box, retrieving instead the little black notebook in which she recorded comings and goings on the canal. She had lived here, on this boat, for six years, and she had learned that you had to be vigilant. All human life was here: good, decent, hard-working, generous people, mixed in with drunks and druggies and thieves and all the rest. You had to keep your wits about you. You had to keep your eyes peeled. You had to watch out for predators. (Miriam knew that better than most.)

So, she noted things down. She had, for example, noted the time on Friday evening when Mad Laura from the launderette had shown up with Daniel Sutherland; she had made a note, too, of when Carla Myerson, the boy's aunt, with her good haircut and her nice coat and her straight teeth, had come knocking. Last Wednesday, it was. Two days before Daniel died. Bottle of wine in hand.

Next, she picked up the key – Mad Laura's key, the one she'd taken from the floor of the dead man's boat – and turned it over in her fingers, feeling its edges, still tacky with blood. Miriam had the sense that, whatever the girl might have done, Laura should be protected. After all, she was another one without power, wasn't she? Oh, she was pretty, bright-eyed and slender, but she was poor too, and troubled. There was something wrong with her: she walked with a limp, and had something mentally wrong too. Not quite right. People could take advantage of someone like that, a small, powerless young thing like Laura, just as they had taken advantage of Miriam.

But power shifts, doesn't it? Sometimes in unexpected ways. Power shifts, and worms turn.

What if, contrary to what she'd written down in her little book, Miriam hadn't seen Laura at all? What if, as she'd told the police, she'd only seen Carla Myerson with Daniel Sutherland? And what if, now she came to think about it, she might even have seen Carla Myerson more than once? The detective had asked her to get in touch if she thought of anything else, hadn't he? If she remembered something, it didn't matter how small, that might be significant? What if – oh, now it was coming back to her! – she remembered overhearing something – raised voices, she'd thought merriment at first, but perhaps it was something else, perhaps it was an argument?

Miriam made herself a cup of tea and soaked her feet, working her way methodically through half a packet of digestive biscuits while she considered what she needed to tell the detective inspector. Should she mention, for example, her encounter with Myerson that morning? Or was that card best held back, kept in reserve to play another time? She was acutely aware that she needed to be careful about how she handled things, that she should not be reckless, should not let this new power of hers go to her head.

She rang the detective's mobile phone, listened to his voice-mail greeting.

'Hello, Detective Barker? It's Miriam Lewis. You said I should call you, if I thought of anything? Well, it's just that . . . it's occurred to me that the woman I saw, the one I told you about, the older woman? I've just remembered that I saw her on the Friday night. You know, I was thinking it was the Thursday, because I'd just come back from work when I saw her going past, she was carrying a bottle of wine, you see, not that that's important, but the thing is that I'd just come back from work, but I didn't go to work last Thursday because I had a bit of a stomach bug, which is unusual for me because I've got the constitution of an ox generally, but in any case I wasn't feeling well on Thursday and so I did my shift on Friday instead . . .'

Miriam ended the call. She leaned forward to take another biscuit from the packet and then reclined, swinging her legs up on to the bench. How satisfying this was, to hold something over Myerson! She imagined for a moment the great man him-self, standing in his study, holding the phone – a call from the detectives perhaps, telling him they were taking her in for questioning, his darling Carla. She imagined his panic. What would such an ordeal do to him? And just think about the bad press!

That would teach him, wouldn't it, for taking what wasn't his? For treating Miriam as though she were nothing, as though she were *material*, to be used and discarded as he wished.

And if Carla suffered too, well, that wasn't ideal, but just as my enemy's enemy is my friend, sometimes my enemy's friend is also my enemy, and that just couldn't be helped, that was the way of the world. That was how this sort of thing happened; it wasn't fair. In any sort of conflict, there were bound to be innocent casualties.

Miriam closed her notebook. She put it back into the box and placed Laura's key on top of it, nestling against the mahogany with Lorraine's gold hoop earrings, the silver cross her father gave to her on her confirmation when she was fourteen, and an ID from a dog collar, inscribed with the name *Dixon*.

The One Who Got Away

The sobbing has stopped. There are different noises now.

The girl uses the cover of these new sounds to break the window. Then, working quickly, she clears as much glass as she can before trying to climb out. Nevertheless she cuts herself badly, on her shoulders, her torso, her thighs, as she forces her solid flesh through the small square of the window frame.

On her haunches, she sits, back to the wall. Blood flows from her wounds, soaking into the hard ground beneath her feet. When she runs, she will leave a trail. Her only salvation will be to get to town before he comes after her: if she goes now, she stands a chance, perhaps.

It is dark now, moonless. Save for the rhythmic croak of a frog, the night is still. She can, however, still hear them inside. The noises he makes, the noises she makes in return.

She closes her eyes, admits the truth to herself. There is another chance of salvation: she could go back into the house, through the front door and into the kitchen, she could find a knife. Surprise him. Cut his throat.

She imagines, for a moment, her friend's relief. How they would cling to each other. She imagines telling the police what happened, she imagines a heroine's welcome at school, how grateful her friend's family would be!

How grateful would they be?

She pictures her friend's beautiful face, her long limbs, her nice parents, her expensive clothes. She is overwhelmed by the thought of her life, her happiness.

The girl imagines herself entering the room, the knife raised, imagines him turning, catching her, punching her in the throat. She imagines him crouching over her, his knees pressing against her chest, she imagines his weight on top of her, imagines the blade pressed against her collarbone, against her cheek, against her lip.

She doesn't even know if there is a knife in the kitchen.

She could try to help, she could fight. Or she could take advantage of his preference for her beautiful friend. She could run.

This is not her fault. She didn't even want to get into the car.

She is sorry. She really is. She is sorry, but she runs.

10

Detective Barker, his bald pate shining like a new penny in the bright morning sunlight, watched as the uniformed policewoman pushed a plastic stick into Carla's mouth, scraping it along the inside of her cheek, withdrawing it, dropping it into a clear plastic bag. When she was done, he nodded, satisfied. He asked the policewoman to wait for him in the car outside. The boat on which Daniel Sutherland had been staying, Barker had already explained to Carla, was a rental, and it was filthy. There were traces of at least a dozen people on it, probably more, so they were collecting DNA and fingerprints from any-one and everyone, he said, in order to rule out as many people as possible.

Carla, sitting at her dining-room table, wiped her mouth with a tissue. 'Well,' she said, rolling her shoulders back to ease the tension at the top of her spine, 'there is every chance you'll find mine.' Detective Barker raised his eyebrows, crossing his arms in front of his chest. 'I lied,' Carla went on, 'about not knowing that Daniel was living on the boat. I lied about not seeing him.' Barker said nothing; he crossed the room and sat down opposite Carla at the table, lacing his fingers together. 'Only you already know that, don't you? Someone's said something to you, haven't they? That's why you've come, isn't it? Did someone see me?' Still Barker said nothing. That old trick again, to make you talk, to press you into filling the silence.

It was irritating in its obviousness, but Carla was too tired to resist – she'd not slept more than an hour or two at a stretch since the detectives had been here last, five days ago. She kept seeing things, kept starting at shadows, black spots moving in the corners of her vision. That morning, she had passed a mirror and been startled to see her sister's face looking back at her, cheeks hollow, expression fearful.

'Daniel told me he'd rented a boat when he came to pick up his things. He told me to drop by. Told me not to expect much. I went there. Twice. Don't ask me when exactly, because I honestly wouldn't be able to tell you.' She paused. 'I lied to you because I didn't want to admit in front of Theo that I'd been there.'

Barker leaned back a little in his chair. 'And why,' he said, flexing his fingers so that the knuckles cracked in a disgusting way, 'was that?'

Carla closed her eyes for a moment. Listened to the sound of her own breath. 'Do you know what happened to my son?' she asked the detective.

He nodded, his expression grave. 'I do,' he said. 'I read about it at the time. A terrible thing.'

Carla gave a stiff little nod. 'Yes. My sister was looking after him when it happened, I'm not sure if they reported that? She was supposed to be looking after him, in any case. Theo never forgave her. He's had nothing to do with her since, not from the day our son died until the day she did. He wouldn't have her in our lives. He wouldn't have her in *his*, in any case, which at the time was also *mine*. Do you see what I'm saying? I saw my sister and Daniel in secret. Of course, Theo suspected that I saw her occasionally, and there were some arguments about it, but we divorced and I moved here, and it didn't seem to matter so much any longer. But I still never mentioned them to him. There it is, I suppose. I've been lying to Theo so long about that side of my life that sometimes I forget when it's necessary and when it isn't. I didn't want him to know that I'd visited Daniel on the boat.'

The detective scrunched his face into a frown. 'So you lied to us, to the police, *during a murder investigation*, just because you didn't want your ex-husband to know you'd seen your nephew?' He opened his palms to her, his fingers spread wide. 'That seems extraordinary to me, it seems . . .' He raised his eyebrows. 'Are you frightened of your ex-husband, Mrs Myerson?'

'No.' Carla gave a brief shake of her head. 'No, I just . . . I didn't want to upset him,' she said quietly. 'I try my best not to upset Theo, and me having a relationship with Daniel would upset him.'

'Does Mr Myerson have a temper?'

Carla shook her head again. '*No*,' she insisted, exasperated, 'it's not . . . it's not like that.'

'What is it like?' Barker asked. He'd the air of someone genu-inely *interested*, he was looking at her as though she were a specimen, a curiosity. 'Did Mr Myerson think you were trying to replace your lost child? With your nephew? Is that why your relationship with Daniel upset him?' he asked.

Carla shook her head again, but said nothing. She turned her face from the detective and stared at the sad, paved back yard, with its padlocked shed and its blackened plants, dead in their pots.

The shed was empty save for a little red tricycle, bright blue tas-sels still attached to the handlebars. It had been a present for Ben's third birthday. They'd had a party at their home on Noel

Road, just family – Theo's parents, Angela and Daniel, Theo's older brother and his wife, their kids. After the cake, after the candles, they took the tricycle out on the towpath, Carla's chest aching with tenderness as she watched Ben try it out, his chubby legs pumping up and down as he pedalled as fast as he could. Theo's face! His *pride*. 'He's a natural, see that?' And Angela, smoking, one eyebrow arched. 'It's a *tricycle*, Theo. Everyone can ride a tricycle.' And on the way home, dusk falling, the crowds thinning, Daniel pushing Ben along. Theo's mother saying, 'Careful, Daniel, not too fast,' while Ben and Daniel ignored her completely, the pair of them shrieking with laughter as they careened around a corner, almost toppling over.

When Ben was gone, when the funeral was over and the godawful mourners finally banished, Carla went to bed and stayed there. Theo rarely came to bed at all. He remained fiercely, angrily awake; through her medicated haze Carla used to hear him pacing in his study off the landing, stomping down the stairs and through the kitchen to the garden to smoke and then stomping back again. She heard him turning the radio on and off, flicking through the channels on the television, playing half a track of a record before sending the needle skittering across the vinyl.

Sometimes he came upstairs and stood in the doorway, not watching her but staring out of the window opposite, his hand across his face, fingers working at his stubble. Sometimes he said things, statements that seemed to lead towards questions at which they never quite arrived. Sometimes he talked about Angela, about how she had been as a child. 'You said she had a temper,' he'd say, or: 'You always talked about her crazy imagination. *Bloodthirsty*, you said. She had a bloodthirsty imagination.'

Occasionally, he asked direct questions. 'Was she jealous, do you think? Of the way Ben was?'

It had been discussed between them, when Ben was alive, how difficult it must be for Angela not to draw comparisons between their son and her own. Ben hit all his milestones early, he was talkative and agile, empathetic and numerate before his third birthday. 'He'll be reading before his fourth,' Theo liked to tell people. Carla had to tell him not to boast.

Daniel hadn't been like that. He was a fussy baby, a poor sleeper, he'd taken for ever just to crawl, he was two and a half before he started to talk. He was a clumsy, frustrated little boy, prone to epic tantrums.

'Do you think it bothered her,' Theo asked, 'how special Ben was? Because Dan's a bit of a weird kid, isn't he? I know I'm not objective, no one is, not about their children, but even so, in this case, I think, objectively speaking, Ben was just the most wonderful little boy. He was—'

'What are you saying?' Carla's voice sounded like it belonged to someone else, to an old woman. 'What are you trying to say?'

He drew closer to the bed, his eyes wide, face flushed. 'I'm asking you whether you think Angela was jealous? If, on some level, she—'

Carla clutched at the bedsheets and drew herself painfully up to a sitting position. 'You're asking if I think my sister left that door open on purpose? Because she thought our son was more special than hers? You're asking if I think she wanted Ben to die?'

'No! Christ, no. Not that she *wanted* him to die, no. Jesus. I'm not saying she did anything on purpose, I'm just wondering if on some subconscious level she—'

Carla collapsed back to her side, drawing the duvet up over her shoulders, over her head. 'Leave me alone, Theo. Please leave me alone.'

*

It was a year before Carla redeveloped the habit of getting up every day, showering, dressing herself. It was eighteen months before she saw her sister again, in secret. She told Theo she had decided to join a yoga class, she dressed her weak, fleshy body in tracksuit bottoms and a T-shirt and walked over to her sister's house on Hayward's Place. When Angela opened the door to her, Carla recoiled in shock: her sister had aged not by eighteen months but by decades. She was emaciated, her sallow skin stretched tight over her skull. She looked hollowed out, desiccated.

Angela's hair went white overnight. That's what she said, in any case. Both sisters went grey young, but Angela claimed that she'd gone to bed on Tuesday a brunette and woken up on Wednesday almost completely grey. Just like that. She kept her hair long and didn't dye it. 'I look like a witch in a fairy tale, don't I?' she said. 'I terrify children in the supermarket.' She was joking, but Carla didn't find it funny. Carla didn't dye her hair either, she chopped it all off when it started to go grey. 'You're lucky,' Angela told her, and Carla flinched. 'You've got a nicely shaped head. If I cut all my hair off, I'd look like an alien.'

It was a compliment, but Carla was annoyed. She didn't like the sound of the word *lucky* in her sister's mouth, certainly didn't appreciate it being applied to her. 'You can't go grey overnight,' she said crossly. 'I looked it up. It's a myth.' True, although it was also true that she had read about young women, much younger than she and her sister, Soviet women fighting for the motherland in the Second World War, who'd faced such unspeakable terror they had greyed overnight. She'd read about Cambodian women who witnessed such horror they lost their sight.

'It happened to me,' Angela said. 'You can't say I didn't experience what I experienced. You wouldn't know, you weren't around.'

'Yoga classes' became a weekly thing, an exercise in determination on Carla's part. She believed in hard work; in fact, she believed that the most worthwhile goals were often the hardest to realize. She believed that if you worked hard enough at something, most often you would achieve it. Call it the ten-thousand-hours theory: if she spent ten thousand hours trying to forgive her sister, would she succeed? No way of telling, but it seemed a reasonable course of action. After all, her parents were gone, her son was gone. There was precious little left for her in the world: only Angela, and little Daniel, and Theo, of course, although she knew, in the saddest part of her heart, that she and Theo would not survive what had happened to them.

Once, when Carla came to visit Angela, she heard noises as she approached the front door, voices raised. She had barely finished knocking when the door flew open, her sister yanking at it as though she were trying to pull it off its hinges. 'Oh, Christ,' she said, when she saw Carla. 'Forgot it was our day. Daniel's off school. He's . . .' She broke off, shrugged. 'He's just . . . off school.'

They sat in the living room as they always did, and after a while Daniel came down to say hello. In their eighteen months of separation, Angela had aged by a decade and Daniel not at all. At nine years old he was still small for his age, dark and uncertain. He had a habit of sneaking around, appearing suddenly and without warning, wringing his hands together in front of his belly. 'Like a little animal,' Carla commented with a smile.

'A little savage,' his mother said.

That day, when he appeared, as if from nowhere, in the doorway and said, 'Hello, Aunt Carla,' he bared a mouthful of metal at her.

'Jesus, Daniel, don't make that face!' Angela snapped. 'It's his fucking braces,' she said. 'He can't smile normally any longer.

Most kids, when they get them, they try to hide their teeth. Not him – he pulls that awful expression all the time.'

'Angela,' Carla hissed, as Daniel slunk away as quietly as he'd arrived, 'he can hear you.'

Her heart, the bit of it that was left, broke for him.

The next time she came, she brought him a huge set of coloured pencils, which she took up to his room. His eyes shone when he saw the gift. 'Oh,' he breathed, delighted almost beyond words, 'Aunt Carla!' He smiled his ghastly smile, wrapping his skinny arms around her waist.

Carla froze. She was unprepared for how it took her, the feeling of a child's body against hers for the first time in so long; she could scarcely breathe, could hardly bear to look down at his small head, at the rich chestnut of his hair, at the nape of his neck, on which she noticed two bruises. Around the size of a finger and thumb, as though someone had grabbed him there and pinched hard. When Carla looked up, she caught her sister watching them.

'He gets into fights at school all the time,' she said, turning away. Carla heard her clumping down the stairs, her tread strangely heavy for one so light.

Carla let the child hold her for a little longer, and then, gently, she removed his arms from around her waist and crouched down so that her eyes were level with his. 'Is that true, Daniel?' she asked him. 'Have you been fighting?'

He wouldn't look at her for a moment. When he did, his expression was grave. 'Sometimes,' he said quietly, 'sometimes people don't . . . they don't . . .' He blew out hard through puffed cheeks. 'Oh, it doesn't matter.'

'It does matter, Dan. It does.'

'No, it doesn't,' he said, shaking his head gently, 'because I'm going away. I'm going to a new school. I'm going to live there, not here any more.' He hugged her again, his arms around her neck this time. She could hear his breathing, quick and light, like cornered prey.

Angela confirmed it; he was going to boarding school. 'His father's paying. It's the same one he went to, somewhere in Oxfordshire. It's quite good apparently.'

'*Somewhere in Oxfordshire? Angie, are you sure about this?*'

'You've no idea how difficult things are, Carla.' She lowered her voice. 'How difficult he is.' Her voice had that hard edge again. '*Don't*. Don't look at me like that. You don't see it, you don't . . . You're here once a fucking week, you don't see how he behaves when it's just me and him, you don't . . . He was traumatized. *Severely* traumatized by what happened to him.'

Carla gave a swift shake of the head and Angela said, 'I know you don't want to hear this, but it's true.' She reached for her cigarettes, fumbled one out of the pack. Angela's hands shook all the time now. Before, she'd been a little shaky the morning after the night before, but now it was constant, a tremor in hands that were always moving, always reaching for something to occupy them: a glass, a book, a lighter.

'Yes, of course he's traumatized.'

'The psychologist says,' Angela said, lighting her cigarette, taking a drag, 'that now he's telling her that he saw . . . you know, that he *saw* him fall, that he saw Ben fall. He's saying that it wasn't just that he found him, but that he actually saw it.' She closed her eyes. 'He's saying that he screamed and screamed, that no one came. He's saying—'

Carla held up her hand – Angela was right, she didn't want to hear this. 'Please,' she said. She took a moment to allow her breath to steady. 'But surely they can't think – *you* can't think – that the answer to his trauma is to separate him from his mother?'

'*His mother* is the whole problem,' Angela said, crushing her half-smoked cigarette in the ashtray. 'He blames me, Carla, for what happened.' She looked up at her sister, wiping tears from her cheeks with the back of her hands. 'He told his psychologist that what happened was my fault.'

It was *your fault*, Carla thought. *Of course, it was your fault.*

11

Could you open your mouth a bit wider, please, sir? There was a young woman, brisk and uniformed, bending towards him, inserting a plastic stick into his mouth; and while the experience ought to have been intrusive and unpleasant, Theo was disappointed to admit to himself that he found it stirring. He closed his eyes, but that only made it worse. He tried not to look at her while she was taking his fingerprints, but when finally he met the young woman's eye he could tell that she sensed something, something that made her uncomfortable, and he felt like a total shit. He wanted to say to her, *I'm sorry, I really am. I'm not like that. I'm not one of those. I'm a one-woman man.*

Theo had only ever loved Carla. There were women before and there had been the occasional one since, but Carla was without question the one. The one and the many, he supposed, because there was this Carla and there was the previous Carla; it seemed as though over the course of his life he'd known multiple Carlas and loved them all, would continue to love them in whatever incarnation they appeared.

Carla was all he had. There had been Ben, of course, for that short, glorious interlude, those three years and forty-seven days of joy, but now there was just Carla. Carla, and his work.

Fifteen years ago, when Ben died, Theo had been deep into his third novel. He abandoned it without much thought, he simply couldn't bear to read words he'd written while Ben played on the lawn outside, or sang with his mother in the kitchen. For a year or two, he couldn't write at all, he barely even tried, and then, when he did try, nothing came. For months and months, for *years*, nothing came. How to write, when his heart hadn't been broken but removed from his body? *What* to write? Anything, his agent told him. It doesn't matter. Write anything. So he did. He wrote a story about a man who loses his child but saves his wife. He wrote a story about a man who loses his wife but saves his child. He wrote a story about a man who murders his sister-in-law. It was awful, all of it. 'It's like pulling teeth,' he told his agent. 'Worse than that. It's like pulling fingernails.' With his heart gone, everything he did was worthless, sterile, inconsequential. 'What if,' he asked his agent as he sat, terrified, in front of a blank screen, 'I cannot work any longer because the man who wrote books is gone?'

All the while, Carla slipped away from him. She was there but not there, a wraith in the house, slipping out of rooms when he entered them, closing her eyes when he crossed her field of vision. She went to yoga classes and returned not at all Zen-like but unsettled, angry, crashing through the house and out into the garden, where she would sit, scratching at the skin on her forearms until it bled. His attempts to reach out to her were clumsy, he saw later, ill-judged. The idea they should try for another baby was met with cold fury.

Theo began to spend less and less time at home. He travelled to writers' festivals, he gave lectures at far-flung universities. He had a brief and unsatisfying affair with his much younger publicist. Finally, Carla left him, although her desertion lacked conviction. She bought a house five minutes' walk away.

Theo tried non-fiction; he tried to write about the low value assigned to fatherhood, he questioned the truths of female liberation, he pondered a return to more traditional (sexist) values. He *hated* himself. And he could not begin to find the words for the scope of his loss, the depth of his anger.

Without his son, his wife, his work, Theo became desperate.

After the police had left, Theo went out for a walk. It was his habit to take a quick turn around the neighbourhood about this time, just before lunch, to prevent himself from eating too early. He had a tendency towards gluttony. In the hallway, he reached for his coat and, instinctively, for the dog's lead, only to withdraw his empty hand. The odd thing wasn't that he reached for it – he still did that every other day, he wasn't yet used to Dixon's absence. No, the odd thing was that Dixon's lead wasn't there. He looked about, but couldn't see it anywhere. The cleaner must have moved it, he thought, though he couldn't for a second think why.

Usually he'd head along the towpath but, given that it was still cordoned off by the police, he headed up over the bridge on Danbury Street instead. There was a man in uniform there, too – a young man with a shaving rash, who grinned when he saw Theo, raising his hand in greeting before self-consciously pulling it away.

Theo saw an opening.

'Still searching, are you?' he said, walking over to talk to the young man. 'Looking for clues?'

The officer's face flushed. 'Uh . . . yes, well. Looking for a weapon, actually.'

'Of course,' Theo said. 'Of course. The weapon. Well . . .' he said, looking up and down the canal as though he might spot the knife from up there on the bridge, 'best let you get on with it. Good luck!'

'And to you, too!' the policeman said, and he blushed furiously.

'I'm sorry?'

'Oh, it's just . . . your writing and that. Sorry. I . . .'

'No, that's quite all right.'

'I'm a fan, that's all. Yeah. I'm a big fan of *The One Who Got Away*. I thought it was so interesting, the way you turned the whole thing around, you know, telling the story all backwards and forwards, letting us see inside the killer's head – that was so brilliant! At first you don't know what's going on, but then it's just like . . . *woah*. So cool. I loved the way you turned everything on its head, playing with our sympathies and empathies and all that business . . .'

'*Really?*' Theo laughed, faking incredulity. 'I thought every-body thought that was a terrible idea!'

'Well, I didn't. I thought it was clever. A new way to tell a story like that, makes you think, doesn't it? Will you be writing another one, do you think? Another crime novel, I mean. Another,' he paused to air quote, ' "*Caroline MacFarlane*"?'

Theo shrugged. 'I don't know. I'm thinking about it, cer-tainly.' He waved an arm vaguely in the direction of the water. 'I could take inspiration from this mess, couldn't I? I could call it *The Boy on the Boat*.' They both laughed awkwardly.

'Is that where you get your ideas from, then?' the policeman asked. 'From real life?'

'Well, now there's a question . . .' Theo said, tailing off in the hope that the policeman didn't really expect an answer to this.

There was a moment's uncomfortable pause before the young man said, 'Because, you see, if you ever wanted, you know, to discuss ideas for crime novels, like, maybe aspects of police work, or forensics, or anything like that,' – the policeman was talking to him, Theo realized, he ought to be paying attention – 'I might be able to help out with things like that. For example—'

'That's very good of you,' Theo said, beaming at him. 'Very kind indeed. I, uh, well, for now I suppose I was just wondering, you know, how much progress you're making at the moment? On this case, my, uh, my nephew's case?' The policeman pursed his lips. Theo stood back, spreading his fingers, palms upwards. 'Look,' he said, 'I understand you can't give *details*. I was just wondering, because, you know, this has been so upsetting for us, for my wife, for Carla, she's been through an awful lot lately, and if an arrest were imminent, well, it would be a huge relief for both of us, of course . . .'

The officer inhaled sharply through his teeth. 'We-ell,' he said, ducking his head a little, 'as you say, I can't give details . . .'

Theo nodded sympathetically, his expression rueful. He fished around in his jacket pocket and extracted a packet of cigarettes. He offered one to the policeman, who accepted.

'Look, I can tell you,' the policeman said as he leaned closer to Theo to light his cigarette, 'that there's some forensic testing going on at the moment, and as I'm sure you know, these things take a little while, we don't get the results overnight, it's not like *CSI* or any of that rubbish . . .'

'Forensic tests . . . ?' Theo prompted.

'Clothing,' the young man said, his voice low. 'Bloody clothing.'

'Ah.' That was reassuring. 'Bloody clothing belonging to . . . that girl? The one you questioned? Because, you know, I saw her. Running from the scene. That morning, I saw her, and I didn't do anything. So stupid. I just thought, you know, she was a drunk or something.'

'Mr Myerson' – the policeman arranged his face into an expression of deep concern – 'there was nothing you could have done. There was nothing anyone could have done for Mr Sutherland, his injuries were much too severe.'

Theo nodded. 'Yes, of course. Of course. But, to return to this girl, she's the primary focus, is she, for the moment? There's not . . . oh, I don't know, a drugs connection, or theft, or . . . ?'

The young man shook his head sadly. 'I can't tell you that as yet,' he said. 'We're pursuing a number of leads.'

'Of course,' Theo said, nodding vigorously, thinking about how *pursuing a number of leads* was really code for *we haven't the faintest idea what's going on*. He made to walk away, but he could see as he did that this policeman, this spotty young man, was desperate to give him *something*, to prove his importance, his worth, and so Theo asked, 'Can you tell me anything about her? The girl? Not her name, of course. I was just wondering, you know, because I assume she's local, they said in the papers she was a resident of Islington, and now she's out there, wandering around, and of course because of my . . . my public profile, it's not difficult to find out who I am and who my wife is, and the thing is, well, perhaps I'm being paranoid, but what I want to know is, is she dangerous, this person? Well, evidently she's dangerous, but is she a danger to me? To us?'

The young man, clearly intensely uncomfortable and at the same time filled with the desire to impart top-secret information, leaned towards Theo. 'She does have a history,' he said quietly.

'A history?'

'Of violence.'

Theo shrank back, aghast.

'Look, it's nothing to panic about. She's just . . . she's unstable. That's all I'm telling you. That's all I can say. Look, I want to reassure you here, I do – we're dragging the canal again this afternoon. We're still searching for the weapon, and once we've got that, then Bob's your uncle. Once we've got that, an arrest has got to be imminent.'

*

94

Back at his desk, feeling somewhat reassured, Theo sorted through his mail, including the few fan letters forwarded on from his agent's office. Time was when there were dozens of these a day and they were dealt with by one of his agent's minions, but the flow had stemmed somewhat over the years. Theo didn't do social media, he didn't reply to emails, but if someone bothered to put pen to paper, he tended to reply to them personally.

> Dear Mr Myerson/Miss MacFarlane,
> I hope you don't mind me writing to you, I am a big fan of your crime novel *The One Who Got Away*, and I was wondering where you got your ideas from?

Theo released a groan of exasperation. *Good God.* Were *ideas* really such a hard thing to come by? Putting them into words, on to paper, that was another story, but ideas were ten a penny, weren't they?

> Specifically where did you get the idea for this book? Was it from a newspaper report or from talking to the police? I am thinking of writing a crime thriller myself and I enjoy reading crime reports on the internet. Do you sometimes ask the police for help with plots, specific crimes, working things out etc?
> Also I was wondering why in the One who Got Away the characters aren't given names. That is quite unusual isn't it.
> Please could you reply to me by email because I am eager to hear your answers to my questions.
> Yours sincerely,
> Henry Carter
> henrycarter759@gmail.com

PS I disagreed with the reviews that said the book was 'mis-ogynist' and 'pretentious', I think they didn't understand the story properly.

Theo laughed at that, and slid the letter on to the top of his in-tray, promising himself that he'd get to it tomorrow. He stood up, reaching across the desk for his cigarettes, and as he did he looked up and out of the window, across the garden towards the towpath, where, standing stock still and looking right at him, was Miriam Lewis.

'Jesus Christ!' He jumped backwards, almost falling over his desk chair in fright. Swearing loudly, he hurried down the stairs, rushed out into the garden and flung open the back gate, look-ing desperately around. She was gone. Theo walked up and down the towpath for a few minutes, his hands clenched into fists at his sides, passers-by skirting around him with nervous expressions. Had she really been here? Or was he seeing things now, was this where he'd got to?

Without his wife, his son, his work, Theo had become desperate, and in desperation he wrote a crime novel. It was his agent's suggestion. 'When I said write anything,' he said, 'I meant it. *Anything*, just to get back into the habit. Try sci-fi, romance, whatever – you won't believe some of the swill that gets pub-lished under the banner of commercial fiction. It doesn't matter if it's any good, it doesn't need to have worth. We'll slap some-one else's name on it. Just write *something*.' And so he tried. Romance was a bust and he didn't have the brain for sci-fi, but crime? Crime he could see working. He loved *Morse*, he'd read Dostoevsky. How hard could it be? All he needed was the right hook, the right concept, and he'd be away. And then an idea came to him, landed right on his doorstep, and he took it and ran with it, he worked with it, crafted it, made it into something distinctive.

The One Who Got Away, published under the pseudonym Caroline MacFarlane, was a highly experimental book, the plot unfolding backwards in some sections, forwards in others, with the point of view occasionally swinging 180 degrees so that the killer's innermost thoughts were revealed to the reader. It was a book that exposed the way the sympathies of the reader might be manipulated, laying bare how quickly we jump to conclusions about guilt and innocence, power and responsibility.

The experiment was not an *unqualified* success. Although Theo had carefully hidden his identity, using a woman's name for his pseudonym ('Women love crime!' his agent told him. 'They enjoy the catharsis of victimhood'), the secret didn't keep. Someone let the cat out of the bag, which meant of course that the book became an instant bestseller, but it also had the critics sharpening their knives (some of the reviews were quite vicious), and it brought all the crazies out of the woodwork. ('You stole my story!') It achieved its central aim, however. It got Theo writing again. That was the thing: when the muse fell silent, Theo refused to give up, he seized upon a scrap of a story and he made it his own. That was the truth of it.

The One Who Got Away

Anticipation. Sometimes it's the best part, because things don't always turn out like you want them to, but at least you should be grateful, shouldn't you, for the sunshine, hot on your back, and the girls going out in their short skirts and crop tops?

At the pub he sees a girl sitting with her ugly friend and she's wearing a skirt, not a crop top but a white T-shirt and no bra, and she's beautiful.

She hitches up her skirt to give him a better look and he's grateful for that, so he smiles at her, but instead of smiling back she makes a face and says to her ugly friend, as if.

As if.

He feels all wrong, like he's being hollowed out from the inside, like something's eating him up, and he feels a terrible craving, a longing left by the place her smile should have been.

12

Miriam thought she might not make it back to the boat. She thought she might pass out right there on the towpath; she could feel it coming, the crashing wave of panic, her field of vision narrowing, darkness crowding in, chest tight, breath coming in gasps, heart pounding. She crashed down the stairs into her cabin and collapsed on to the bench, head hanging, chin to chest, elbows on her knees, trying to regulate her breathing, trying to slow her racing heart.

Stupid, stupid, stupid. She should never have gone over there to see him – who knows what might have happened? He might have called the police, he might have claimed she was harassing him – she could have ended up jeopardizing everything she'd been working towards.

She had given in to her desire, her impatient desire to see Myerson, just to catch a glimpse of him. She was getting no joy at all from the news: two days had passed since her call to Detective Barker and she'd yet to hear anything about anyone new being questioned in connection with Daniel's death.

She had started to wonder – perhaps they hadn't taken her seriously? It wouldn't be the first time someone had claimed to have her interests at heart, had pretended to listen to her and had then dismissed her out of hand. Perhaps Myerson had said something about her, something to discredit her? That was why she'd needed to see him, to see his face, to see written on it fear or stress or unhappiness.

And she knew exactly where to direct her gaze: up at the window looking out over the garden. That was the window to his study, in front of which stood the stout mahogany desk at which Theo Myerson toiled, head bent over his laptop, cigarette burning down in the square glass ashtray as he crafted sentences and conjured images. As, in an affront that felt like an act of violence, he wrote Miriam out of her own story.

When Miriam pictured Myerson in his home, at his desk, wandering down to the kitchen to fix himself a snack, pausing, perhaps, in front of the framed picture in the hall of him and his wife, young and vital and wreathed in smiles, she was not conjuring these details out of thin air. She had visited Theo's beautiful Victorian house on Noel Road, she had walked through the entrance hall and into a dark corridor, painted some fashionable shade of ash or stone, mole's breath or dead fish. She'd admired the paintings on the walls, the jewel-coloured Persian rug laid over original wooden floorboards, the drawing room lined with bookshelves groaning under the weight of glossy hardbacks; she'd noticed, with a sharp twinge of pity, the silver-framed photograph on the table in the hall of a smiling, dark-haired toddler.

Miriam had been working at the bookshop for no more than six months the first time Myerson appeared, strolling along the towpath with his dog, a small terrier, a tiresome yapper that he would tether to a mooring while he browsed the books. Myerson and Nicholas, Miriam's boss, would gossip about what was selling well and what was bombing, about who was getting savaged on the pages of the *London Review of Books* and who was in the running for the Booker. In the shadows behind a shelf, Miriam eavesdropped, unseen.

She'd read his books – most people had. His first, published back in the mid-1990s, had moderate sales and good reviews; the second was a runaway bestseller. After that, he disappeared, not just from the bestseller lists but from bookshops altogether; his name would crop up in the odd Saturday supplement feature, the great literary success story of the Nineties undone by personal tragedy.

Miriam had always considered his writing overrated. But she found that even she was not immune to the glamour of a brush with celebrity – it was odd how quickly one began to reassess the quality of someone's work once its creator was no longer an abstract, no longer just a smug photograph on a book jacket, but a living, breathing person with a shy smile and a smelly dog.

One day, a Wednesday morning in early summer, perhaps six months after he'd first started visiting the shop, Myerson turned up while Miriam was minding the shop alone. He tethered the dog as usual, and Miriam brought it a bowl of water. He thanked her graciously, asking whether they had in any copies of the new Ian Rankin. Miriam checked and discovered that it wasn't published yet, it was due in the following week. She'd set aside a copy for him, if he liked? He replied that he would, and they began to chat. She asked if he was working on something new and he said that he was, that in fact he was thinking of trying his hand at crime. 'Really?' Miriam was surprised. 'I wouldn't have thought that was your cup of tea.'

He bobbed his head from side to side, a wry smile on his face. 'We-ell,' he said, 'it's not, really, but I seem to find myself in something of a rut.' It was true, more than a decade had passed since he'd published anything substantial. 'I was thinking I might try something completely different,' he said, tapping the side of his temple with his forefinger. 'See if I can shake something loose.'

The following week, when the new Rankin duly arrived, Miriam set aside a copy. Only Theo didn't turn up to fetch it, not that day, or the next, or the next. She had his address – they'd mailed books to him in the past – and she knew exactly where he lived, it wasn't very far from her narrowboat, less than a mile further along the canal, so she decided to deliver it by hand.

She wasn't sure if this would be an intrusion, but in fact, when he opened the door, he seemed genuinely pleased to see her. 'That's so kind of you,' he said, inviting her in. 'I've been a bit under the weather.' He looked it. Dark circles under his eyes, whites yellowing around the pupils, his face flushed. The house reeked of smoke. 'Difficult for me,' he said, his voice cracking, 'this time of year.' He didn't elaborate and Miriam didn't probe. Awkwardly she laid a hand on his arm and he pulled away, smiling, embarrassed. Miriam had felt such tenderness towards him, when first she got to know Theo Myerson.

They took their tea out on to the little patio outside his kitchen and talked books. It was the start of summer, evenings lengthening, the smell of wisteria heavy in the air, music playing softly on a radio somewhere. Leaning back, eyes closed, Miriam felt an immense sense of contentment, of privilege. To be sitting here, in this gem of a London garden, right in the middle of the city, conversing on myriad topics with this distinguished writer at her side! She glimpsed, opening up in front of her, the possibility of a quite different life from the one she currently led, a far richer (in the cultural sense), more *peopled* life. Not that she imagined anything romantic, not with Theo. She wasn't stupid. She had seen pictures of his wife, she knew that she did not compare. But here he was, treating her as an equal. As a friend. When she left that evening, Theo shook her warmly by the hand. 'Drop by any time,' he said with a smile. And, foolishly, she took him at his word.

The next time she came to see him, she had an offering. Something she thought might draw them together. A book, *her* book, telling her own story, a memoir she had been working on for years, but which she had never had the courage to show to anyone, because she had never trusted anyone enough to let them see her secret truth. Until she met Myerson, a real writer, a man who also lived with tragedy. She chose him.

She chose badly.

She believed she was entrusting her story to a man of integrity, a man of good character, when in fact she was baring her soul to a charlatan, a predator.

You'd have thought she'd be able to recognize them by now.

The first predator Miriam ever met was called Jeremy. Jez for short. On a stifling Friday afternoon in June, he picked them up, Miriam and her friend Lorraine, in his pale blue Volvo estate. They were hitchhiking – people used to do that in the 1980s, even in Hertfordshire. They'd bunked off the last two periods at school and were headed into town to hang out, smoke cigarettes, try on clothes they couldn't afford to buy.

When the car pulled up, Lorraine got into the front seat, because why wouldn't she? She was the slim one, the prettier one (although to be honest they were neither of them lovely). She was the one he stopped for. So she got the front seat. Miriam climbed into the back, she sat behind Lorrie's head. The driver said hello and told them his name and asked for theirs, but he never looked at Miriam, not once.

In the footwell of the car, empties rattled around Miriam's feet, beer cans and a whisky bottle. There was an odd smell, underneath the smoke from Jez and Lorraine's cigarettes, something sour, like old milk. Miriam wanted to get out of the car almost the second she got in. She knew they shouldn't be doing this, she knew it was a bad idea. She opened her mouth to speak, but the car was already moving, accelerating hard. Miriam wondered what would happen if she opened the door – would he slow down? Most likely he'd think she was mad. She wound down her window, breathed in the hot summer air.

A song came on the radio, a slow one, and Jeremy reached out to change the station, but Lorraine put her hand on his arm. 'Don't,' she said. 'I like this one. Don't you like this one?' She started to sing.

'For the time I had with her, I won't be sorry
What I took from her, I won't give back.'

Jez didn't take them into town, he took them back to his place, 'for a smoke'.

'We have cigarettes,' Miriam said, and Lorrie and Jez both laughed.

'Not that sort of smoke, Miriam.'

Jez lived in a shabby farmhouse a few miles outside town. The house was at the end of a long lane, a winding road to nowhere, the tarmac getting narrower and narrower until by the time they'd got to the gate it had dwindled all the way to nothing and they were bumping along a dirt track. Miriam's stomach was in knots, she thought she might actually shit herself. Jez got out of the car to open the gate.

'I think we should go,' Miriam said to Lorraine, her voice quivering, urgent. 'This is weird. He's weird. I don't like this.'

'Don't be such a wuss,' Lorrie said.

Jez drove the car into the driveway and parked next to another car, an old white Citroën; when Miriam saw it, her heart gave a little leap. Her mother used to have a car like that. It was the sort of car middle-aged women drove. Perhaps *his* mum was here, she thought, and then she noticed that the car's tyres were flat, the chassis resting on the ground. Despite the heat, she shivered.

Jez got out of the car first, Lorraine followed him. Miriam hesitated for a moment. Perhaps she should just stay in the car? Lorraine looked back at her, widening her eyes. *Come on!* she mouthed, gesturing for Miriam to follow.

She climbed out, her legs trembling as she walked towards the house. As she stepped from bright sunlight into shadow, she saw that the house wasn't just shabby, it was derelict. The windows to the upstairs rooms were broken, the downstairs ones boarded up. 'You don't live here!' Miriam said, her tone indignant. Jez turned and looked at her for the first time, his face blank. He said nothing. He turned away, taking Lorraine by the arm as he did. Lorraine glanced back over her shoulder at Miriam, and Miriam could see that she was frightened too.

They walked into the house. It was filthy, bottles and plastic bags and cigarette packets strewn over the floor. There was a strong smell of shit, and not animal shit either. Miriam put her hand over her nose and mouth. She wanted to turn back, to run back outside, but something prevented her from doing so; something kept her moving forward, one foot in front of the other, walking behind Lorraine and Jez, down a hallway, past a staircase, into what must once have been a living room, because there was a broken-down sofa pushed up against a wall.

Miriam thought that if she acted normal, then maybe everything would just *be* normal. She could force it to be normal. Just because this *felt* like the kind of thing that happened in a horror movie didn't mean it would *be* like a horror movie – quite the opposite. In horror movies, the girls never saw it coming. They were so stupid.

They were so stupid.

The One Who Got Away

She wakes.

Joints stiff, hip aching, part blind, unable to breathe. Unable to breathe! She jolts, rocks herself upright into a sitting position, her heart thundering in her chest. She is dizzy with adrenaline. She inhales sharply through her nose. She can breathe, but there is something in her mouth, something soft and wet, a gag. She retches, tries to spit it out. Hands behind her back, she struggles, pushing through pain. Finally, she pulls her right hand free, takes the rag from her mouth. A T-shirt, she sees, faded blue.

In another room, not too far away, someone is crying.

(She can't think about that now.)

On her feet. Her right eye will not open. With her fingernails, the girl delicately picks a crust of blood from her eyelashes. That helps, a little. It opens, a little. Now she has perspective.

The door is locked, but there is a window, and she is on the ground floor. The window is small, granted, and she is not slender. It is not quite dark. Towards the horizon, over to the west, a murmuration forms, dissipates, re-forms. The sky fills with birds, empties, fills again, and it is beautiful. If she stays right here, the girl thinks to herself, right here on this spot, if she watches, it will never grow dark, and he will never come for her.

The sobbing grows louder and she steps back from the window. She can no longer see the birds.

Like the door, the window is locked, but the glass is a single pane, breakable. Breakable, but not silently breakable – will she have time to get out before he comes? Will she be able to force her flesh through that small space at all? Her friend would be able to. Her friend is slender, she did ballet until she was thirteen, her body bends in ways the girl's does not.

(She cannot think of her friend now, of the way her body bends, of how far it might bend before it breaks.)

The crying stops, starts again, and she can hear a voice, saying, please, please. The funny thing is (not funny, not really) that it's not her friend's voice, it's his voice. He is the one who is begging.

13

Laura woke up on the sofa, fully dressed, her mouth dry. She rolled over and on to the floor, grabbing her phone. She'd missed calls: from Irene, from two different numbers she didn't recognize, from her father. She dialled her voicemail to listen to his message.

'Laura,' a voice that was not her father's said, 'it's Deidre here, I'm calling from Philip's phone. Mmmm.' Among the many teeth-grindingly annoying things about Deidre was her habit of punctuating her speech with a weird humming sound, as though she was about to burst into song, if only she could find the right note. 'We got your message, and the thing is, Laura, the thing is that we already agreed, didn't we, that we wouldn't just be handing over money every time you get yourself into trouble. You need to learn to sort these things out for yourself. Mmmm. My Becky is getting married this summer, as you know, so we've considerable demands on our finances as it is. We have to prioritize. Mmmm. All right, then. Goodbye, Laura.'

Laura wondered if her dad had even heard the message, or whether Deidre listened to them first and screened out the ones she didn't deem important. She hoped that was the case; it was less hurtful that way, to imagine that he didn't even know she was in trouble. She *could* call him. She could find out for sure. She just wasn't quite sure she could stand to.

Her heart in her mouth, she scrolled through the BBC News site looking for stories about Daniel's murder, but was disappointed. No updates since yesterday, the police were pursuing a number of different lines of enquiry, they were appealing for witnesses to come forward. She wondered how many there would be, how many people had seen her that morning, down on the towpath with blood on her lips?

She distracted herself by texting Irene.

So so sorry I've had some problems ☹

on my way now get yr shopping list ready see you v soon ☺

Usually, she'd ask Irene to text her shopping list so she could pick up the groceries on her way over, but this time she was going to have to ask for the money up front.

A woman, familiar in some vague way, opened Irene's door when Laura knocked.

'Oh,' Laura said. 'Is . . . is Mrs Barnes in? I'm Laura, I'm . . .'

She didn't finish her sentence because the woman had already turned away and was saying, 'Yes, yes, she's here, come in,' in a tone that suggested annoyance. 'Looks like your little helper has turned up, after all,' she heard the woman say.

Laura stuck her head around the living-room door. 'All right, gangster?' she said, grinning at Irene, who usually laughed whenever she said this, but not this time. She looked quite anxious.

'Laura!' she exclaimed, raising her crooked little hands into the air. 'I've been so worried. Where *have* you been?'

'Oh, I'm sorry, mate.' Laura crossed the room to give Irene a kiss on the cheek. 'The week I've had, like, you would not *believe*.

I'll tell you all about it, I will, but how are you? You doing all right, yeah?'

'Since your *friend* is here,' the other woman was saying, her voice clipped, cut-glass, 'I think I'll get on. Is that all right?' she asked, tilting her head to one side. 'Irene?' She slung what Laura judged to be a very expensive handbag over her shoulder, collected a couple of shopping bags from the doorway and thrust a piece of paper in Laura's direction. 'Her list,' she said, fixing Laura with a withering look. 'You'll see to that, will you?'

'I will, yeah,' Laura said, and she glanced at Irene, who pulled a face.

'I'll show myself out,' the woman said, and she stalked smartly from the room, slamming the front door behind her. A moment later, Laura heard another door slam.

'Who is *that*?' she asked.

'That's Carla,' Irene said, raising an eyebrow. 'Carla Myerson, my friend Angela's sister.'

'Warm, isn't she?' Laura said, giving Irene a wink.

Irene harrumphed. 'Somehow, in Carla's presence I always feel looked down upon, and I don't just mean because she's tall. She talks to me as though I'm a fool. An old fool. She drives me potty.' She paused, gently shaking her head. 'But I shouldn't be unkind. She may not be my favourite person in the world, but she's had an awful time of it. Her sister passing away, and then her nephew . . .'

'Oh *yeah*,' Laura said, as the truth dawned on her. *That* was why she looked familiar – she looked a bit like him. Something around the eyes, the set of the mouth, the way she tilted her chin up a little when she spoke. 'Oh God. I didn't think about that. So she's his aunt?'

'That's right,' Irene said, her eyebrows knitting together. 'I take it you heard about what happened to Daniel, then?' she asked, and Laura nodded.

'Yeah. Yeah, you could say that.'

'It's been all over the news, hasn't it? And they haven't caught the people who did it . . .'

'Early days, I suppose,' Laura said, her gaze slipping away from Irene's, gratefully casting her eye over the list that the woman had given her, frowning as she did. 'Is this your list? Did she write this?'

Irene nodded. 'Oh yes, she didn't have the patience to wait for me to think of the things I needed, she just went into the kitchen and looked in my cupboards and *deduced*.'

Laura rolled her eyes. '*Muesli?* You don't like muesli, you like Crunchy Nut Cornflakes.'

'I did tell her that,' Irene said, 'but she wasn't having it.'

'Wild rice? What the actual . . . Jesus *Christ*.' Laura ripped up the list, tossing the pieces into the air like confetti. 'What you should do, yeah, when you think of something you need, is make a note on your phone . . .'

'Oh, I can't type on those things, it's all too small and I can't see what's going on even with my glasses and half the time the damn thing changes your words without you asking, so you end up with gibberish.'

'No, no,' Laura protested, 'you don't have to *type* anything. What I do, see, is record stuff. I've got a terrible memory so as soon as I think of something I need to do or buy or whatever, I just use the voice recorder. So you don't need to type, you just need to say stuff.'

Irene shook her head. 'Oh, no, I don't think so. I've no idea how that works. I'm not even sure I have one of those on my phone.'

'Course you do.' Laura picked up Irene's handset and swiped the screen. She located the voice-recorder app and clicked on it. 'Crunchy Nut Cornflakes,' she enunciated loudly. 'Not sodding muesli.' She winked at Irene. 'Then, see here, you can play it back.

'*Crunchy Nut Cornflakes. Not sodding muesli,*' the phone intoned.

'Oh, that does look easy.' Irene laughed. 'Show me again.'

After they'd put together a new list, Irene told Laura to take a twenty-pound note from her purse to cover the shopping. Irene paid her five pounds per time to fetch her groceries, which was pretty generous since it generally took her all of fifteen minutes, but this time Laura helped herself to two twenties anyway. She spent fourteen pounds and pocketed the rest, losing the receipt on the way home.

While she unpacked the groceries, she filled Irene in on what had been going on – how she'd lost her key and had to break into her flat, how she'd hurt her arm and then lost her job on top of that. She left out the part about Daniel. Irene didn't want to hear about that, didn't want to hear about the fucking and the argument and the getting arrested.

'I'm really sorry I didn't get in touch earlier,' Laura told her, once she'd finished putting everything away, once she'd made them both a cup of tea and laid some chocolate biscuits out on a plate. 'I've just been all in a spin, you know?' Irene was sitting in her favourite chair and Laura was leaning up against the radiator under the window, her legs stuck out in front of her. 'I didn't mean to let you down.'

'Oh, Laura.' Irene shook her head. 'You didn't let me down, I was just worried about you. If something like that happens again, you must let me know. I might be able to help you.'

Laura thought of the money she'd taken and hated herself. She should give it back. She should slip it back into Irene's purse, and then just ask her, straight out, the way a normal person would, for a loan. For help, just like Irene said. It was too late now, though, wasn't it? Irene's bag was right there next to her chair, she couldn't put the money back now, there was no way she could do it without Irene noticing. And anyway, if ever there was a time to ask for help it had just passed, a few seconds back, when Irene offered it.

She stayed for a little while longer, time for another cup of tea, a couple more biscuits, but she'd barely any appetite; her dishonesty curdled within her, souring everything.

She made her excuses. She left.

On her way out, she noticed that the door to number three – Angela Sutherland's house next door – was slightly ajar. She pushed it open, very gently. Peering inside, she saw Carla Sutherland's coat draped over the banister, the expensive handbag hanging from the newel post, and the other bags, the shopper and the tote, just slung on the floor. Just lying there, within reach of an open door! Fucking rich people. Sometimes they just asked for it.

Back at home, she emptied the contents of the tote bag on to her living-room floor, her heart racing as, along with the crappy old scarf and the decent but ancient Yves St Laurent jacket, out came tumbling two small leather boxes. She grabbed the first, the purple box, and opened it: a gold ring, set with what looked like a large ruby. In the second, a slightly larger brown leather box, there was a St Christopher's medal, also gold, with the initials *BTM* engraved on the back, along with a date: *24th March 2000*. A christening present, maybe? Not for Daniel, the initials were wrong. Some other child. She snapped the box shut. It was a shame about the engraving, she thought, it made the medal less sellable. But the ring, if it was real, that must be worth a bit.

What a piece of shit she was.

In the kitchen, she emptied her pockets and counted out all

the cash she had to her name: thirty-nine pounds fifty, twenty-six of which she'd stolen from her friend, Irene.

What a lying, thieving lowlife.

Laura listened to the voice recordings on her own phone, listened to her own voice reminding her to contact the council about her housing benefit, to contact the building's maintenance people about the boiler (again), to call the nurse at the doctor's surgery to talk about renewing her prescription, to buy milk, cheese, bread, tampons . . .

She paused the recording, exhausted at the very prospect of all the things she had to do, at the obstacles she could already see rising in front of her. She scrolled quickly through her messages, from boys she'd been chatting to, prospects she'd been cultivating whom she now had no interest in and no energy for. She listened to her voicemails, one of them a cold call about insurance, the other a message from her psychologist.

'You've missed two appointments, Laura, so I'm afraid if you don't make the next one we're going to have to take you off the service, do you understand? I don't want to do that, because I think we've been making good progress and keeping you on a nice, even keel and we don't want all that hard work to go to waste, do we? So I'm expecting to see you on Monday afternoon at three, and if you can't make it, please ring me back today to reschedule.'

Laura slid lower into her chair; she gently massaged her scalp with the tips of her fingers, squeezing her eyes shut, tears sliding out from under her lids and across her cheekbones. *Stop stop stop*, she said quietly to herself. *If only it could stop.*

She had been referred to the psychologist after the fork incident. The psychologist was a nice enough woman with a small face and large eyes, she reminded Laura of some sort of woodland creature. She told Laura that she needed to stop *reacting*.

'You seem to spend your entire life firefighting, Laura. You keep lurching from one crisis to the next, so what we need to do is to find some way to break this pattern of reaction, we need to see if we can devise some strategies . . .'

Psychologists were always big on devising strategies: strategies to stop her acting out, lashing out, losing control. To make her stop and think, to prevent her from picking the wrong course of action. *You know your problem, Laura? You make bad choices.*

Well, possibly, but that was only one way of looking at it, wasn't it? Another way of looking at it might be to say, You know your problem, Laura? You were hit by a car when you were ten years old and you smacked your head on the tarmac, you suffered a fractured skull, a broken pelvis, a compound fracture of the distal femur, a traumatic brain injury, you spent twelve days in a coma and three months in hospital, you underwent half a dozen painful surgeries, you had to learn to speak again. Oh, and on top of all that, you learned, while you were still lying in your hospital bed, that you had been betrayed by the person you loved most in the world, the one who was supposed to love and protect you. Is it any wonder, you might say, that you are quick to take offence? That you're angry?

The One Who Got Away

In the place where her smile should have been there is a question: so, where are we off to, then? Now there's no space where her smile should have been, because now she is smiling and he's not angry any more, he's thinking of how it's going to be, he's wishing the friend wasn't there in the back, but if he just doesn't look at her doesn't think about her then maybe it'll be OK.

He doesn't like the way the friend looks at him. The way she looks at him reminds him of his mother, who he should have forgotten all about, but he hasn't. She was ugly, too, bitten by a dog when she was a girl and yapping about it ever since, her mouth scarred, lip twisted like she was sneering at you, which she usually was.

Scarred inside and out, always yelling, at him or at his dad, wanted him to be miserable, just like her, couldn't stand it whenever he was laughing or playing or happy.

Now look. He's thinking about his mother again. Why is she always in his head? It's the other one's fault, isn't it, the ugly one in the back, she's made him think of his mother, he thinks of her when he's doing things, all sorts of things – driving his car, trying to sleep, watching TV, when he's with girls, and that's the worst, makes him feel all hollow inside, like he's not got enough blood to fill him up. Makes it so he can't do anything. Can't see anything, except for red.

14

Irene was very worried about Laura. In her kitchen, gently heating a saucepan of baked beans to pour over her toast (Carla would not approve), she thought about phoning her up to make sure she was all right. She'd said she was ('Golden! You know I am!'), but she'd seemed distracted and anxious. Of course, she'd just lost her job, so she was bound to be worried, wasn't she? But it seemed like more than that. Today, Laura had seemed uneasy in Irene's company in a way Irene had never noticed before.

Not that she'd known her very long. Just a couple of months they had been in each other's lives, and yet Irene had quickly come to care for the girl. There was something so terribly raw about her, so unguarded, that Irene feared for her. Someone like that seemed so vulnerable to the worst the world had to offer. And Irene had come to rely on this vulnerable young woman, because without Angela she found herself alone. She was aware, of course, that there was a danger in allowing herself to see Laura somehow as a replacement for Angela.

They were, in their way, quite similar: both funny, kind, visibly fragile. The best thing about both Angela and Laura, from Irene's point of view, was that they didn't make assumptions. Laura didn't just assume Irene would be incapable of learning how to use a new app on her mobile phone; Angela didn't assume Irene would have no interest in the words of Sally Rooney. Neither of them assumed that Irene wouldn't laugh at a dirty joke (she would, if it were funny). They didn't assume that she would be physically incapable, or small-minded, or uninterested in the world. They did not see her, as Carla did, as a busybody, an old fool.

Irene was eighty years old, but she didn't feel eighty. Not just because she was, sprained ankle notwithstanding, a spritely, trim woman, but because it was impossible to feel eighty. Nobody *felt* eighty. When Irene considered it, she thought that she probably felt somewhere around thirty-five. Forty, maybe. That was a good age to feel, wasn't it? You knew who you were by then. You weren't still flighty or unsure, but you had not yet had time to harden, to become unyielding.

The truth was that you felt a certain way inside, and while the people who had known you your whole life still probably saw you that way, the number of *new* people who could appreciate you as that person, that *inside* person, rather than just a collection of the frailties of age, was limited.

And Irene no longer had too many people around who'd known her her whole life. Almost all of her old friends, hers and William's, had moved out of the city, many of them years ago, to be nearer to children or grandchildren. At the time it hadn't bothered Irene all that much, because as long as she had William she never felt remotely lonely. And then one bright March morning six years ago, William went off to get the newspaper and he never came home; he dropped dead in the newsagent's from a heart attack. Irene thought he was strong as an ox, she thought he'd go on for ever; she thought she might die from the shock, at first, but then that wore off, and the grief came, and that was worse.

A door slammed and Irene jumped. It was next door. Irene was well accustomed to the particular timbre of the front door slamming. She struggled to her feet, leaning forward to see out of the window, but there was no one there. Carla, presumably, doing God knows what. Angela had been gone for two months and still Carla came to the house, day after day, 'sorting through things', though Irene struggled to imagine what there was to sort – Angela hadn't had much. They came from money, Carla and Angela, but somehow Carla seemed to have ended up with most of it. Angela had the house, of course, but nothing else. She eked out a meagre living doing freelance editing and copy-writing work. She'd had her child young, that was the thing; his father was one of her university professors. There was an unhappy affair, an unexpected pregnancy, and Angela's life was derailed. She'd had a difficult time of it, Irene was aware, she'd struggled a great deal, with the money and the child-rearing and all of her demons.

People assumed you couldn't have much of a life without children, but they were wrong. Irene and William had wanted kids. It hadn't worked out for them, but Irene had had a perfectly good life anyway. A husband who loved her, a job as a dental receptionist that she'd enjoyed more than she'd ever expected to, volunteering at the Red Cross. Trips to the theatre, holidays in Italy. What was wrong with that? She could do with a bit more of it, if she were honest. And she wasn't done yet, despite what people thought; she wasn't in death's waiting room. She'd the Villa Cimbrone she wanted to visit, in Ravello, and Positano, where they'd filmed *The Talented Mr Ripley*. Oh, and Pompeii!

Irene had read in a newspaper article that the happiest people on earth were unmarried, childless women. She could see why, there was a lot to be said for that sort of freedom, for not being answerable to anyone, for living exactly how you pleased. Only, once you'd fallen in love you could never be truly free, could you? It was too late by then.

After William died, Irene fell into one of her moods. Depression, they called it now, though when she was younger it was just moods. Angela called it the Black Dog. Irene had been visited, infrequently, by the dog ever since she was a young woman. Sometimes she took to her bed, sometimes she plodded through. The moods took her suddenly, sometimes triggered by an obvious sadness (her third miscarriage, her last), though sometimes they descended without warning on the brightest of days. She kept her head above water and she never went under, because William didn't let her. William always saved her. And then when William was gone, miraculously, Angela stepped in.

The year William died, 2012, Christmas crept up on Irene. Somehow she'd managed to miss the gradual appearance on shop shelves of decorations and festive food, she'd turned a deaf ear to the annoying music, and then suddenly it was freezing cold, and it was December and people were carrying trees along the lane.

Irene received invitations – one from her friend Jen, who'd moved to Edinburgh with her husband, and another from a cousin she barely knew who lived in *Birmingham*, of all places – but she declined them with barely a thought. She couldn't face the Christmas travelling, she said, which was quite true, although the real reason she felt she ought to stay at home was that if she didn't spend Christmas alone this year, then next year would be the first one without William, or the one after that. All the Christmases for the rest of her life were going to be without William. She thought it best just to get the first one over with.

Angela, who was sensitive about this sort of thing, said that at least Irene should pop round on Christmas Eve. 'Daniel and I will be having a takeaway curry from the Delhi Grill,' she said. 'Delicious lamb chops. Won't you join us?'

Irene said that sounded very nice indeed. On the afternoon of the twenty-fourth, she went out to get her hair set and her nails painted, and to buy some small gifts: a copy of *The Hare with the Amber Eyes* for Angela and a voucher for art supplies for Daniel.

On returning home, she'd barely had time to put down her things when she heard the most peculiar sound, a kind of moaning, a lowing, almost. That strange, animal sound was interrupted sharply by another: something shattering, glass or china. Shouting came next. 'I cannot deal with you! It's four o'clock in the afternoon and look at you! Just look at you. Jesus!' Daniel's voice was high and strangled, the voice of someone at the end of their tether; Angela's was the voice of someone way past that. 'Get out!' she was screaming. 'Just get out, you . . . you *bastard*. God, how I wish—'

'What? What do you wish? Go on! Say it! What do you wish?'

'I wish you'd never been born!'

Irene heard the sound of someone crashing down the stairs, the front door slamming so hard the whole terrace seemed to shake. From the window she watched Daniel storm past, his skin livid, his hands balled into fists at his sides. Angela came reeling out into the street a few moments later, she was falling-down drunk. Literally – Irene had to go outside to help her up. She managed – after a fashion, after a great deal of consoling and cajoling and gentle and then not so gentle persuasion – to get Angela inside and up the stairs to bed.

Angela talked all the while, mumbling to herself, scarcely audible at times. Irene heard this, though: 'Everyone told me to get rid of it, you know that? I didn't listen. I didn't listen. Oh, I wish I'd had your good fortune, Irene.'

'My good fortune?' Irene repeated.

'To be barren.'

It was Boxing Day before Irene saw Angela again. Angela came round with a book (a collection of Shirley Jackson stories) and a box of chocolates, apologizing for the missed dinner. 'I'm so sorry, Irene,' she said. 'I feel awful, just awful, but . . . the thing is, Daniel and I had a row . . .'

She didn't seem to have any recollection of her fall, of what she'd said afterwards. Irene was still angry, she'd half a mind to repeat what Angela had said, to tell her how hurt she had been. Angela must have seen something in her face, perhaps had a flash of recollection, because her own face coloured suddenly, she looked ashamed and she said, 'It isn't me, you know. It's the drink.' She exhaled a short, painful breath. 'I know that's not an excuse.' She waited for a moment for some response and, when none came, stepped forward and kissed Irene lightly on the cheek. Then she turned away from her, towards the door. 'When they're born,' she said, her hand resting on the door handle, 'you hold them, and you imagine a glorious, golden future. Not money or success or fame or anything like that, but happiness. Such happiness! You'd see the world burn if only it meant they would be happy.'

15

Carla stood, distracted, in Angela's kitchen, which was empty save for an ancient kettle on the counter next to the stove top. Her mobile phone was buzzing; it kept buzzing, on and on. She didn't bother to look at it – it would either be Theo or the police, and she wasn't in the right frame of mind to talk to either. She'd already had the estate agent on the phone, wanting to set up a time to see the place so they could get it on the market in time for the peak home-buying season of late spring. She'd found the act of engaging in conversation – with the agent, with Irene next door – almost overwhelming.

She opened the cupboards above the sink and then closed them again, she checked down below. The cupboards were empty. She knew they were empty. She'd emptied them. What on earth was she doing? She was looking for something. What was it? Her phone? No, that was in her pocket. The tote bag! Where did she put the tote bag?

She left the kitchen and went back into the hallway, only to discover that she'd left the front door open. Jesus. She really was losing her mind. She gave the door a good kick, slamming it shut. She turned back, and stood, aimless, staring at the point on the wall just next to the kitchen doorway where the ghost of a picture hung. What used to hang there? She couldn't remember. What did it matter? What was she doing? What had she come in here for?

This forgetfulness was new. It came from sleep deprivation, she supposed, there was a reason why they used it as a form of torture, it robbed you of all capacity. She remembered this feeling, vaguely, from just after Ben was born. Only then the distraction had been suffused with joy, like being stoned. This was like being sedated. Or held underwater. This was more like after he died.

Carla wandered back into the kitchen and stood at the sink, looking out into the lane; she leaned forward, her head against the glass, and caught a glimpse of the girl – the one she'd met at Irene's – disappearing from view. Walking with a strange shuffle. There was something off about that girl. Weaselly. Pretty, but sharp-toothed. Sexually available. She put Carla in mind of that cart-wheeling young woman who'd been all over the newspapers a few years back, the one who murdered her friend. Or didn't murder her friend. Somewhere in France? No, Italy. Perugia, that was it. Jesus, *what on earth* was she thinking about now? She knew almost nothing about *this* girl – in fact, the only thing she did know was that in her spare time she visited old ladies to help them with their shopping. And here was Carla, casting her as one of the Manson family.

In her pocket, her phone buzzed again, an angry insect trapped in a jar, and she ground her teeth. Ignored it. *Tea,* she thought. *I'll have a cup of tea. Lots of sugar.* She went back into the kitchen, flicked on the kettle. She opened the cupboard above the sink. Still empty. *Oh, for God's sake.*

Carla turned off the kettle again and walked slowly upstairs; she felt exhausted, legs leaden. At the top, she paused, turned and sat, gazing down the stairs at the front door, at the space on the floor beside the radiator where once had lain a small Qashqai rug. Next to her, on the top stair, there was a tear in the carpet. She plucked at it, running her finger along the length of its neat slit, an inch or two long. Wear and tear. From the end of her nose, a tear dropped. *Worn and torn, Angie,* she thought. *That about sums us up.*

Wiping her face, she got to her feet and walked directly into Daniel's old room at the back of the house, empty save for the old single bed and the wardrobe with its door hanging off that the house-clearance firm had rejected. She placed the notebook she was carrying on top of the pile of papers at the bottom of the wardrobe and closed the door as best she could. Then she took the dog's lead from her pocket, shuffling her coat off her shoulders as she did so. She closed the bedroom door and looped the leather end of the lead over the coat hook, giving it a good tug. She left it hanging there, opened the door once more and wandered slowly, taking her time, along the hall to Angela's room, dragging her fingertips over the plasterwork as she went.

After Angela sent Daniel away to boarding school, Carla went round to visit less and less, until one day she stopped going altogether. There wasn't a reason – or rather, there wasn't just one reason, she simply found that she couldn't face it any longer. Fake yoga was over.

Years passed. Then one night, a good six or seven years after Ben's death, Carla was woken by a phone call, sometime after midnight, the allotted hour of dreaded telephone calls. She took a while to answer, to shake off the fug of chemically assisted sleep.

'Can I speak to Carla Myerson, please?' a woman said.

Carla's heart seized – Theo was in Italy, holed up in some

remote Umbrian farmhouse, trying to write – and people drove so badly there. *Theo* drove so badly there, he seemed to feel the need to join in.

'Mrs Myerson, could you possibly come down to Holborn police station? No, no, everything's all right, but we have a . . . Miss Angela Sutherland here, your sister? Yes, she's OK, she's just . . . she's had a bit to drink and got herself into a bit of trouble, she needs someone to pick her up. Could you do that, do you think?'

Carla called a taxi and threw on some clothes, then stumbled out into freezing London rain, unsure whether to feel terrified or furious.

The police station was quiet and brightly lit. In the waiting area a woman sat alone, crying softly to herself, saying, 'I just want to see him. I just want to know he's all right.'

The woman on reception, quite possibly the one she'd spoken to on the phone, nodded at Carla. 'Domestic,' she said, indicating the crying woman. 'He lumps her one, she calls us, then decides that she doesn't actually want to press charges after all.' She rolled her eyes. 'What can I do for you, love?'

'I'm here to pick up Angela Sutherland. She's my sister. I was told she was here.'

The woman checked her computer screen and nodded, called out to someone in a room somewhere behind her desk. 'Could you bring Mrs Sutherland out for me, John? Yeah, her sister's here.' She turned back to Carla. 'She'd had too much to drink and caused a scene at the taxi rank.'

'A scene?'

The woman nodded again. 'She was being abusive to a man in the queue, a man who by all accounts had it coming, but in any case your sister was extremely vocal, and when one of the cabbies tried to intervene he got it in the neck, too. He called for assistance, and when a couple of our officers turned up, they were called a bunch of effing c-words for their troubles.'

'Jesus.' Carla was appalled. 'God, I'm so sorry. She's . . . I've never known her behave like that, she's not that sort of person at all, she's . . . quite civilized, usually.'

The woman smiled. 'Ah, well, the drink does funny things, doesn't it? If it's any consolation, I think she's feeling pretty ashamed of herself. And no charges have been brought, so there's no harm done, really.' She leaned forward, lowering her voice. 'I think she's given herself a bit of a fright, if I'm honest.'

Carla's overwhelming memory of that night was of shame, too. The shame of being called in the middle of the night to pick up her drunk and disorderly little sister, completely dwarfed by the shame of seeing what her sister had become in Carla's absence. Emaciated, hollow-eyed, her smooth cheeks spidered with veins, her shoulders hunched.

'Angela!'

'I'm so sorry, Cee,' she said, her eyes lowered, her voice a whisper. 'I'm so sorry, I don't even remember doing it. They said I was shouting at people, shouting and swearing and . . . I don't remember doing it.'

They sat side by side in the back of a black cab on the way back to Angela's house. Neither said a word, but Carla wrapped an arm around her sister's bony shoulders and held her close. The sensation shamed her again: it was like holding a child, like holding her sister when she'd been a little girl – tiny and fierce and funny. Infuriating. Lifetimes ago. It felt like lifetimes since she had loved her, since they had been each other's best friend. Carla started to weep.

She was still weeping when they reached Hayward's Place. She wept as she handed the money to the taxi driver, as she followed her sister to the front door, as she took in the mess of the house, its dank smell of damp and ashes.

'Please stop,' Angela said as she took herself upstairs. 'Please, for Christ's sake, stop.'

Carla could hear her running water for a bath. She made tea – black, there was no milk in the fridge, there was nothing in the fridge save for some ancient cheese and an open bottle of white wine. She took two mugs upstairs, and sat on the loo seat while her sister soaked.

'I didn't even mean to get drunk,' Angela said. She was sitting up, dabbing gently at her bloody knees with a flannel. Carla could see her shoulder blades moving, they looked ready to break through the skin. 'I had a couple of glasses, three, maybe? Something else in the pub afterwards? It was a work thing, you know. No one saw me, I don't think. At the taxi rank. God, I hope nobody saw me. It was just so sudden. One moment I was fine and then I sort of just . . . *woke up* and there was this man towering over me, calling me a drunk . . .'

I thought you didn't remember being in the taxi queue, Carla thought. She said, 'You weigh nothing, Angie. Had you eaten anything before you went out?' Angela shrugged. 'How long . . . have you been like this?'

Angela looked back over her shoulder, her expression dulled. 'Like what?' She turned her face to the wall and picked at the mould on the grouting between the yellowing tiles.

Carla helped her out of the bath, fetched paracetamol from her handbag, found some antiseptic in the bathroom cupboard, which she applied to Angela's cuts. She helped her to bed, then lay at her side, holding one cold hand, her thumb gently stroking the backs of her sister's fingers. 'I should have known that things had got so bad,' she said. 'I should have known.'

I should have forgiven you, she thought. *I should have forgiven you by now.*

They fell asleep.

Angela woke hours later, a cry in her throat. Carla jerked awake in fright.

'Is he here?' Angela whispered.

'Is who here? Who? Angie, who are you talking about? Is who here?'

'Oh. No, I don't know. I was dreaming, I think.' She turned her face to the wall, and Carla settled back down, closing her eyes, trying to return to sleep.

'Did you know,' Angela whispered, 'that I was seeing someone?'

'Oh. Were you? I didn't know. Has something happened? Did you break up?'

'No, no. Not now,' Angela said, her lips smacking. 'Then. I was seeing someone *then*. I never told you this, did I? He was married. He came to the house sometimes.'

'Angie,' Carla put her right arm around her sister's waist, pulling her closer, 'what are you talking about?'

'Lonsdale Square,' Angela said. Carla withdrew her arm. 'When I was living in Lonsdale Square with Daniel after Dad died, I was seeing someone. The night before . . . the night before the accident, we were together in the study. Watching a film on the screen there, you remember?' The projectionist's screen their father had had installed, for watching home movies. 'We were drinking, and . . . *well*. I thought the kids were asleep, but Daniel wasn't. He came downstairs, he caught us.' Her breathing was slow, ragged. 'He was so upset, Cee . . . he was just so *angry*, he wouldn't calm down. I told him – my friend – to go. I told him to leave and I took Dan upstairs. It took me a long time to calm him down, to get him to sleep. Then I went to bed. I went straight to bed. I never went back downstairs again, to the study. I never went back down to close the door . . .'

'Angie,' Carla interrupted, 'don't. Don't do this. We always knew – *I* always knew – that you left the door open. It was—'

'Yes,' Angela said quietly. 'Yes, of course you knew. Of course.'

16

Laura pressed her phone to her ear, hunching up her right shoulder so that she could hold it there, hands free. She was in her bathroom, searching through the medicine cabinet for some antiseptic to put on the cut on her arm. In the sink, dampening, its ink blurring, lay a letter she'd received that morning, informing her of a change of date for the hearing about the fork thing. As she swept little bottles off the shelves and into the sink, on to the letter, she started to laugh.

'The fork? The fork, the fork, the fork! The fork is a red herring!' She laughed harder, at the connection her mind had made. 'Perhaps the fork was a herring fork?' (It wasn't, it was a cocktail fork, she knew perfectly well.)

She released the phone from her shoulder-grip and dropped it into her hand, looking at the screen to remind herself who she was talking to. She was on hold: that was it; she was on hold with the court people, because she wanted to tell them that the date they were now proposing was not convenient for her. It was her mother's birthday. They might go out for lunch! She laughed harder, laughing at herself. When had her mother last taken her for lunch?

Perhaps she could explain, though. Perhaps she could explain the whole fork thing to whoever would be, at some point, on the end of the line. Perhaps she could tell them the story, perhaps they'd understand. It was an easy story to tell, she'd told it before, a number of times, a number of versions: to the police, to the duty solicitor, to her psychologist (*We need to develop strategies, Laura, to help you control your anger*), to Maya at the launderette.

Tell it again!

She'd been in a bar, not far from where she was right at that moment. It was very late, she was *very* drunk, and she was dancing, slowly, on her own. Encouraged, perhaps, by the small group of people who had gathered to watch her, she performed, slowly and impromptu, a fairly professional-looking striptease. In the middle of this routine and without so much as a by-your-leave, an aggressively bearded twenty-something – drunk, too, but less drunk than she – stepped forward, right into her space, reached out and grabbed her left breast, hard.

His friends cheered and everyone else laughed, except for one girl who said, 'Fucking *hell*.'

Laura was thrown off her rhythm; she stumbled backwards, grabbing on to the bar to steady herself. Everyone laughed harder. Suddenly, blindly furious, she lunged over the bar, groping for a weapon. She happened upon a cocktail fork, a two-pronged affair used for skewering olives, which she grabbed, lurching forward. The man dropped his shoulder, dodged to the right, lost his balance, flailed with his left hand, grabbed the bar with his right and there, she stabbed him, right through the centre of his hand. The fork went in, it really went *in*, sank into his flesh as though it were butter, and it stuck.

There was quite a scuffle then, with lots of pushing and shoving and the young man screaming in pain. The bouncers waded in, one of them wrapping half-naked Laura in his jacket and ushering her towards the back of the bar. 'Did that bloke do this to you, love?' he asked. 'Did he attack you? Did he take your clothes?'

Laura shook her head. 'I took off my clothes,' she said, 'but then he grabbed me. He grabbed my tit!'

The police were called, and while they were waiting, the two protagonists – the man with the fork in his hand and the half-naked woman with a bouncer's jacket around her shoulders – were forced to sit almost side by side. 'Fucking mental,' the man kept muttering. 'She's fucking *mental*. She wants locking up.'

He was trying to extract a cigarette from the pack with one hand but he kept dropping the pack on the floor, which was making the bouncers laugh. 'You can't smoke in here anyway,' the jacketless one said.

All this while, Laura was silent – the outbreak of mayhem had sobered her up, frightened her – until the man said, 'You're going to get done for assault, you mad bitch, you know that? You're getting locked up.'

At this point, she turned to look at him and replied, 'No, I'm not. I defended myself.'

'You fucking *what*?'

'When did I say you could touch me?' Laura demanded. 'You assaulted me,' she said. 'You put your hands on me.'

The man's jaw dropped. 'You took your top off, you mental bitch!'

'Yes, I'm aware of that, but when did I say that *you* could touch *me*?'

'She's got a point,' the bouncer said. Fork boy squeaked in disbelief.

Laura smiled sweetly. 'Thank you,' she said.

'Yeah,' the bouncer went on, 'it's a fair point, love, but still.

You can't just stab people in the hand with a fork. It's dispropor-
tionate, innit?'

Laura held her gaze in the mirror. She was still in the bathroom,
still holding the phone to her ear. There was no sound from the
other end. No one said anything. No one was listening. Laura
took the handset from her ear, tapped the screen and scrolled to
her mother's number. She listened to a familiar beeping sound,
to a woman's voice telling her, *You have no credit available for this
call*. She placed the phone on the edge of the basin. She tried to
smile at herself in the mirror, but her facial muscles didn't seem
to be working properly. She could only grimace at her ugliness,
at her loneliness.

17

Theo knocked on the door of Angela's house again, louder
this time. 'Carla? Are you in there?' There was an edge to his
voice; his mood had been veering all morning between irritation and panic. He'd not been able to reach Carla for two days
now – she'd not responded to his messages, and if she was at
home she'd not answered the door to him. So, irritation: because
she did this sometimes, she dropped out of circulation without
thought for the consequences, without caring how much
others – himself, mostly – might be worrying about her. Once,
she disappeared for a whole week. It turned out she was in
France, she wouldn't say who with.

On the other hand, panic. Her sister was gone. So too, Daniel. And in a week's time it would be Ben's birthday. Would have
been Ben's birthday, had he lived. His eighteenth. Their little
guy, an adult. An actual adult. Talking about going off to university, bringing home girls. Or boys. It hurt to think about – who
he might have been, who they might have been, if not for the
accident.

If not for Angela.

Theo had been to Carla's home, he'd been to the graveyard,
he'd called her friends. If he failed here, he might have to call

the police. It had crossed his mind more than once that she might be with the police already. That she might be sitting in a room, right now, answering questions. Because if they'd come for his fingerprints, his DNA, then they'd have come for hers too, wouldn't they? And what might they have found?

He knocked again, more loudly still, and called out, desperate: 'For God's sake, Carla, let me in!'

The front door of the next-door house opened a fraction. An elderly woman poked her wizened face through the crack. 'There's no one there,' she said curtly. 'It's empty.'

The nosy neighbour. Carla had mentioned her; Theo couldn't remember her name. He beamed at her. 'Oh, hello. I'm *so* sorry to bother you,' he said, stepping away from Angela's front door and walking towards the old woman. 'I'm looking for my wife. Carla Myerson? She's Angela's sister. I was just wondering if you'd seen her at all . . . ?' She narrowed her eyes at him. 'Carla?' he repeated loudly, enunciating clearly. The woman's brow furrowed. He had the feeling she might not be quite all there. 'It's all right,' he said, smiling again. 'Don't worry, never mind.'

'*You*,' the crone said suddenly, pulling the door open and pointing one gnarled finger at his chest. 'It was you. Of course! I should have recognized you.'

'I beg your pardon?' Theo said.

'Wait here,' she said. 'Don't go anywhere.' And off she went, disappearing down her hallway, leaving the door wide open.

Theo stood for a moment, unsure what to do. He looked up and down the lane. He called out, 'Hello? Mrs . . . uh . . .' What *was* her name? *Senile old goat*, he seemed to remember Carla calling her. He stepped into her dark hallway, glancing briefly at the pictures on the walls: cheap prints, naval scenes. Perhaps the husband was into ships? He took another step further into the house.

Suddenly, out of the gloom, she appeared, and he jumped. With a pair of glasses perched on the end of her nose she peered at him, eyes narrowing again.

'It *is* you! You were here before. You were out in the lane, with Angela.'

'Uh, no . . . I . . .'

'Yes, yes, it was you. The police officer asked me who the man was and I couldn't say, I didn't recognize you at the time, or I didn't remember anyway, but it was you. You were here, with Angela. You made her cry.'

'I did not,' Theo said emphatically. 'You have me confused with someone else, I'm afraid,' and he turned away, heading quickly back down the path.

'You had a dog with you!' the old lady called out behind him. 'A little dog.'

Theo walked briskly along the lane, around the corner and straight into the Sekforde Arms. He ordered himself a whisky. He drank it swiftly and went outside to smoke. Breaking the rules: no spirits before six p.m., this cigarette disallowed under his own regime. Still. Extenuating circumstances, he thought, crushing the half-smoked cigarette against an ashtray, turning to look back towards Hayward's Place, as though the old woman might be following him.

Would she tell Carla, he wondered? Would she tell Carla that she'd seen him today, or that she'd seen him before? *Jesus Christ.* He went back inside and, raising a finger to the young woman behind the bar, ordered another drink. The barmaid raised an eyebrow, almost imperceptibly. Almost. *Mind your own business,* he wanted to say. She placed the second drink in front of him with a smile. 'There you go.' Maybe he'd imagined the eyebrow. Maybe he was being paranoid.

Maybe he was being paranoid about the old woman, too. If she did say something to Carla, then what? Would Carla even believe her? Surely it was paranoia to believe that she would; didn't Carla think the old dear was losing her marbles? Wasn't that what she'd said?

Still. What if she *did* believe her? What would she think? If she knew that he had been with Angela, in what direction would that take her? Impossible to tell. Theo had known Carla close to thirty years and still he was never quite sure which way, in any given situation, she might jump. He knew this: he had forgiven her all her trespasses and would continue to do so, always. But he was by no means certain that she would reciprocate.

He pulled his mobile from his pocket and called Carla again. Still she did not pick up. He was tempted to order another drink, but the buzz from the first was already drifting into the dangerous fog of the second, and what if she *did* pick up? What was he going to say then? What was he going to tell her?

The last time he'd seen Angela, they had been standing out in Hayward's Place, the exact spot where he'd just been speaking to the neighbour. A grey day, a heavy sky, all of London monochrome. Theo had been looking for Daniel, but instead he'd found Angela. The old woman was right: Angela had cried, although he wasn't sure it was accurate to say he'd *made* her cry. She'd just burst into tears the moment she saw him. She'd invited him inside, but he'd preferred to talk in the street. He couldn't be in a room with her alone, he didn't trust himself.

She looked shocking: painfully thin, spidery blue veins tracing their way through papery skin. Her hair was grey and very long, she looked like the wicked witch from a fairy tale, she looked hollowed out, a husk. Theo tried to ignore her appearance and her distress, he tried to speak to her matter-of-factly, to convey as directly as possible why he was there. That Daniel had come to his house, asking for money; that he'd said he'd lost his job and had no one else to turn to. He didn't want to bother Carla, he'd said. Theo thought that was probably a lie, he assumed there was something else at play, but he didn't want to know what. Theo had written him a cheque for a thousand pounds. A couple of weeks later, Daniel came back. Theo was out, but he'd left a message.

'Can I listen?' Angela asked.

'It wasn't a phone message,' Theo said. 'He pushed a note under the door.'

'What sort of note? What did it say?' Angela's eyes were wide, the whites a jaundiced yellow. *She's ill*, Theo thought. *She might even be dying.*

'It doesn't matter what it said,' Theo replied. 'I just need to talk to him about it.'

Angela said she didn't know where Daniel was, but that if she saw him she would talk to him. 'Won't do any good,' she said, shaking her head. 'He doesn't listen to me. Carla's the one.' Her eyes filled with tears again. 'He'll usually do what Carla asks.'

Theo stood there for a while, watching her cry; he tried to feel pity for her, but failed. She clearly felt so much for herself already, his own seemed superfluous. He walked away from her before he could say something he regretted.

That wasn't the last time he saw her, of course. That was the second to last.

18

In the corners of the room, bodies of gathering shadows formed, faceless, shifting, approaching and receding, dissipating back to nothingness. Irene lay awake, listening to her breath come short and ragged in her chest, the sound of blood thick in her ears, dread weighing on her, pressing her body down into the bed.

Something had woken her. A fox in the churchyard? Or some drunkard out in the lane, shouting at nothing, or – there! No, there it was again, a sound. A creak on the stair? Irene held her breath, too afraid to reach over and turn on the light. A few seconds passed, a few more. Perhaps she had imagined it? Perhaps she had been dreaming? She exhaled slowly, turning on to her side. There! Again! A tread. No doubt about it, and not – thankfully – on her stairs, but next door. She knew the sound well, she'd listened to Angela go up and down those stairs at all hours for years. The walls of these terraced houses were paper thin.

Was it an echo of Angela's footsteps she was hearing? Was this a normal response to grief? Just like her visions of William coming whistling along the lane in the evenings, or standing over by the window when she woke, always on the point of turning, always on the point of saying, *Fancy a cuppa, Reenie?*

Around the edges of her vision, something moved; Irene gripped the bed covers so tightly her fingers ached.

How would Angela appear to her, Irene wondered, if she came? Would she be herself, always a little jittery, her knee forever bouncing as she sat, one skinny leg crossed over the other, chatting about the book she'd just finished, her hands always working away at something, rolling a cigarette or pulling at a thread in her linen shirt? Would she be herself, or would she be something else? Would she come crooked, her neck broken, her sweet wine breath mingling with rot?

Then – there was no doubt about this now – Irene heard someone walk along the landing on the other side of the bedroom wall. A soft tread, not like Angela's drunken shuffle, and not some muffled, indistinct, *imagined* noise, but footsteps. Careful and unmistakable.

There was someone next door, and it was not a ghost. It was an intruder.

More than most things, Irene dreaded an intruder. She dreaded the moment when the intruder would realize that there was someone at home, a witness they would have to deal with. She dreaded the moment of reckoning, the moment when she, the frail pensioner alone in bed, would come to understand the sort of intruder this was: an opportunist, out to snatch a wallet or a laptop computer, or something else. Someone in search of a plaything. Those terrible pitiful stories you heard, of old ladies beaten, assaulted, eyes blackened, nightdresses soiled.

There, again! Another noise, someone moving back and forth, perhaps, along the corridor. Looking for something? *Myerson*, Irene thought. The man who'd made Angela cry. The man who'd lied about having ever been there at all. She'd not liked the look of him, not liked the way his eyes slid over her, underestimating her all the while. *Stupid old fool*, he'd thought. She could almost hear him muttering. *Nosy old cow.*

Well. She might as well fulfil her curtain-twitching destiny then, mightn't she? She felt in the darkness for the light switch and clicked on the lamp, blinking as her eyes adjusted to the light. Manoeuvring herself into a sitting position, she reached for her spectacles. Her mobile phone, inevitably, was not next to her bed. The blasted phone was never where she needed it to be, no matter where she was or what she was doing, it was always in another room.

She crept down the stairs, feeling her way in the dark, not wanting to attract attention by turning on the downstairs light. 'Stupid,' she muttered to herself. 'Blundering around in the darkness. Never mind twisting an ankle, you'll break a hip.'

As Irene reached the last step, as she carefully tested with one slippered foot that she had quite definitely reached the ground floor, she heard from next door a louder sound, a sudden *whump!*, as though someone had stumbled, and she cried out, 'Who is that? I can hear you. I'm calling the police! The police are coming!' She sounded laughably indignant, even to her own ears. 'Do you hear me?'

Silence answered.

Two police officers – one a young man, stocky, fresh-faced; the other older, a woman in her thirties, weary-looking – stood outside Angela's house, hands on hips.

'The door's locked,' the stocky one told Irene. He tried the door handle again, just to show her. 'No sign of anyone tampering with it. No sign of any damage to the windows . . .' He shrugged, apologetic. 'There's no sign of a break-in.'

'There's someone in there,' Irene, huddling in her own doorway, insisted. 'I heard them. I heard them walking around . . .'

'And you say the house is empty? You're sure it hasn't been rented out?'

'No, it's definitely empty, they haven't even finished clearing it. And the thing is, there was a man here today, and he lied about the fact that he's been here before, and I just . . . I just . . .'

The policewoman pursed her lips. 'So someone's been hanging around the property, then?'

'Well . . . no, that's not what I'm saying, but a woman died here. A couple of months ago, a woman died, and you – not you, but the police – said it was an accident, only I'm not sure that's right, because now the son's died, and doesn't that seem strange to you?'

The woman blinked slowly. 'Sorry,' she said. 'You're saying there have been two suspicious deaths at the property?'

'No, no, only one, the son died somewhere else. I just . . . I'm not some time waster,' Irene said. 'But there's someone next door, and . . . frankly, I'm frightened.'

The stocky policeman nodded. 'Right you are,' he said, giving Irene a smile. He raised his fist and thumped it firmly against the door. They all waited. He thumped again. And then a light came on.

Irene almost fell over in her haste to back away from the door. 'There *is* someone there!' she cried, at once terrified and triumphant.

A few moments later, the door swung open, and there stood Carla, her expression thunderous.

Later, after they'd sorted everything out with the police, after Carla had explained who she was and how she'd every right to be there, she accepted Irene's offer of a three a.m. cup of tea.

'You shouldn't be crashing around in there,' Irene said to her, aggrieved. 'Not in the middle of the night.'

'With respect, Irene,' – as Carla accepted a mug of tea she

144

raised her chin a little, so that she was looking down the bridge of her nose as she spoke – 'I can go there whenever I want. It's my house. I mean, it will be. So I will go there whenever it suits me.'

'But—'

'I'm sorry I disturbed you,' Carla went on, her tone betraying not one iota of contrition, 'but I've been sleeping badly, if at all, of late, and so sometimes, instead of lying in bed staring at the ceiling, I get up and I get on with things, whether that be correspondence, or cleaning, or in this case coming here to look for something I mislaid earlier.'

'What?' Irene snapped, infuriated by Carla's manner, by her blithe disregard for Irene's peace of mind. 'What on earth did you need so urgently at two o'clock in the morning?'

'None of your business!' Carla slammed her mug down on to the kitchen counter, spilling tea on the floor. 'Sorry,' she said, reaching for a sheet of kitchen towel and crouching down to mop up the spill. 'God!' She stayed down there, hunched over, her arms hanging loose at her sides, her face pressed against her knees. 'I'm sorry,' she mumbled. 'I'm sorry.'

Irene reached out a hand, placed it gently on Carla's shoulder. 'It's all right,' she said, a little taken aback by this display of weakness. 'Come on, up you come.'

Carla stood. She was crying – not loudly or demonstratively, but in a quiet, dignified, *Carla* sort of way, tears sliding elegantly down her cheeks, dripping from her jawline on to the collar of her crisp white shirt. She closed her eyes and pressed the heels of her hands against her cheekbones.

'Come on now,' Irene said gently, coaxing her, as though Carla were an animal, or a small child. 'Take your tea, there, that's right,' she said, and she led Carla from the kitchen to the living room, where they sat, side by side, on the sofa.

'I had some things,' Carla said after a while, 'in a bag. Some clothes and a couple of jewellery boxes. I had them with me when I came here today – I mean, yesterday . . . whenever it was. I'm sure I did.'

'And now you can't find them?'

Carla nodded.

'Were they valuable?'

Carla shrugged. 'Not terribly. I don't know . . . My mother's engagement ring, that's probably worth a bit, but the medal, a St Christopher . . . It belonged to my son.'

'Oh, Carla.'

'I can't lose it, I can't. We bought it for his christening, we had it engraved . . .' She shook her head, blinking away tears. 'He never wore it, of course, he was too little, but he *loved* to look at it, to get it out of the box, he wanted to play with it, you know how kids are. But I always said that he couldn't keep hold of it, that it was precious, that he had to put it away, and that I would look after it for him, I would keep it safe for him . . . I promised to keep it safe for him, and I did, for all this time, and now . . .' She broke off, turning her face away.

'Oh, I'm so sorry,' Irene said. 'But why bring it to the house? Were you on your way somewhere? Did you stop off anywhere, perhaps? A shop, perhaps you set them down . . .'

'No, no. I didn't go anywhere else. I was just . . . I wanted them with me, those things. I wanted them with me when . . .' She turned her head away.

'When what?' Irene didn't understand.

'I was . . . I was in despair,' Carla said. She turned back and their eyes met.

Irene's hand flew to her mouth. She understood now. 'Oh, Carla,' she said. 'Oh *no*.'

Carla shook her head again. 'It doesn't matter,' she said. 'It doesn't matter.'

'It matters. Of course it does.' Irene rested her hand gently on top of Carla's. 'Your son, and then your sister and Daniel, so close together – it feels like too much to bear.'

Carla smiled, withdrawing her hand, wiping the tears from her cheeks. 'We've not had much luck,' she said.

'You're grieving,' Irene said. 'You can't think straight when you're grieving. I was the same when I lost my husband. I thought about it – putting an end to it. There didn't seem much point in going on, just me, you know, no one else. Your sister pulled me out of it, you know. She just kept coming round, bringing those little pastries she liked, the almond ones, Swedish? Danish, that's it. Or sometimes some soup, or just coffee, whatever, and she'd be chattering away, about what she was reading, you know, that sort of thing. She saved my life, did Angie.'

Carla's face seemed to darken, she turned her head away.

'I know that things weren't always good between you and her, but she loved you,' Irene said. 'And . . . well, I know you loved Daniel, didn't you? He meant a great deal—'

Carla got to her feet. 'You need to go back to bed,' she said briskly, carrying her mug back to the kitchen. 'I've kept you up.'

'Well, I don't sleep terribly well anyway,' Irene said. 'It's all right, if you'd like to rest here, if—'

'Oh, no,' Carla said, as though the idea were abhorrent. She was back from the kitchen, all trace of emotion wiped from her face. She stood in the doorway, back straight, chin tilted towards the ceiling, her mouth a line. 'Don't get up, Irene, please,' she said. 'Thank you for the tea. And I'm sorry about the disturbance. I'll be going home now, so I won't bother you again.'

'Carla, I . . .' Irene paused. She wanted to say something reassuring, something hopeful, something conciliatory. She couldn't think of a single thing. Instead, she asked, 'You will be all right, won't you?'

For a moment, Carla appeared not to understand that question, and then she blushed. 'Oh, God. Yes, of course. You don't have to worry about that. I'm not sure I ever would have gone through with.it. The imagining of it is one thing, isn't it, and then the reality . . .' She tailed off. 'I brought the dog's lead,' she said. Irene shuddered, her skin crawling from her tailbone to the nape of her neck at the thought of it, of *another* body next door, waiting undiscovered behind those paper-thin walls.

'Not my dog, of course,' Carla was saying. 'I don't have one. My ex-husband did, though, and I think that somewhere in my subconscious I was ensuring that I wouldn't go through with it.' She smiled, a strange, private smile. 'I think I must have known that I would look at the lead and I would think of his little dog, I would think of how much he loved the dog, and of how much he loved me, and that would pull me back.' She shrugged, her expression soft. 'That's what I think now, anyway.'

'Oh!' Irene said, remembering all of a sudden. 'I forgot to say. Your ex-husband, he came looking for you. He was here—'

'*Here?*'

'Well, outside, in the lane, knocking on Angela's door. I didn't recognize him at first, but then I remembered that he'd come before, I'd seen him out there talking to Angela, so—'

Carla shook head. 'No, that couldn't have been Theo.'

'It was, it was definitely—'

'You're mistaken, Irene, there is no way that my husband—'

'I saw him with her,' Irene insisted. 'I saw them out there, in the lane. She was crying. Angela was crying. I think they were arguing.'

'Irene,' Carla's voice rose, two spots of dark colour appearing in her cheeks, 'Theo didn't speak to my sister. He would never—'

'He had his little dog with him. A little terrier of some sort, black and tan.'

Carla blinked slowly. 'You saw him with Angela?' she asked. Irene nodded. 'When?'

'I'm not sure, it was . . .'

'How many times?'

'Just the once, I think. They were outside in the lane. Angela was crying.'

'When, Irene?'

'A week or two,' Irene said, 'before she died.'

Back upstairs in bed, Irene lay awake, watching a grey light creep through the gap in the curtains. It was almost morning. She'd returned to bed feeling exhausted, knowing it was unlikely she would sleep. It was true what she'd said to Carla about her wakefulness, short sleeping being yet another side effect of old age. But she doubted she'd have slept anyway, no matter how old she was or how she'd been feeling; the stricken look on Carla's face when Irene had mentioned Theo Myerson's visit would have kept her awake, no matter what.

19

'Will you just. Fucking. Let me in?'

Half past nine in the morning in the pissing rain and Laura stood on the pavement outside the launderette, her breath ragged, only vaguely conscious of wage slaves beneath umbrellas hurrying past, giving the nutcase on the street a wide berth, the one who was now swinging her backpack around in the air, who was hurling it at the launderette door as hard as she could. 'It's not about the job,' she yelled. 'I don't care about the job, you can stick your fucking job! I just want to talk to Tania! Maya, for fuck's sake! Let me in!'

On the other side of the glass door, Maya stood, square-shouldered and impassive, her arms folded across her chest. 'Laura,' she called out, 'you need to calm down. I'm going to give you thirty seconds, all right, to calm down and walk away. And if you don't, I'm going to call the police. Do you understand me, Laura?'

Laura crouched down and bit down hard on her lip. She felt a wave of nausea hit her as adrenaline flooded her system, her mouth filling with saliva, her heart pumping fit to explode. She grabbed an empty beer bottle lying in the gutter and raised her arm.

A hand grabbed her, pulling her arm sharply back behind her torso. She felt a painful twist at her shoulder and she cried out, dropping the bottle. The hand let go.

'What on earth do you think you're doing?' a woman's voice asked and Laura turned, left hand rubbing her painful right shoulder, to find she'd been apprehended by the hobbit.

That's what they called her in the launderette, because she was short and hairy and she looked like she might live in a burrow or a warren or something, although it turned out she actually lived on a boat, which was in itself quite weird.

'Well?' The woman was frowning at her, more confused than angry. Like when her dad got cross with her, only he tried to deny it and said, *I'm not angry, chicken, I'm disappointed.*

'They won't let me in,' Laura said limply, the red mist burning off as quickly as it had descended. 'She won't let me in, and I didn't even want to start any trouble, I only wanted to talk to Tania about something. It's not even anything to do with the shop, it's not even . . .' Laura stopped talking. It was pointless. All of it, pointless. She sank down on to the edge of the pavement, her knees up under her chin. 'I didn't want to cause any trouble.'

The hobbit leaned heavily on Laura's shoulder as she sat down at her side. 'Well,' she said gruffly, 'I'm not certain chucking bottles about is the best way to not cause trouble.'

Laura glanced at her and the hobbit smiled, baring a mouth full of crooked, yellowing teeth.

'I can't remember your name,' Laura said.

'Miriam,' the woman replied. She patted Laura on the knee. 'I take it you're not working there any longer? I'd noticed you'd not been around.'

'I got fired,' Laura said miserably. 'I didn't turn up for two shifts on the bounce, and it wasn't the first time I'd missed, and

I didn't call Maya to tell her, so she missed her grandson's birthday, which is really shit, but the thing is that I didn't mean to do it, I didn't mean any of it. It wasn't my fault.'

Miriam patted her knee again. 'I'm so sorry. That's horrible. Horrible to lose a job. I know how that feels. Would you like to go somewhere, to drink a cup of tea? I'd like to help you.' Laura shifted away from her slightly. 'I've had to rely on the kindness of strangers myself, once or twice,' Miriam said. 'I know what it's like. It can be disconcerting at first, can't it?' Laura nodded. 'But I think,' Miriam said, smiling at her benevolently, 'I think you'll find that we're really quite alike, you and me.'

No we're fucking not, Laura thought, but she managed not to say anything, because she could see the woman was only trying to be kind.

'So then, four years after I got run over, my mother married the man who knocked me off my bike.' Laura paused, adding milk to the mugs of tea she'd made. She handed the less chipped mug to Miriam. 'It fucks you up, stuff like that, no question. I mean, obviously, being knocked down by a car fucks you *physically*, it leaves you with pain and scars and all sorts of *impairments*, doesn't it?' She gestured downward, to her gammy left leg. 'But the other stuff's worse. The emotional stuff is worse, the mental stuff. That's what fucks you up for good.'

Miriam sipped her tea and nodded. 'I couldn't agree more,' she said.

'So now,' Laura said, collapsing into her chair, 'I do stuff – stupid stuff – sometimes, like this morning, or like . . . whenever, and it's not like I even mean to, or sometimes I do mean to, only it's like something's been set in motion and I can't stop it, and all I can do is react, try and minimize the damage to myself, and sometimes when you do that you end up damaging other people,

152

but it's not *deliberate*. Not premeditated.' The hobbit nodded again. 'People scoff, you know? People like my stepmother or my teachers or the police or Maya or whatever, when I say it's not my fault. They're like, well, whose fault is it then?'

Janine, Laura's mother, stood in the driveway in front of the house, looking over at the bird feeders in the apple tree. They needed filling up. She wasn't sure they had any more feed, but she didn't want to go to the shops now, it had been snowing for a while and the roads would be horrible. She closed her eyes and took a deep breath, enjoying the pull of cold air into her lungs and the almost perfect quiet – which was broken suddenly and violently by a squeal of brakes. There followed a long, swooping silence and then a horrible, sickening crack. The drive was about two hundred yards long and tree-lined, and there was a hedge at the edge of the property, so there was no way of seeing what had happened in the road, but Janine knew. She told the police when they came that she just knew something terrible had happened.

The car was gone. Laura lay in the road with her legs twisted around at a strange angle. As Janine sank to her knees at her child's side, she saw a slow trickle of blood dripping from the back of Laura's helmet on to the slick, wet tarmac. She reached into her pocket for her phone and found that it was not there and she started to scream and scream, but no one came, because the next house along was half a mile away.

The police wanted to know what she had seen and heard, was she sure she didn't glimpse anything of the car, perhaps a blur of colour? Janine shook her head. 'This was my fault. It was my fault.'

'It is not your fault, Mrs Kilbride. This is the fault of the driver of the car that hit Laura,' the policewoman said to her. The policewoman put her arm around Janine's shoulders and squeezed her. 'We'll find him. Or her. We'll find whoever did this. Don't you worry, they're not going to get away with this.' Janine pulled away from her, she gazed at her in pale, wordless terror.

They did find him. CCTV half a mile away captured two cars going past within minutes of Laura's accident: the first belonged to an elderly woman whose car was found to be immaculate, without any sign of a collision. The second belonged to Richard Blake, an art and antiques dealer who lived a few miles away in Petworth and whose car, he said when the police tracked him down at work, had been stolen the night before. He had not reported it. As the police officers were leaving, Richard asked in a strangled voice, 'Is she going to be all right?', and the policewoman asked, 'Is *who* going to be all right?'

'The little girl!' he blurted out, wringing his hands in front of him.

'I mentioned a child, Mr Blake. I didn't say she was female. How did you know the victim was a girl?'

A criminal mastermind Richard Blake was not.

That's how it happened. That's what Laura believed. That's what she was told, so – she was ten years old, remember? – that's what she believed.

At first, of course, she didn't believe anything at all, because she was in a coma. Twelve days unconscious, and then, when finally she woke, it was to a new world, one in which she had a broken pelvis and a compound-fractured femur and a smashed skull, a world in which, it seemed, someone had done a full factory reset, sent her all the way back to zero. She had to learn to speak again, to read, to walk, to count to ten.

She'd no memory of the accident, or of the months preceding

it – the new school, the new house, her new bicycle: it was all gone. She had a vague memory of their old house in London, of the next-door neighbour's cat. After that, everything went blurry.

Gradually, though, as time passed, things began to come back to her. A few weeks before she left hospital, she said to her father, 'The house we live in now, it's at the foot of a hill. Is that right?'

'That's right!' He smiled at her. 'Good girl. Do you remember anything else?'

'Bungalow,' she said, and he nodded. She frowned. 'The car. It's green.'

Her father shook his head, a rueful smile on his lips. 'Red, I'm afraid, chicken. I've got a red Volvo.'

'No, not *our* car. The car that hit me. It was green. It turned out of our driveway,' she said. 'It was leaving our house, just as I was coming home.'

The smile slid from her father's face. 'You don't remember the accident, chicken. You couldn't possibly remember the accident.'

A few days after that, when her mother came to visit (they never visited together any longer, which seemed odd), Laura asked about the car that hit her. 'It was green, wasn't it?' she asked. 'I'm sure it was green.'

Her mother busied herself with tidying the Get Well cards on the windowsill. 'You know, I'm not sure. I didn't actually see the car.'

Liar.

Janine, Laura's mother, stood in the driveway in front of the house, shivering, wearing Ugg boots and wrapped in a bathrobe of chartreuse silk. Her skin was flushed with sex. They'd lost track of time, they were still entangled with each other when she looked over at her husband's watch on her bedside and said, 'Shit, Laura's going to be home soon.'

Richard had dressed in a hurry; he almost fell over putting his trousers on, the pair of them laughing, making plans for next time. She saw him out and kissed him as he got into his car, he told her he loved her. She stood on the driveway, her head tilted back, watching the snow come falling down, opening her mouth so she could feel the flakes on her tongue. His words echoed in her head and then she heard it and she knew: something terrible had happened to Richard.

She sprinted to the road. The first thing she saw was his car, his dark green Mercedes parked at an odd angle in the middle of the road, and then, beyond that, Richard himself. He was kneeling with his back to her, his shoulders heaving, and as she reached him, she saw that he was sobbing, his tears falling on to the broken body of her child. 'Oh God oh God oh please God no, please God no. She was in the road, Janine, she was in the middle of the road. Oh please God no, please God.'

Janine grabbed his arm and started to pull him to his feet. 'You have to go,' she was saying, her voice sounding weirdly matter-of-fact even to her own ears. 'You have to get in the car and go, go right now. Go, Richard, I'll take care of her. Go on!'

'She's bleeding, Janine. It's bad. Oh Christ, it's bad.'

'You have to go,' she said again, and when he didn't move, she started to shout. 'Now, Richard! Leave! Just go now. You weren't here. You were never here.'

Liar, liar.

All that would come out later. Everyone told Laura (everyone being her parents and the doctor and her counsellor) not to google what had happened, that it wouldn't help, it would only

156

upset her, frighten her, give her nightmares. Which Laura, who might have only just turned eleven but wasn't *born yesterday*, thought was bollocks, but also quite suspicious, and she was right about that, wasn't she?

The first thing she found when she googled herself was a news story with the headline 'MAN JAILED FOR HIT AND RUN' and a picture of her looking like a twat in her school uniform, grinning goofily at the camera. She started reading:

Art dealer Richard Blake was yesterday sentenced to four months in prison for the hit-and-run accident which seriously injured local schoolgirl, Laura Kilbride, 11.

Laura read that sentence again. *Richard?*

But that couldn't be right. She knew Richard. Richard was the man who taught the art classes her mum went to, Richard was nice. He had an open, friendly face, he was always laughing. Laura liked Richard, he was kind to her, they'd played football together once in the car park when she was waiting for her mum to finish up in the supermarket. Richard wouldn't have done that to her. He would never have driven away without calling an ambulance.

The revelation about Richard Blake was quickly forgotten though, in the shock of what was to come:

Mr Blake, 45, who pleaded guilty to failing to stop and failing to report an accident, was conducting a relationship with the child's mother, Janine Kilbride, at the time of the accident. Mrs Kilbride, 43, who arrived on the scene shortly after the accident, called an ambulance to attend to her child, but told police she did not see the vehicle that struck her. Janine Kilbride was fined £800 for giving false information to the police.

When Laura looked back on that period, she identified the moment that she read that paragraph as the beginning of the end. Her body was already broken, of course, her brain function already affected, but a person can recover from that sort of damage. But *this*? The knowledge that she had been lied to – by both of her parents, by everyone who'd been caring for her – that was a knockout blow, the sort that lays you out, the sort from which you do not get back up. That knowledge, the sense of betrayal that came with it, that changed her. It left her marked.

It left her *angry*.

20

Miriam could recognize damaged goods when she saw them. People always went on about the eyes, about guarded expressions, haunted looks, that sort of thing. Possibly, Miriam thought, but it was more about movement, about the way you carried yourself. She couldn't see it in herself, of course, but she could feel it – she might be old and heavy and slow now, but she was still on the balls of her feet. Still wary. Ready for that rush of blood to the head.

Miriam saw Laura creating havoc outside the launderette and seized her opportunity. She stepped in quickly, picked up Laura's rucksack, apologized to the exasperated owner and escorted the girl smartly away. She offered her a cup of tea on the boat, but Laura turned her down. Understandable, under the circumstances. When you consider the mess she got herself into last time she went down there.

They went to Laura's place instead. An ordeal, to put it mildly. Laura lived in a council flat in a tower block over by Spa Fields, up on the seventh floor, and the lift was out. Miriam was unsure she'd make it all the way up, she had to stop several times, her breath short and the sweat pouring off her. Little toerags in the stairwell laughing, making jokes. *'Shit, bruv, your nan's having a heart attack.'*

When she got up there, though, the climb felt almost worth it. A stiff breeze, none of the stink of the canal, and a view – a glorious view! The spire of St James's in the foreground, behind that the hulking brutalist towers of the Barbican, the quiet splendour of St Paul's and, further still, the City's shining glass facades. London, in all its glory, the one you forgot about when you lived with your nose so close to the ground.

Laura hardly seemed to notice. Used to it, Miriam supposed, and clearly in pain – the limp seemed to get worse with every floor they climbed. When finally they reached Laura's front door, Miriam asked about it, politely, as a simple expression of concern, fully expecting a banal response – a twisted ankle, a drunken fall – and instead received a tale of woe she could scarcely believe. Awful parents, a terrible accident, virtual abandonment to her fate. Miriam's heart went out to her. A start like that in life? No wonder she was such an odd fish.

Her sympathy for the girl swelled when she saw her pitiful little flat. Cheap, ugly furniture on a grey acrylic carpet, walls the yellow of nicotine. This was the home of a child *without*: no colourful throws or cushions, no ornaments or trophies, no books on the shelves, no posters on the walls – nothing whatsoever save for a single framed photograph, of a child with its parents. A relief from the bleakness until you got closer, as Miriam did, stepping over a pile of clothes lying in the middle of the living-room floor, to see that the picture had been defaced, the child's eyes crossed out, its mouth bloodied. Miriam peered at it and flinched. When she turned around, Laura was looking at her, a strange expression on her face. Miriam's skin goosefleshed. 'Shall we have that cup of tea, then?' she asked with forced jollity.

(Damaged goods, odd fish – who knew what was going on behind those pretty eyes?)

In the kitchen, tea drunk and an uncomfortable silence hanging over them, Miriam decided to take a risk, to speak up. 'I know you, you know,' she said. In her pocket, she fiddled with the key, the one she'd taken from the floor of the boat, with the keyring attached.

Laura gave her a look. 'Yeah. From the launderette. Duh.'

Miriam shook her head, a small smile on her lips. 'It's not just that. I know why you didn't want to go down to the canal.' She saw the girl's expression change, from boredom to consternation. 'It's nothing to worry about,' Miriam said. 'I'm on your side. I know it's you the police are talking to about him. About Daniel Sutherland.'

'How did you know that?' There it was: the girl's body tensed, ready for the off. Fight or flight.

'I was the one who found him,' Miriam said. 'My boat – the pretty green one, with the red trim, the *Lorraine*, you've probably seen it – it's moored just a few yards from where his was.' She smiled at Laura, letting this information sink in. 'I was the one who found him. Who found his body. I was the one who called the police.'

Laura's eyes widened. 'Are you serious? *Fuck*. That must have been grim,' she said. 'Seeing him . . . all . . . bloody like that.'

'It was,' Miriam said. She thought of the gash in his neck, the whiteness of his teeth. She wondered whether, at that moment, Laura held the same image in her mind, whether for a moment or two they found themselves in alignment. She tried to meet the young woman's eye, but Laura was in the process of pushing her chair from the table, getting to her feet, reaching over Miriam's shoulder to pick up her empty mug.

'Have you . . . have you been in touch with the police since?'

Laura asked her, her voice strangely high. 'Since you found him, I mean. Are they, like, giving you updates or anything? Because I keep looking at the news and nothing really seems to be happening, and it's been more than a week, now, hasn't it, since he ... well, since he was found, so ...' She tailed off. She was standing with her back to Miriam, placing the mugs in the sink.

Miriam didn't answer the question, but waited until Laura had turned to face her again before she spoke. 'I saw you leaving,' she said. 'The day before I found him. I saw you leaving the boat.'

Laura's eyes widened. 'And?' Her expression was defiant. 'It's not a secret I was there. I told the police I was there. Everyone knows I was there. I didn't lie.'

'I know you didn't,' Miriam said. 'Why would you? You did nothing wrong.'

Laura turned away again. She turned on the tap, rinsing the mugs under the stream of water, her actions jerky, a little frantic. Miriam's heart went out to her, she could see victimhood written all over her, in every flinch and every twist. 'Do you want to tell me what happened?' Miriam asked gently. 'Do you want to tell me what he did?' Breath held, blood singing, Miriam felt herself teetering on the edge of something important: a confidence. An allegiance. A friendship? 'I'm on your side,' she said.

'My side?' Laura laughed, a scornful, brittle sound. 'I don't have a side.'

But you could have, Miriam wanted to say. *You could have an ally. It could be us against them! Those people who think they have all the power, who think that we have none, we could prove them wrong. We could show them that we can be powerful, too. You up here in your shabby tower, me down there on the water, we may not live in elegant homes, we might not have expensive haircuts and foreign holidays and good art on the walls, but that doesn't make us nothing. So many* things Miriam wanted to say, but she had to be careful, she had to approach this thing slowly, she couldn't rush it.

A slight change of tack, to test the ground. 'Do you happen to know anything about his family? Daniel Sutherland's family?'

Laura shrugged. 'His mum's dead. She died quite recently. She was an alkie, he said. He has an aunt. I met her at Irene's.'

'Irene's?'

'My friend.'

'Who's your friend?' Miriam asked.

'Just a friend. None of your beeswax.' Laura laughed. 'Look, it was nice to have a chat and everything, but I think—'

'Oh, well.' Miriam cut her off. 'I know quite a bit about his family, and I think you might find what I know quite interesting.' Laura was leaning against the counter now, picking at her nails, she wasn't even paying attention. 'The thing is, you see, I think it might have been *her*,' Miriam said.

'Her?' Laura looked up.

'I think his aunt might have had something to do with it.'

Laura's brow crinkled. 'With what?'

'With his death!'

Laura gave an abrupt bark of laughter. 'His *aunt*?'

Miriam felt her face redden. 'This isn't a joke!' she snapped, indignant. 'I saw her there, I saw her visiting him, just like you visited him, and I believe that something happened between them.' Laura was watching her, a crease at the top of her nose. 'I think,' Miriam went on, '– and this is the important thing – I think that her husband – her *ex*-husband, I mean, Theo Myerson – I think he might be trying to cover the whole thing up, because . . .' Miriam kept talking, but as she did she could see the girl's expression change, from scepticism to disbelief to suspicion, she could see that she was losing her trust. How could this girl be so obtuse? Couldn't she see, at the very least, that it was in her own interest to point the finger at someone else? Wasn't it obvious that Miriam's theory was beneficial to her? 'It may sound far-fetched,' Miriam said at last, 'but I think you'll find . . .'

Laura smiled at her, not unkindly. 'You're one of those people, aren't you?' she said. 'You like to get involved in things. You're lonely and you're bored, and you don't have any friends, and you want someone to pay attention to you. And you think I'm like you! Well, I'm not. Sorry, but I'm not.'

'Laura,' Miriam said, her voice rising in desperation, 'you're not listening to me! I believe—'

'I don't care what you believe! Sorry, but I think you're a nutter. How do I even know that you're telling the truth? How do I even know that you saw me at the boat? How do I even know that you're telling the truth about finding him? Maybe you didn't find him at all. Maybe he was alive and well when you went down there! Maybe it was you stuck a knife in him!' Laura sprang towards Miriam, her mouth wide open and red. 'Hey,' she was laughing, prancing around the table, 'maybe I should be calling the police right now!' She mimed making a call. 'Come quick! Come quick, there's a mad woman in my house! There's some psycho hobbit woman in my house!' She threw her head back and cackled like an insane person, she danced about, she was up in Miriam's face, invading her space. Miriam struggled to her feet and lurched away from Laura.

'What is wrong with you?'

But the girl was laughing, manic, lost in her own world, her eyes glistening, sharp little teeth shining white in her red mouth.

Miriam felt tears stinging her eyes. She had to get away, had to get out of there. Horrible laughter ringing in her ears, she walked from the flat with as much dignity as she could muster.

She shuffled exhaustedly down the walkway and down all those stairs, her legs as heavy as her heart.

Miriam was tearful by the time she arrived home, which was a dramatic overreaction to unkindness from a stranger, but not unusual. She overreacted to slights, that's how she was, and knowing a thing about yourself didn't stop it from happening. Miriam had lost the talent for friendship when she was young and, once gone, it was a difficult thing to recover. Like loneliness, its absence was self-perpetuating: the harder you tried to make people like you, the less likely they were to do so; most people recognized, right away, that something was off, and they shied away.

The worst part of it wasn't the end, it wasn't the jeering and the mockery, the insulting her appearance, it was what Laura had said earlier. *You're lonely and you're bored . . . and you think I'm like you.* And Miriam did, she did think Laura was like her. That was the worst part of it, being seen for what she was, what she felt. Being read and being rejected.

In the cabin of her boat, in her sleeping quarters, Miriam had an annotated copy of *The One Who Got Away*, a copy on which she'd marked up relevant sections, on which she'd noted key similarities to her own memoir. The pages towards the back of the book were thick with her scrawl, blue ink soaking through the pages where she had pressed her pen against them, her notes all but unreadable to anyone but herself, where she railed against Myerson's twisting of her tale, against all the things he'd got wrong, all the things he'd got right.

Small things throw your life off course. What happened to Miriam wasn't a small thing, it was a very big thing, but it started with a small thing. It started when Lorraine said she couldn't stand two hours of Mr Picton's coffee breath, and Biology was so boring anyway, and there was a sale at Miss Selfridge. Miriam didn't even want to bunk off, she thought they'd get into trouble. 'Don't be such a wuss,' Lorraine said.

Miriam didn't want to argue – they'd only just made up from the last fight, over a boy called Ian Gladstone who Miriam had liked for ages and who Lorrie had got off with at a party. Miriam found out about it later. 'I'm sorry,' Lorrie said, 'but he's not interested in you. I asked if he liked you and he said no. It's not my fault he chose me.'

They'd not spoken for a week after that, but neither of them really had any other friends, and it wasn't like Ian Gladstone was even worth it. 'He kisses like a washing machine,' Lorrie said, laughing, making circles in the air with her tongue.

A small thing, then.

At the farmhouse, Jez rolled a joint. He was sitting on a leg-less sofa in the main room of the house, his long legs bent, knees up by his ears. He licked the paper, running his fat tongue along the glue-tipped edge, rolling the cigarette gently between fore-finger and thumb. He lit it, took a hit and handed it to Lorraine, who was standing awkwardly to one side of the sofa. Miriam loitered near the door. Lorraine took a toke, two, then waved it at Miriam, who shook her head. Lorraine widened her eyes, *Come on*, but Miriam shook her head again. Jez hauled himself up to his feet, took the joint from Lorraine and wandered slowly out of the room, heading deeper into the house, away from the front door. 'Anyone want a beer?' he called out over his shoulder.

'Let's go,' Miriam hissed to Lorraine. 'I want to get out of here.'

Lorraine nodded OK, she looked out of the dirty window, towards the car, and then back at Miriam. 'Maybe I should say we need to go back to school?' she said.

'No, let's just—'

Jez came back, too quickly, holding two beers. 'I think,' he said, not looking at either of them, 'Lorraine and I are going to spend a bit of time on our own.'

Lorraine laughed and said, 'Nah, that's all right, I think we actually have to get going now,' and Jez put the bottles down on the floor, stepped quickly over to Lorraine and punched her in the throat.

Miriam's legs were jelly, they wouldn't work properly. She tried to run but she kept stumbling over things, and he caught her before she reached the front door, grabbing hold of her ponytail and pulling her back, ripping the hair out of her head. She fell to the ground. He dragged her back into the heart of the house, through the filth on the floor, the cigarette packets and the mouse shit. Lorraine was lying on her side, her eyes open, wide and wild; she was making a weird, rasping sound when she breathed. Miriam called out to her and Jez told her that if she opened her fucking mouth one more time he was going to kill her.

He took Miriam into another room, an empty one, at the back of the house, and shoved her to the ground. 'Just wait here,' he said to her. 'It won't be long now.' He closed the door and locked it.

(*What won't be long?*)

She tried the doorknob, pulling at the door, then pushing it, running at it, crashing against it.

(*What won't be long?*)

She couldn't be certain, but she thought she could hear Lorraine crying.

(*What won't be long?*)

Behind her, there was a sash window, big enough for her to climb through. It was locked, but the thin pane of glass was old and cracked. It wasn't double-glazed. Miriam took off her T-shirt and wrapped it around her hand. She tried to punch through the glass, but she was too tentative. She didn't want to make too much noise. She didn't want to hurt herself.

She told herself that whatever was coming, it was going to be worse than a cut hand. She told herself that she didn't have a lot of time. She had only as long as he took with Lorraine.

She hit the window again, harder this time, and then she really went for it and her hand went smashing through, one jagged peak tearing into her forearm, causing her to cry out in shock and pain. Desperate, she stuffed the bloody T-shirt into her mouth to stifle her own cries. She stood stock still, listening. Somewhere in the house she could hear someone moving around, a creaking, a heavy tread on the floorboards.

Miriam held her breath. Listening, praying. She prayed he hadn't heard her, that he wouldn't come downstairs. She prayed and prayed, tears seeping from her eyes, the smell of her own blood in her nostrils; she prayed that he would not come for her.

It was still light out. Miriam ran to the car first, but he'd taken the key from the ignition. She ran on. She ran along the winding dirt road, blood dripping from the cuts on her arm and her torso where she'd scraped herself climbing through the window. Blood ran down her neck and face, it oozed from the wound on her scalp where he'd pulled out her hair.

After a while, she was too tired to run, so she walked instead. She still seemed a long way from the main road, she hadn't remembered the drive to the farmhouse being this long – she wondered if she might have taken a wrong turn. But she couldn't remember a turn, couldn't remember any junction at all. There was this road and only this road and it seemed to go on and on, and no one would come.

It was dark by the time she heard thunder. She looked up at the cloudless sky, at the bright stars above, and realized it wasn't thunder at all, it was a car. Her knees buckled with the relief. Someone was coming! Someone was coming! Joy clouded her mind, only for a brief moment before a howling gale of cold fear blasted the clouds away. The car was coming from behind her – not from the main road but from the farm – and she started to run blindly off the road. She scrambled over a barbed-wire fence, cutting herself again in the process, and flung herself into a ditch. She heard the car's gears grind as it slowed, its lights illuminating the space above her. It passed.

Miriam lay in the ditch for a while after that, she couldn't really be sure for how long. Eventually, though, she got up, and she climbed back over the fence, the flesh of her arms and legs and torso torn, her knickers soaked with urine, her mouth sticky with blood. She started to run, she fell, she got up. She kept going. After a while, she reached a petrol station. The man there called the police.

They were too late.

The One Who Got Away

She has been crying for a while now, this girl, crying out. She calls for help and bangs on the door until her fists bleed. She says her friend's name. Quietly at first and then louder, and louder still, over and over, she calls her friend's name until it echoes through the house and silences the birds and silences everything but her pitiful cries.

In this silence, a door slams and the sound of it is deafening, earth-shattering, a sonic boom. Louder than anything the girl has ever heard in her life.

Her crying stops. She hears movement, footfall, quick and urgent and coming her way. She scrabbles backward, falling, twisting, ferreting into the corner of the room, where she presses her back to the wall, braces herself with either hand. Bares her teeth.

The footsteps slow as he approaches the door. She hears the scrape of boots against the stone, the rattle of the key in the lock, a click as it turns. Her blood is roaring and she is ready, she is ready for him now. She hears him sigh. Hush, now, big girl. Hush, now, ugly girl. It's not your turn. There is another rattle, another click, and her blood subsides, her insides seem to shift, a wave breaking a dam. Hot piss drips on to the floor.

As he leaves, he hums a tune, and in a voice full of tears he sings. What I took from her, I won't give back.

21

Carla moved through her house, from room to room, checking and re-checking wardrobes, cupboards, the backs of doors, anywhere she might have hung the bag with the St Christopher in it. Light-headed with exhaustion, she moved slowly and carefully, as if through mud. Every now and again, her phone rang. Every time it did, she looked at the screen and saw that it was Theo and sometimes she hovered her finger over the green button, she willed herself to accept the call, but every time she wavered at the last minute, either replacing the phone in her pocket or pressing red instead.

What would she say to him, if she answered now? Would she ask him the question, straight out? *What were you doing with my sister? What were you doing at her home?* Those weren't the questions she really wanted to ask, though. She hadn't formulated the real question yet, she hadn't allowed herself to do so.

She opened the storage cupboard on the landing. Why would the tote bag be here? She never opened this cupboard, hadn't opened it in months. It was filled with clothes she never wore: silk dresses and tailored suits, clothes that belonged to a woman she hadn't been in years. She stared stupidly at it all, took none of it in. Closed the cupboard door.

In her bedroom, she lay down on the bed. She pulled a woollen blanket over her legs. She was desperate to sleep, but every time she closed her eyes, she pictured it: she saw Theo with Angela, arguing outside her house. Then there was a cut, and they were inside the house, shouting at each other. In her mind, they had gone back in time. Carla saw them the way they were the day Ben died: Theo raging, wild-eyed; Angela cowering, her delicate hands raised above her head, pale wrists exposed. She heard Theo's voice asking, *Was she jealous, do you think? Of the way Ben was? You said she had a temper. Bloodthirsty*, his voice said. *You said she was bloodthirsty.* That wasn't what she'd said, was it? *A bloodthirsty imagination*, maybe? Carla's own imagination now took her elsewhere: to Angela's house on Hayward's Place, where Theo appeared in her mind as he was today, his comfortable bulk pressing against Angela's frailty, grappling at the top of the stairs. Carla saw him walking down the stairs, stepping over her sister's broken body. She saw him out in the lane, lighting a cigarette.

She opened her eyes. What would it have done to him, Carla wondered, to see Angela again, after all this time? Had it been all this time? Or had there been other meetings that she didn't know about? It hurt her to think about it, the two of them together, keeping things from her. She simply couldn't fathom *why*. All this, on top of Daniel, it was too much. She was becoming numb, her mind fogged with misery.

She rolled herself off the bed. The St Christopher her son had never worn, she needed to find it. It *must* be in this house somewhere, since it wasn't in Angela's. She started again, moving from room to room, black spots appearing in front of her eyes, a slow buzz in her ears, her limbs liquid, as she tramped downstairs and back up again, back to the cupboard on the landing, to the silk dresses, the well-cut suits. The shelf at the bottom of the cupboard was lined with a row of pale blue shoeboxes; she opened them one by one, revealing grey suede boots, red-soled stilettos, bright green sandals with black heels, and, in the last one, no shoes but a plastic bag full of ash. Carla sat back on her haunches, breath leaving her lungs in a stuttering sigh.

There you are. She'd never made up her mind what to do with her. With Angela.

After the funeral, she and Daniel had come back here, to Carla's home. They sat side by side on the sofa, drinking tea in virtual silence, the plastic bag in front of them on the coffee table. The air in the house felt heavy, the atmosphere thick with shame. Daniel was pale, thin, hollowed out, drowning in a dark suit that smelled of smoke.

'Where was she happy?' Carla asked him, staring at the bag in front of them. 'It should be somewhere she was happy.'

Next to her, she felt Daniel's shoulders rise and fall. 'I don't remember her happy,' he said.

'That isn't true.'

He sniffed. 'No, you're right. I remember her happy at Lonsdale Square. But we can't very well scatter them there, can we?' His head bent, his mouth opened, his shoulders heaved. 'She was alone for *days*,' he said.

'Daniel' – Carla put her hand on the back of his neck, leaning closer to him, her lips almost against his cheek – 'you couldn't watch her all the time.'

She meant it, but she also meant: *I* couldn't watch her all the time. 'You have to live your own life, Dan. You have to. We cannot *all* be ruined.'

He turned his face to hers then, buried it in her neck. 'You're not ruined,' he whispered.

Carla leaned forward, carefully lifting the bag of ashes from the shoebox, weighing it in her hands.

I am now.

22

Sorting through his mail, Theo discovered another letter from his fan, Mr Carter, who, Theo could tell, not just from the somewhat peevish tone but from the force with which the writer's pen had been pressed into the paper, was irritated not to have received a reply.

I did leave my email address, because I thought that meant you might respond to me quickly.

I understand that your probably busy.

In my last letter I talked about the fact that people said it was sexist that you put the point of view of the man forward and what would you say about that? I think its sexist when you only see what the female point of view is. Lots of crime books now are written by females so you often have only their point of view. I read in lots of amazon reviews that your book is 'victim blaming' but isn't the point that 'he' has also been treated badly by many people in his life, including 'the friend' and 'the girl' so in some ways he is a victim too so he can't be blamed one hundred percent? I think that maybe you made him too weak though by the end. Do you sometimes wish you had written a story a different way?

Please could you reply to my questions by email.
Thank you, kind regards,
Henry Carter.

Theo tossed the letter on the 'to do' pile with the others; he considered, briefly, what the most polite way might be to tell Mr Carter that, while he agreed that many, many Amazon reviewers had misunderstood his intentions in telling his story the way he had, it looked very much as though Mr Carter himself hadn't a clue what Theo was trying to do either. He considered this, and then he forgot about it. He was, as Mr Carter pointed out, very busy.

Not with work – he'd not done any proper work for days, he was too busy worrying about life. Eleven days had passed since Daniel died, five since he'd last spoken to Carla. She hadn't been in police custody – he'd spoken to DI Barker on the phone; the detective told him that they were 'pursuing a number of leads' (that again), but he also said they'd had no one new in for questioning, not since the girl they'd picked up and then released, and they had made no arrests.

Theo was at once relieved and disappointed – what about the girl, he'd wanted to ask. What about the bloody girl? He was relieved, though, that Carla did not appear to have fallen under suspicion.

And he knew that she was all right, that she was up and about, moving around the top floor of her home – he'd caught a glimpse of her through the window when he had been round that morning, to knock once more on her door. He'd knocked and waited and then stepped quickly back, looking up, to catch her slipping back behind the curtains. He was furious then, he wanted to scream at her, to beat his fists against the door. He couldn't, obviously. There had been an incident, last year, when the neighbours complained about him making a racket outside. They'd had a row, he couldn't remember what it was about now.

He wouldn't care about the neighbours, didn't give a damn about disturbing them, only he had to be cautious: he was a (semi) public figure, there were consequences these days to everything you did. Everything was recorded and committed to cyberspace for eternity; if you stepped out of line you'd be shamed on the internet, pilloried on Twitter, 'cancelled'. It was mob rule, not that you were allowed to say it. Saying it would get you cancelled, too.

Theo was certain now that the old woman, the nosy neighbour, must have spoken to Carla, she must have told her that he'd met Angela. And so Carla was angry because he hadn't told her. He wasn't surprised, but he was annoyed. She'd lied to him dozens of times over the years. He wasn't a complete fool, he knew that she used to see Angela occasionally. He hadn't known about the relationship with Daniel – that had come as a shock, and he was upset, not least because of the nature of its revelation. But he'd not frozen her out, had he? He hadn't ignored her calls or barred his door. He'd done as he always did, as he always would: he had stood by her. He had directed his anger elsewhere.

The last time he'd seen Angela – the very last time – Theo had raised his hand to her. He'd never struck a woman, never in his life, but he had thought about it with her, for a second, two. Then the moment passed and, instead of hitting her, he told her what he thought of her, and that was worse.

She had called him, left a message saying there was something she needed to tell him, and that she'd prefer to do it face to face. No tears this time, not at first, anyway. She invited him in, and this time he accepted. He had things to say to her, and he didn't want to say them in the street.

The previous time he'd seen her, he'd been thrown by her appearance; this time, he was taken aback by the state of her home, its carpet stained and windows filthy, the surfaces thick with dust, the pervading air of neglect made somehow worse by the fact that there were prints on the walls, carefully framed, as though Angela must once have made an effort to make her home look nice.

'Love what you've done with the place,' Theo said and Angela laughed, a throaty rumble that tore at his heart. He turned away from her, running his eye over the books on the shelf next to the fireplace, his eye coming to rest on *The One Who Got Away*. 'I hear this one's good,' he said, removing it and waving it over his head. She laughed again, half-heartedly. He tossed the book on to the coffee table, collapsing heavily into a dark leather arm-chair. He took out his cigarettes. 'I take it you don't mind?' he asked, without looking at her.

'No, I don't mind.'

'You want one?'

She shook her head. 'I'm trying to give up.' She smiled at him, glassy-eyed at eleven thirty in the morning. 'You want a coffee?'

'Is that what you're having?' he replied, and she shook her head.

She sat down in the chair facing his. 'This is hard for me, you know,' she said, and Theo barked a loud, mirthless laugh. Angela passed her hand over her eyes; her smile had become fixed, her expression strained. She was trying not to cry. 'I spoke to him,' she said eventually. 'To Daniel. I finally got him on the phone. Most of the time he just ignores my calls.' Theo said nothing. 'I asked him to leave you alone, I told him that you wouldn't be giving him any more money.'

'When was this?' Theo asked. He leaned forward to flick his ash into the ashtray, missed.

'A few days ago,' Angela said. 'He didn't say much, but he listened, and I think he . . .'

Slowly, Theo got to his feet. He took an envelope from his inside jacket pocket and handed it to Angela. She opened it, extracting the single piece of paper within, took one look at it and blanched. She closed her eyes, folded the paper, put it back into the envelope. She offered it back to Theo.

'No, that's all right,' he said coldly, 'you keep it.' He didn't want to see it again, the pencil drawing of his wife, so finely made, perfectly capturing her oddly rapturous expression in sleep. Daniel had sketched her lying on her side, the covers thrown back, her body exposed. 'I received that in the post this morning,' he said, 'so I'm not convinced your little chat did much good.' Angela bent forward, her head in her hands; she was muttering something under her breath. 'What was that?' Theo snapped. 'I didn't hear you.'

'It's monstrous,' she said, looking up at him, her eyes swimming with tears. 'I said, it's monstrous.' She bit her lip, looked away. 'Do you think,' she asked, her words catching in her throat, 'do you really think they've—'

'*They* haven't done anything!' Theo snapped, viciously grinding his cigarette into the ashtray. 'This is not about *them*, it's about him. It's all him, it's his perverted little fantasy. And do you know what?' He was towering over her now, and she was so small, so fragile, like a child at his feet. 'I can't even blame him. I mean, you can't, can you? Look at the life he's had! Look at the place he grew up! Look at the state of his mother!'

'Theo, please.' She was looking up at him through huge eyes, she was begging, and he raised his hand to strike her, to wipe the self-pity off her face.

He watched her cower, terrified, and then he stepped back, appalled at what Angela had provoked in him. 'I feel sorry for him,' he said. 'I do. Look at the life you made for him. He has no idea of what love is supposed to be, no idea of what a mother's love is. How could he?'

'I tried,' she sobbed, 'I tried . . .'

'You tried!' he roared at her. 'Your laziness, your neglect cost my child his life. And then you neglected your own son, too, sent him away because he got in the way of your drinking. Is it any wonder he ended up a sociopath?'

'He didn't end up a—'

'He did, Angela. That's what he is. He is grasping, calculating and manipulative. That's what you've done to him.'

She fell silent for a few moments, and then rose unsteadily to her feet. Hands trembling, she picked up the copy of Theo's book and tucked the envelope he had given her inside it, before replacing it on the bookshelf. She turned to face him again, drawing in her breath, as though summoning her energy for some onerous task. 'I need . . .' she said, wringing her hands together in front of her chest, 'I want to tell you something.'

Theo spread his hands, eyebrows raised. 'I'm listening.'

Angela swallowed hard, she seemed to be wrestling with something.

'Well?' He'd no patience for this, for her amateur dramatics.

'I think it's best if I show you,' she said quietly. 'Would you . . . would you just come upstairs?'

23

Laura found herself fixating on all the things she'd done wrong, but not necessarily the obvious things. She didn't wake up in a cold sweat thinking about Daniel Sutherland lying dead on his boat, she didn't fixate on the guy with the fork sticking out of his hand. No, the thing that kept coming to her, the thing that made her cringe, made all the blood rush to her face, made her insides squeeze up like a fist, was the incident on the bus, that time she'd shouted at that woman, calling her a stupid fat cow. She couldn't stop seeing the expression on the woman's face, her hurt and her embarrassment; every time she thought of it, it brought tears to her eyes.

She'd thought of going back and riding the same route in the hopes of finding her, so she could apologize and explain that she had this problem, that when she was stressed or tired or angry she said things she didn't mean (which, of course, wasn't true, the problem was that she said things she *did* mean, but the woman didn't have to know that). The thing was, she couldn't remember what bus it was.

Still, thinking about the woman on the bus made her think about Miriam, about the look on *her* face, how shocked and hurt she had seemed when Laura had taunted her, when she had laughed at her. Miriam was strange and off-putting and Laura didn't feel bad about what she'd done in the same way as she did about the woman on the bus, she certainly wasn't crying over it, but still. It had been pretty fucking uncalled for. There had been no need to be cruel, she hadn't really meant to be, she'd just got carried away. And since she couldn't apologize to the person she wanted to apologize to, she may as well apologize to Miriam. She knew, at least, where Miriam lived.

She found the *Lorraine* moored exactly where Miriam had said it would be, just a few yards further along from where Daniel's boat had been. That boat was gone now, there was another in its place, a much smarter, tidier one with an expensive-looking bike attached to the roof. It was strange, going back down there, it was like he'd been erased, every trace of him. Strange in a good way: it was like that thing had never happened, like it had been a dream – look, there's no dirty blue boat here! That thing you thought happened? It didn't. It was a nightmare. You can wake up now.

The *Lorraine* wasn't like the dirty blue boat at all, it was long and sleek, painted green with a red trim, there were well-tended pot plants on the roof, solar panels at one end, it looked tidy and clean and lived-in. It looked like somebody's home.

Laura stood outside it, on the towpath, wondering where exactly it was that one knocked when one wanted to attract the attention of whoever lived in a boat (on the window? That seemed intrusive), when Miriam emerged, stepping through the cabin doors on to the back deck. Her frizzy hair was down, it hung limp on her shoulders, echoing the shape of her tent-like linen dress. Miriam's legs and feet were bare and startlingly white, as though they'd not seen the sun in a very long time. Her toenails were long, yellowing slightly. Laura wrinkled her nose, stepping back a little; the movement caught Miriam's attention.

'What the hell do *you* want?' she snarled.

'Your home is really lovely,' Laura said, staring dumbly at the boat before her. 'It's really pretty.' Miriam said nothing. She folded her arms across her chest, glowering at Laura from beneath her lank hair. Laura bit a nail. 'The reason I came is that I wanted to say sorry for how rude I was. I wanted to explain—'

'I'm not interested,' Miriam said, but she didn't move or turn away, she remained on the back deck, looking Laura directly in the eye.

'I say stupid things. I do it all the time, it's not even . . . I mean it *is* my fault, but it's not always something I can control.' Miriam cocked her head to one side. She was listening. 'It's a thing I have, a condition. It's called disinhibition. It's from the accident. You know I told you about the accident I had when I was younger? Please,' Laura said, taking a step towards the boat. She hung her head. 'I only wanted to say I was sorry, I was horrible to you, and you were only trying to help me, I see that now. I'm really sorry.'

Miriam glowered a little longer. She turned away, as if to go back into the boat, then turned to face Laura again. At last, she relented. 'Come on, then,' she snapped. 'You'd better come in.'

'This is nice, isn't it?' Laura walked up and down the cabin space. 'It's so . . . *homey*, isn't it? I didn't think these boats could be so *cosy*.'

Miriam nodded, her mouth a firm line, but Laura could tell, from the glow in her cheeks, the expression in her eyes, that she was pleased. Miriam offered tea, she put the kettle on and collected mugs from a cupboard. Laura continued to look around, running her fingers over book spines, picking up the framed photograph of Miriam with her parents. 'This is you! You can see it's you, can't you? You haven't changed that much,' she said, thinking, *You were minging then and all*. 'Your mum and dad look like nice people.'

'They were,' Miriam said. She hoisted herself up on to the bench opposite where Laura stood.

'Oh.' Laura turned to look at her. 'They're not around any more? Sorry. My parents are a dead loss. I told you that, didn't I? My dad means well, but my mum's a nightmare, and the thing with her is, no matter how shit she is, right, I always end up forgiving her, don't know why. I can't help myself.'

The kettle whistled. Miriam got up and removed it from the hob. She folded her arms once more across her chest, watching Laura with a thoughtful expression on her face. 'You're damaged, that's why,' she said at last. 'I don't mean that as a criticism, it's an observation. Things were done to you when you were younger that left you with scars, inside and out. Isn't that right?'

Laura nodded. She backed away a little, so that she was leaning right up against the bookshelf.

'When I came to your home and you laughed at me and mocked me – no, no, don't say anything, just listen – when that happened, I told you that we were similar, and you said that we weren't, but you were wrong. I recognize the damage in you, because I've been damaged too, you see. Something happened to me when I was a girl, something that marked me.'

Laura sidled along the back of the cabin, towards the bench that ran along one of its sides. She hopped up on to it, crossing her legs as she did, leaning forward, her curiosity piqued. 'How do you mean?' she asked. 'What happened?'

Miriam reached for the kettle, she picked it up and then put it down again. She turned to face Laura. 'When I was fifteen years old,' she said quietly, her expression grave, 'I was abducted.'

Laura was so surprised she almost laughed. She covered her

mouth with her hand just in time. 'You . . . you were *abducted*? Are you being serious?'

Miriam nodded. 'I was with a friend. We bunked off school one day, we were hitchhiking. A man picked us up and he . . . he took us to a house. A farm. He locked me in a room.' She turned away again, her fat little fingers holding on to the edge of the counter. 'He locked me in, but I managed to break a window, I managed to escape.'

'*Jesus.* That is, like, unbelievable.' Laura meant it literally – she couldn't be sure whether to believe Miriam. 'That's really horrible. Were you hurt?'

Miriam nodded.

'Fuck. Man, I'm sorry, that is . . . that is properly scary. Was your friend hurt too?'

Miriam said nothing. She didn't move, but Laura could see her knuckles whitening.

'Miriam?'

'I couldn't help her,' Miriam said quietly. 'I ran away.'

'Oh, God. Oh my God.' Laura, for once, was lost for words. She shook her head, her hand covering her mouth, tears springing to her eyes. 'But then . . . ?'

Miriam gave a cursory nod.

'Oh, God,' Laura said again. 'When was this? I mean, you were fifteen, so this was like . . . the Seventies?'

'Eighties,' Miriam said.

'And . . . what happened? I mean, afterwards. Jesus. I can't even imagine this. I can't even begin to imagine what it must have been like for you.'

For a long moment Miriam stood and looked at her, and then, without speaking, she turned away, squeezing through the door from the main cabin into what Laura assumed must be the sleeping area at the end of the boat. When she returned, she had in her hands a sheaf of papers. 'If you're really interested,' she said, 'you could read this. It's the book I wrote about it. What happened, how it affected me.' Miriam held out the papers, which had been bound into a hefty manuscript. 'You could . . .' Miriam's face was flushed, her eyes shining. 'I suppose you could read it if you want.'

Without thinking, Laura shook her head. 'I'm not much of a reader,' she said. She watched Miriam snatch the manuscript back to her chest, all the warmth disappearing from her eyes, her mouth turning down, her expression souring. 'I mean . . . I really would like to read it,' Laura said, holding out her hand. Miriam pulled away. 'Only it might take me a while, because, like, I'm really, really slow. I mean, not like I'm slow in the head, though some people might say that too, although actually when I was little they said I was gifted and I used to read, like, all the time, but then after the accident I just couldn't concentrate on anything and I kind of lost the habit, do you know what I mean?' Laura bit her lip. 'I would really like to read it, it sounds like . . .' What did it sound like? It sounded awful, devastating. 'It sounds like such an interesting story.'

Warily, Miriam handed over the manuscript. 'You can take your time. But please be careful with it,' she said.

Laura nodded vigorously. 'I won't let it out of my sight,' she said, and she shoved the manuscript into her backpack.

They slipped back into awkward silence. Laura gazed hopefully at the kettle.

'Have the police been in touch with you?' Miriam asked her. Laura shook her head. 'Good. That's good, isn't it?'

Laura chewed her lip. 'I suppose. I don't really know. I keep looking on the news to see if there's been any . . . progress, but there doesn't seem to be.'

'No, there doesn't, does there?'

And the silence descended again.

'I could murder a cup of tea,' Laura said.

'Oh, yes!' Miriam looked relieved to have something to do. She resumed tea-making duties, only to discover that she had no sugar (Laura took two and a half spoons), so she said she'd nip along the towpath to the café to borrow some.

Laura slipped off the bench and started to inspect Miriam's accommodation. It was a lot nicer than she'd been expecting. Then again, what *had* she been expecting? Something sad and dirty and dreary, like Daniel's place? This wasn't *that*, this was a lot nicer than her own flat. Here there were plants and pictures and cookbooks, there were blankets, old and threadbare but colourful still, folded neatly in the corner. It smelled lovely, of woodsmoke and lemon. All the surfaces were spotless.

On the bookcase next to the wood burner sat a little gold carriage clock. Laura picked it up, felt its pleasing weight in her hand. Above the bookcase, there was a shelf on which sat a wooden box. Laura tried the lid and was surprised to find it unlocked. She took the box from the shelf and placed it in front of her on the bench. Inside, she found a pair of gold hoop earrings, which didn't look like Miriam's taste at all. She slipped them into her pocket and continued to sift through the box. There was a silver cross with a tiny crucified Jesus, a dog tag, a smooth grey pebble, a letter addressed to Miriam, a key attached to a keyring.

Laura was so surprised to see it that at first she didn't recognize it. Not *a* key, *her* key! Her front door key, attached to the wooden keyring with a bird on it. She picked it up, holding it up to the light. Behind her, she heard a creak, and she felt the boat rock gently beneath her. Out of the corner of her eye she saw a shadow move and a voice said, 'What do you think you're doing?'

Laura jerked around so quickly she almost fell off the bench. Miriam stood in the doorway, a jar of sugar in one hand, her face thunderous. 'What in God's name do you think you're doing, going through my things?'

'*Your* things?' Laura recovered quickly, squaring herself, ready to go on the offensive. 'This is *mine!*' she said. 'What the fuck are you doing with my front-door key?'

Miriam took a step forward and placed the jar of sugar on the counter. 'I found it,' she said, pursing her lips, as though she were offended that Laura should question her in this way. 'I meant to give it back to you, only I forgot. I—'

'You *forgot*? You were in my flat the other day, and you didn't think to tell me you had my key? Where did you find it? Where . . . this is blood, isn't it?' Laura said, turning the key over in her hand. 'This had . . . *Jesus*, this is covered in blood.' She dropped the key as though it were red hot, wiping her fingers on her jeans. 'Why would you take it?' she asked Miriam, her eyes wide, uncomprehending. 'You were there, you said, you were there after I left, but why would you . . . why would you take it?' Laura was starting to get a bad feeling about this, a very bad feeling, not helped by Miriam, standing squarely in front of her, blocking the entrance to the cabin, a stout, squat block of flesh, arms across her chest, shaking her head but saying nothing, as though she were thinking, as though she were trying to come up with an excuse for her behaviour. Laura's stomach flipped. Before, back at her flat, she'd been *joking* when she'd said that maybe Miriam killed Daniel, but now, now she was thinking maybe she'd been right, now she was thinking all kinds of things. This woman was damaged, this woman was a victim, this woman was fucking *crazy*.

'I saw it.' Miriam spoke at last, her expression blank and her voice even, the anger gone. 'I saw the key lying there, it was next to him. He was pale, and he looked . . . oh.' She sighed, a long sigh, as though all the breath were leaving her body. 'He looked desperate, didn't he?' She closed her eyes, shaking her head again. 'I saw the key, I picked it up . . .' As she spoke she half-mimed the action, bending down, picking up the key, her eyes tightly shut until she said, 'I was protecting you, Laura. I've been protecting you all along, and I may have my own reasons for doing so, but that doesn't change anything.'

Fucking *crazy.*

'I don't want your protection!' Laura could hear the fear in her own voice and it made her feel panicky. 'I don't need anything from you! I just need to get out . . .' She grabbed her backpack and tried to manoeuvre her way through the tight space of the cabin, past Miriam's considerable bulk. 'Let me get out, please . . .' But Miriam was solid, she wouldn't move, she pushed back, throwing Laura off balance. 'Don't you touch me! Don't touch me!'

Laura needed to get out, she needed to get off this boat, she felt as though she were choking, as though she couldn't breathe. She felt as though she had been plunged back into the nightmare from before, the one where she was on Daniel's dirty little boat and he was laughing at her, and she could taste his flesh in her mouth. She was spitting now, screaming, '*Get out of my way get out of my way get out of my way,*' she was wrestling with someone, some other body, grabbing fistfuls of greasy hair, pushing against her, '*Get out of my way,*' she could smell sweat and bad breath, she bared her teeth, '*Please,*' she was crying out, and Miriam was crying too. '*Don't touch me don't touch me don't touch me.*'

The One Who Got Away

Arms linked, they are on their way home from the horrible pub in the middle of town, the girl and her friend, weaving a little along the side of the road. The girl is buoyed by gin and happy, comforted by the warm press of her friend's skinny arm against the roll of flesh at her waist.

A car approaches, and her friend sticks out a thumb, half-heartedly. A battered yellow Golf, its go-faster stripe peeling away from the paint-work, cruises past, and slows. They look at each other and laugh. They run towards the car, and as its door swings open, the girl hears a snatch of music, someone singing, a man's voice, gravelly and low. She catches sight of the driver's neck, red raw.

Don't, she says to her friend. Don't.

But her friend is already getting into the car, sliding in next to him, saying, Where are we off to, then?

24

There were dandelions and daisies around his headstone, sunny yellow and soft cream amid the grass, which was overgrown, but gave the impression of lushness rather than untidiness. Carla longed to lie down on the grass, she longed to lie down right there, to sleep and not wake up. She had brought with her a red cashmere blanket, which she laid out, and instead of lying, she knelt, leaning forward, as though in prayer. She rested her fingertips on top of the black granite headstone, still shockingly new among the greyer, mossier graves, and said, 'Happy birthday, sweetheart.' She leaned back on her haunches and allowed herself to cry for a little while, in small, hiccupping sobs. Then she wiped her eyes, blew her nose and sat down cross-legged, her back straight, to wait. Before long, she saw Theo making his way towards her along the path, as she'd known she would. He raised a hand in greeting. She felt her heart beat feebly in the base of her throat.

He stopped a few paces away from her. 'I've been worried, you know,' he said, but she could tell from the tone of his voice and the cast of his face that he wasn't angry with her. He had a chastened look, the same one he'd worn when she found out about the publicist. So, he knew. He knew that she knew about Angela, that there was something to know about Angela.

'I lost Ben's St Christopher,' Carla said, moving a little to one side to make space for him on the blanket. He sat down heavily, leaned in to kiss her, but she shrank back, saying, 'No.'

He frowned at her. 'Where did you lose it? What were you doing with it?'

'I . . . I don't know. If I knew where I'd lost it, I wouldn't really have lost it, would I? I had it out, because . . . just because I wanted to look at it. I've looked everywhere.'

He nodded, his gaze moving over her, taking her in. 'You look awful, Carla,' he said.

'Yeah, thanks. I've not had a great couple of weeks,' she said, and she started to laugh, just a giggle at first and then a full-throated cackle. She laughed until tears ran down her face, until Theo lifted his hand to brush them away. She flinched away from him again. 'Don't touch me,' she said. 'Not until you tell me the truth. I don't want you to touch me until you tell me what you did.' Part of her wanted to run away from him, part of her ached to hear him deny it.

Theo rubbed the top of his head with his forefinger, his chin dropping to his chest. 'I saw Angela. I went to see her because Daniel had come to me asking for money, and I'd given him some, but then he wanted more. That's it. That's the whole story.'

Carla twisted her fingers into the grass, pulled a clump up with her hands, pushed it back into the soil. 'Why didn't you tell me, Theo? Why wouldn't you tell me that Daniel had come to you, of all people . . .'

Theo threw up his hands. 'I don't know. I don't know! I didn't know what was going on, and frankly' – he looked her dead in the eye – 'I wasn't sure I wanted to.'

Carla felt her skin flush from the base of her neck to her cheekbones. 'So you saw her . . . once? Just that one time? Theo?'

'Twice,' he said quietly. 'She asked to see me the second time, and I went. I couldn't tell you, Cee . . . It was,' he exhaled hard, 'just before she died. I went to see her, and a week or so later she was found at the bottom of the stairs. It looked bad.'

'It looked bad,' Carla repeated. 'And was it?' she asked, her voice soft. 'Bad?'

'Cee . . .' He reached for her hand and she let him take it. 'I don't want to have this conversation here, do you? It's Ben's day. It's his eighteenth. I don't even want to think about her today.'

'Why did she ask to see you?' Carla asked.

Theo didn't answer. He leaned towards her and kissed her on the mouth, and she let him.

'I've missed you,' he said. 'I don't like it when you disappear.'

They sat for a while in silence, hand in hand. Theo had brought cognac in a hip flask and they took turns to sip from it, passing it back and forth between them.

When the alcohol was burning hot in her chest, Carla asked him, 'What would you do differently? If you could. Would you still marry me if you knew what was to come?'

'Of course, I would. I—'

'I don't think I'd have married you,' she said. Theo winced. She squeezed his hand, dropped it. 'I don't mean that to be cruel, but if I had known, I don't think I could have. Only, I suppose it didn't really matter who I married, did it? It might have happened anyway, mightn't it?'

'What do you mean?' He took hold of her wrist, finger and thumb looping around the slender bone; with his other hand he reached out and touched her face. He tried to turn her chin so that she would face him, but she pulled away.

'The poison,' she said. 'It came from me, from *my* family.'

'You are not your sister,' Theo replied.

Then, finally, she met his eye. 'You should forgive her, Theo.'

Theo tried to get Carla to go home with him, but she insisted that she wanted to stay a while. At first he offered to stay with her, but eventually she managed to persuade him to leave. Though not before he'd handed over a USB drive with a draft of his latest novel for her to read.

'Theo, really? I do have quite a lot going on at the moment, you know? I haven't even . . .' Her voice caught. 'I haven't even done anything about the funeral. Daniel's funeral. I have to wait for the coroner to finish the inquest and then I . . .'

'I can take care of that,' Theo said, still pressing the USB stick into her hand. 'I can make those arrangements, I'll talk to the police about where they are with the inquest, but . . . *Cee*. You've always been my first reader. You can't just stop being my first reader, it doesn't work like that.'

Carla watched him weave his way through the gravestones, a little the worse for the cognac, dappled sunlight picking him out as he made his way to the main road. She waited for a while to make quite sure that he was gone, that he hadn't turned back, wasn't loitering somewhere keeping an eye on her, before she took from her pocket a handful of ash and sprinkled it over the grass covering Ben's grave.

She tried to conjure up her sister's lazy drawl, her throaty laugh.

'Do you remember that house in Vaugines, Cee?' Angela had asked her, years ago. They'd been sitting on the sofa in Angela's living room in the house on Hayward's Place, weak sun shining through half-closed curtains, illuminating the room with a dirty yellow glow. Angela sat with her feet tucked up underneath her; she was smoking, picking at her nails. Her hands were steady, which meant she'd already had a drink. 'Do you remember that place, by the olive grove, with all those strange animal-head sculptures on the walls? And Daniel and I stayed in the pool house? Ben was still a baby, he was *tiny*.' She held out her hands to demonstrate. 'Warm and perfect like a loaf of bread.'

'Of course I remember,' Carla said. 'It was the first holiday we ever took him on. Theo and I spent all our time on those day-beds beneath the trees, falling asleep with him tucked in between us.' She closed her eyes. 'What were those trees? Were they oak trees, do you think? Or maybe plane . . .'

'Those incredible sunsets,' Angela said. 'Remember those? All that rosé.'

'And you couldn't get Daniel out of the pool, not for love nor money. Do you remember how cross he got, because he wanted to teach Ben to swim and we kept telling him Ben was way too little?'

Angela shook her head. 'Did he? Did he really?' she asked, bending forward to stub out her cigarette in the ashtray on the carpet. 'It seems impossible, doesn't it? Thinking about it now, from *here*,' – she gestured at the ugly room around them – 'that we were all so happy. It seems unimaginable. All that happiness, wrecked.'

Carla's own hands shook, her arms, her legs, her whole body trembled as she rose to her feet, as she stared down at her sister, lamenting their lost contentment. 'Unimaginable,' she'd croaked. 'It is, isn't it? Just a few moments of carelessness, an hour or two of unthinking neglect, a door left open. And here we are.'

She remembered the way her sister stared at her then, glassy-eyed, her mouth working but making no sound.

Carla took another handful of ash, and brought it to her lips before she pressed it down, into the earth.

The One Who Got Away

They skip school, slipping through the gates unseen. There's a bus to and from town, one an hour, on the half-hour. Hurry up! Her friend hitches up her skirt, sprints ahead, waving frantically to attract the driver's attention. The girl half jogs, book bag slung awkwardly over her shoulder, large breasts bouncing. They board the bus, pass the smirking driver, pass the other sour-faced passengers.

The moment they get off the bus, the girl regrets coming. It is baking hot, pavements crammed with shoppers. There's nothing to do here, nowhere to go. Listlessly they drag their feet from shop to shop, they look at clothes they cannot afford, they buy cigarettes from the corner shop, cheap ones, rough on the back of the throat. They smoke, lighting one from another, until they feel sick.

They go to the pub, but the barman won't serve them. They sit at a table outside, skirts hitched up. Sunning themselves. The old blokes sitting at the next table give them dirty looks. A younger man approaches, he looks at them, looks at the friend, not at the girl, he smiles. He is ugly, his eyes too close together, acne on his neck, red raw. Her friend rolls her eyes. As if, she says, and she laughs.

Music starts to play from somewhere, a radio, a jukebox. The girl has heard this one before, something slow, a man's voice soft and hoarse over acoustic guitar. In the hot afternoon sun, the girl's skin is cold. She feels as though someone has poured petrol all over her, and yet there is a point at the back of her scalp, right where her ponytail is secured, that throbs with a vicious heat.

Something bad is going to happen.

25

The basin almost full, her hands plunged wrist deep into warm, soapy water, Miriam experienced a flashback so pin-sharp she recoiled. It wasn't visual, but a sensation: the sudden, surprising heat of arterial blood bubbling up through her fingers; the shock, immediately afterwards, of disappointment. Of sorrow. *No taking it back.* She stood at the sink in her tiny bathroom, her arms in the water, unable to move for a minute, perhaps even two. Her right hand squeezed a nail brush and her left gripped the handle of a pair of scissors, as if in spasm.

And then the moment passed, her hands relaxed and she came back to herself. She pulled the plug and watched the soapy water run out, she replaced the brush and the scissors on the little shelf beneath the mirror. Carefully, she dried her hands, before tipping a little antiseptic lotion on to a ball of cotton wool, which she applied gently to the scratches on her neck and arms. She took the strips of adhesive bandage she'd cut from the roll and applied it to the worst of the wounds, along the side of her left forearm.

When she was finished, Miriam returned to the main cabin and began to tidy up. She replaced the books that had tumbled from the shelves, she put her wooden box back in its place; with a dustpan and brush she swept up broken pottery and soil, one of her herb pots having fallen from the sill. The plant itself, a little spike of tarragon, was irredeemable. Back aching, knees pressed painfully into the floor, she worked methodically, trying her best to sweep away all traces of her confrontation with that vicious girl. She was angry, but her fury was controlled, simmering, right up until the moment when she discovered one of Lorraine's gold hoop earrings under the table, bent slightly out of shape, and she started to sob.

Why must people take what does not belong to them? Why must they take what is hers, and ruin it?

What Miriam remembered most vividly from the time immediately after her abduction was not the hospital. Not her mother, sobbing so hard she literally had to be propped up by Miram's father when they came to see her for the first time. Not the hours of interviews with the police, not the crowds of people camped outside their home, the journalists and the television cameras.

What she remembered most clearly was the unbearable kindness of Lorraine's parents. Lorraine's father, weeping when he came to her hospital room, squeezing her hand, murmuring, 'Thank God, thank God you're all right.'

Surely, Miriam thought, that could not really be what he was thinking? Surely he must have been thinking, *Why not you? Why wasn't it you?*

After Lorraine's funeral, there was a wake at her parents' home. Miriam asked if she could go upstairs, if she could spend some time in Lorraine's bedroom, and Lorraine's mother, this small, broken woman, managed to smile at her. 'Of course you can,' she said. 'You are always welcome here. You can visit any time you like.'

Upstairs, sitting at Lorraine's dressing table, Miriam looked at all her friend's brightly coloured scrunchies, her lipsticks in dark pinks and reds, her eyeshadow palette in purple, blue and white. There was a jewellery box in front of the mirror, it played 'Greensleeves' when you opened it, Miriam had admired it since they were little girls. Inside the box there were necklaces and bracelets, a ring too small for Miriam's fingers and the earrings, the gold hoops, which she slipped into her jacket pocket.

She left the wake without saying goodbye.

Three days later, Jeremy's car was found in a car park on a cliff in an area euphemistically referred to as a beauty spot, one of those places people go when they have nowhere left to run. Three days after that, in very bad weather, the coastguard called off the search. And three weeks after that, two young children playing on a beach near Hastings came across a severed human foot which was the right size and colour, which contained blood of the right type. Whether dashed against rocks or chewed up in a boat's propeller, Jeremy was gone for good. All that remained of him was the note he'd left in the glove compartment of his abandoned car – a note of apology, a single word, *sorry*.

Sorry.

At school, everyone felt sorry for Miriam. Everyone felt sorry for her, and nobody wanted to be anywhere near her. Everyone looked at her and no one met her eye. Her name was on everyone's lips and no one spoke to her at break time, at lunch. She walked past and they smiled kindly, even the teachers, looking at some point in the middle distance, not at her. She was tainted. People – her parents, her grief counsellor, the police – told her that what had happened to Lorraine wasn't her fault. 'No one would have expected you to do any different, Miriam.' But the fact that they felt the need to say it told its own tale. The fact that they felt the need to say it meant they had thought about it, they had thought, *You might have done something else. No one would have expected you to. But you might have.*

No one ever said that out loud. Not until Theo Myerson came along.

The One Who Got Away

When he catches her, she knows what he is going to do to her. She has come full circle, this girl. Lying in the dirt, she sees herself as she was that morning, at her dressing table, brushing her hair, pulling it back into a ponytail which she secured, tightly, with a band at the nape of her neck.

Still innocent then.

She could have stopped it, couldn't she? She could, when her friend suggested skipping school, have simply shaken her head and walked ahead to Double Maths. She could, when they were in town, have refused the pub and suggested the park. She could have said, I'm not getting in that car. She could have said it louder: Don't.

Even after it had all been set in motion, she could have done something different.

She didn't have to run.

Instead of running, she might have selected a piece of glass from the debris lying on the yellowing grass outside the window she had shattered. She might have slipped this sliver into the pocket of her jeans. She might have crept back into the house, following the sounds of her friend's distress. She might have slunk into the room where he held her, where he pinned her to the filthy floor. With bare feet she might have moved quickly, her breath held. She might have grabbed hold of his hair, pulled his head back and jammed the piece of glass into his throat.

But now it is too late.

26

Irene, dozing in her chair next to the window, a copy of Pat Barker's *Blow Your House Down* open in her lap, was woken by the rain, a sudden downpour so heavy the raindrops drummed like hail against the flagstones in the lane outside, the sound of it so loud that Irene almost missed the sound of someone weeping.

She thought she'd imagined it at first, and then, rising to her feet, she thought with a sinking heart that it might be Carla – despairing, tragic Carla – back to haunt the house next door once more. But then she heard a knocking at her door, so soft, so tentative it might have been the work of a child. She heard a small voice call out, 'Irene? Are you there?'

Laura, on her doorstep, soaked to the skin and in a dreadful state, her jacket torn and a livid bruise the size of a tennis ball marring the left side of her face. She was trembling, weeping like a little girl.

'Laura, good God! Come inside.' Irene reached for her, but Laura drew back.

'Don't,' she sobbed. 'You shouldn't. You shouldn't be kind to me.'

'What on earth are you talking about? Laura, for goodness'

sake!' She grabbed a handful of the girl's sodden coat. 'Come in, come out of the rain.'

In the darkened hallway, the door shut behind her, Laura shook herself like a dog. 'You should turn me away,' she said miserably. 'You should tell me to fuck off – not that you'd ever say that, because you're too nice and polite.'

'Well, quite,' Irene said crossly. 'Stop being silly. Take off that wet coat, put it on the radiator there. Hasn't it got cold? I'll turn the heating on. Now come on, don't dawdle, don't drip. Come into the living room. I'm going to turn the heating on and then I'm going to get us a cup of tea. You can tell me all about it, you can start from the beginning.'

When she returned with the tea, Laura was sitting on the floor in the middle of the living room, her legs crossed and her head in her hands. Irene handed her a mug. 'Come on, then. Let's hear it. What's going on?'

As Irene settled back into her armchair, Laura began. She said that she'd taken money from Irene's purse, which Irene knew, of course, because although she was forgetful, she wasn't a fool. Laura told her that she'd taken something from next door, too, that she'd seen the door open and snatched a bag from the hall-way, and Irene had not known about that.

'Do you still have what you took?' she asked sternly, and the girl nodded. 'Then you'll give it back. Money is one thing, Laura, and I understand you're in a tight spot. But you can't take things that mean something to someone. Can you imagine how you'd feel,' she scolded, 'if someone took William's watch from me? Can you imagine what you'd think of that person?'

Laura cringed in shame. Her expression forlorn, she tipped the contents of her backpack on to Irene's living-room floor, picked up the two little jewellery boxes and handed them to Irene.

'That's not the worst of it,' she said, her voice barely more than a whisper.

Irene's heart quailed. She dreaded what Laura was about to tell her, for what could be worse? What could be worse than stealing from a grieving woman?

'What have you done, Laura?' Her breath catching, she could barely utter the words. 'You've not . . . you haven't hurt someone, have you?'

Laura looked up, eyes bright. 'I don't think so. Unless you count the guy with the fork, but I don't think that's what you mean, is it?' Irene shook her head, confused. 'Daniel,' Laura said, and Irene's hand flew to her mouth.

'Oh no, Laura.' Irene felt her heart might stop.

'I didn't kill him!' Laura cried. She was on her knees at Irene's feet. 'I didn't, I swear. But I was there . . . just before. I was there with him. And I didn't tell you, because you said he was trouble, you—'

'I didn't say he was trouble, Laura. I said he was *troubled*. I think I warned you to be careful with him because he was a troubled boy, didn't I? He had a difficult family life, I told you that, I—'

'And I didn't listen. And I went with him, and I spent the night . . .' Laura tailed off.

Outside, the rain had abated somewhat, but the sky was darkening as if in preparation for a second assault.

'You stayed the night?' Irene repeated, and Laura looked down at the carpet. 'Oh, for God's sake!' Irene snapped. 'There's no need to be so coy. I'm an old woman, not a child.' Laura nodded, but she didn't raise her eyes. 'So, you spent the night with him. And then you left without any breakfast, I'm guessing. But he was fine when you left him?' Laura nodded again. 'And you've no idea what happened to him?' Laura shook her head this time.

'Laura! Did you honestly think, in the light of all that, that it was really a good idea to go stealing from his family? For God's sake. Imagine how it would look, if someone found out, if—'

'Someone *has* found out,' Laura said, her voice small. 'You have.'

Irene rolled her eyes; she felt quite cross. 'Oh, don't be ridiculous, I'm not about to call the police, am I? And none of that explains all this,' Irene said, waving her hand in Laura's direction. 'None of it explains the state you're in now.'

'Oh, well.' Laura sat back down, crossing her legs. 'There's this woman, you see, who lives in one of the boats on the canal, and I know her a bit because she comes in the launderette sometimes, her name's Miriam, and she's a bit weird, she *looks* weird, you know, like she's always wearing a few too many clothes, do you know what I mean? In any case, she's the one who found Daniel – found his body, I mean – she was the one who called the police, and then the other day she showed up outside the launderette, and I was in a bit of a state, nothing terrible, just . . . you know.' Irene didn't know, she had no idea what Laura was talking about. 'Anyway, so I went round to her place, to her boat, you see, because I owed her an apology – it's a long story, you don't really have to know about all this, but the point is, the point is, when I got to the boat, I found out that she had the key to my flat.'

'She had your key?'

'Exactly! Remember I said I lost it? Well, she had it.'

'And she gave it back to you?' Irene wasn't really understanding the point of this story.

'No, no, she didn't give it to me. She hid it from me. I found it in her boat. I was looking through her things, you see . . .'

'You were looking for something to steal!' Irene said.

'Yes, all right, I was, but that's not the point, is it? The point is she had my key. And so when I found it we had a bit of a . . . well . . .'

'An altercation?'

'Exactly.'

'And she hit you? This woman hit you? Gave you that bruise?'

Laura shook her head. 'There was a bit of pushing and shoving, I was basically trying to get out of there, and I tripped. I fell.'

'Do you think we ought to be calling the police, Laura? I mean, if this woman has your key, then—'

'Oh, no – I have the key now.' She delved into her jeans pocket and pulled it out, along with one gold earring, which she peered at, before stuffing it back into her pocket. 'I have the key, and I have this as well.' From the pile where she'd emptied out her backpack, she took a sheaf of papers, a bound manuscript, which she held out to Irene. 'She gave me this. Before we had our . . . whatchacallit – altercation – she gave me this. Her "memoir",' Laura said, air quoting with her fingers. 'Suggested I read it. Which I'm never going to do. You might like it, though. It has a crime in it! She claims she was kidnapped by a madman when she was young. Or something like that, anyway.'

'Good grief,' Irene said, accepting the manuscript with both hands. 'How extraordinary.'

There was a sudden flash of light, accompanied by a particularly vicious crack of thunder, which had them both ducking their heads.

'Fucking hell,' Laura said.

'Indeed,' Irene replied. 'Do you know,' she said, 'I think you ought to go upstairs and get out of those wet things, hang them in the airing closet and run yourself a nice hot bath. I think you should stay here with me this afternoon, don't you?'

Laura smiled, squeezing tears from her eyes. 'I'd like that.'

*

Above the sound of the second downpour, Irene could hear Laura singing, her voice truer and sweeter than Irene would have imagined. She took her time, it was almost an hour before she came back downstairs, wrapped in a pink terrycloth robe that had been folded up in the airing cupboard, unused for the best part of a decade. Something about the sight of this tiny young woman in Irene's old robe was extraordinarily touching to Irene. She felt a wave of emotion come over her, a feeling she imagined might almost be maternal.

She said none of this to Laura, whom she suspected might be embarrassed by such a declaration. Instead, she said, 'Do you know, it's very odd, this book.' She brandished the manuscript Laura had brought with her. 'This memoir. I was reading through it and—'

'You can't have read it already,' Laura said, flinging herself lengthways on to the sofa and rearranging the cushions beneath her head.

'Well, I was just skimming through it. It's actually not badly written – a little overwrought, perhaps, but the odd thing is that some parts of it feel terribly familiar, though of course the idea of someone escaping from a serial killer isn't exactly *original*. Only . . .' She tailed off, frowning, peering up at her bookshelves over the rim of her glasses. 'There's something that's bothering me and I just can't put my finger on what it is.'

Laura closed her eyes and snuggled down on the sofa, pulling Irene's robe down over her knees. 'Oh,' she murmured, 'this is, like, heaven. I am just so knackered, you know what I mean? I just want to lie here for ever.'

'Well, you're welcome to stay. You could even spend the night, if you like,' Irene suggested. 'I could make up the spare bed.'

Laura didn't answer, but with a smile upon her lips said, 'I always feel safe here, you know? I feel like no one can get me here.'

'No one's going to *get* you, Laura,' Irene said. 'Why ever would you think that?'

'Oh, they will,' Laura said, pulling the robe up so that it covered her chin. 'They will. They always do.'

While Laura slept, Irene read. A number of the scenes in the manuscript were terribly familiar – two girls hitchhiking on a hot summer's day, a chance encounter, a sudden descent into violence occurring at a remote farmhouse, tender young limbs slashed on broken windows – it was all standard horror-film stuff, she supposed. But there was something that snagged on her memory, and that was the singing. A refrain, played on the radio, sung by one of the characters (could you call her a character, if this was a memoir?), was familiar to her. It reminded her of something, rang a bell from somewhere.

On the sofa, Laura stirred. She turned over so that she was facing away from Irene and began, very gently, to snore. Irene felt again the pull of affection, a twinge in her stomach which she thought of as maternal, but then what did she know? She couldn't say what it was, only that she felt the same urge to protect the girl as she'd felt towards poor Angela.

She cast her eye once more over Angie's books, the ones she'd not yet finished sorting through. She really ought to get on with that, because those books had been lying around for weeks. Perhaps she might ask Laura to take that first pile up to the Oxfam shop on Upper Street.

And then she saw it. On the top of the charity-shop pile: *The One Who Got Away* by Caroline MacFarlane. Theo Myerson's crime novel! It was staring her in the face. She got out of her chair and picked up the book, a hardback copy, hefty and well-bound. She turned it over, reading the words on the back cover, in bold blood red:

**On their way home from school, a girl and her friend
were abducted.
The girl made it home. The friend did not.
This girl is a victim.
This girl is grieving.
This girl is damaged.
This girl is vengeful.
This girl is guilty?
This girl is The One Who Got Away.**

Irene rolled her eyes – she'd thought it was drivel when she'd
first read it on publication; her view had not changed. Returning
to her chair, she opened the book, flicking through it to find the
passage she felt sure she remembered, something about a song,
a snatch of a lyric. It was there somewhere, though not at all easy
to find in this novel, whose story jumped about all over the
place, the point of view occasionally switching from victim to
perpetrator, the timeline moving backwards and forwards. Very
confusing and, if you asked Irene, irritating. She remembered
hearing Myerson, once he'd been unmasked as the author,
defending it on a radio programme, saying something about
playing with perceptions of guilt and responsibility, challenging
the reader's expectations, all that sort of guff. Nonsense. Experi-
mentation for its own sake, who did that serve? What was wrong
with the traditional crime novel, after all, with good prevailing,
evil vanquished? So what if things rarely turned out like that in
real life?

Irene was interrupted in her reading by an odd buzzing
sound. She looked up and saw a light flashing on Laura's phone.
It quietened and then, after a moment, started up again. On the
sofa, Laura stirred. 'Oh, that's me,' she groaned, rolling over

towards Irene and promptly falling off the edge of the couch. 'Fuck's sake,' she mumbled as she crawled across the carpet to pick up the phone, 'I was completely out.' She squinted at the screen. 'Yeah?' she answered. 'Who? Oh, yeah, sorry. What's that? Oh, no, I'm not there at the moment, I'm with a friend. I can . . . but I . . . but . . . What, *now*?' She closed her eyes for a second. 'Do I have to?'

She ended the call with a heartfelt sigh. She looked sleepily up at Irene. 'Told you,' she said, trying to smile, despite the tell-tale crack in her voice. 'I told you they always get me, didn't I?' Wearily, she dragged herself to her feet. 'I have to get going,' she said. 'That was the police.'

Laura left in a hurry, dismissing Irene's concerns. 'It's nothing to worry about, mate,' she said, as she ran upstairs to get her clothes. 'Nothing to worry about,' she said again when she came back down.

'This is about Daniel?' Irene said and Laura pulled a face.

'Yeah, of course it is! Of course, it's about Daniel, I haven't slept with anyone else who's carked it lately, have I? I'm a wit-ness, that's all. I was the last person to see him, you know, *alive*. It's nothing to worry about.'

Irene saw her to the front door. Helping her into her still-damp coat, she asked if Laura had a solicitor. Laura laughed as she started off down the lane, limping a little more than usual, and then she turned back, a grin on her face, all traces of tears banished. 'Does the pope shit in the woods?'

Irene was thinking, as she popped a couple of slices of bread into the toaster, how much William would have liked Laura. She would have made him laugh. He'd not been overly keen on Angela – he was never unkind to her or anything like that, he was just wary. 'She's on the edge of something, that one,' he'd said. 'And when she goes over, you don't want to be anywhere nearby, she'll catch hold of you and, *whoop*, off you'll both go.' William never really got to know Angela, he never got to see how kind she was.

Toast buttered, Irene sat at the kitchen table with the memoir open in front of her and Theo's novel next to it, for comparison. 'Something about singing,' she was saying to herself, as she flicked through the pages. 'Something about – *oh.*'

Right at the back of Theo's novel, tucked into the flap of the jacket, she discovered an envelope, addressed to Theo Myerson. Odd, since this was Angela's copy. Inside the envelope, she found a sheet of A4, apparently torn roughly from a pad, on which there was a pencil drawing of a woman sleeping, the bedclothes flung back to expose her naked torso. At the bottom of the page, in a spidery hand, was written, *Hello old man, been doing some sketching, thought you'd like to see.* The note was unsigned, but the drawing looked very much like one of Daniel's. And the woman in the picture was unmistakably Carla Myerson.

27

On Carla's bed lay her suitcase, half-full. The wardrobe was open, too, and bits and pieces of clothing were strewn all over the counterpane. She was having trouble making her mind up what to pack: she'd no idea how long she'd be gone for, or what she'd need. The weather had turned cold here, but it would be warm further south, wouldn't it? Mindlessly, she grabbed things from her shelves – T-shirts and jumpers, a dress she'd not worn in years. Somewhere in the house her phone was ringing, but then, her phone was always ringing. It never stopped.

She would have to speak to Theo at some point, she knew that, to ask him to forward her mail to wherever she decided to go, to deal with solicitors, with the estate, with the sale of Angela's house.

There would be an argument, inevitably, which was why she was considering taking the coward's option and calling him from abroad. But she wasn't sure she could do that to him, to just leave without seeing him again. She wasn't sure she could do that to herself.

She needed to tell him that she'd looked at his latest piece of writing, too, that she didn't like it, all the to-ing and fro-ing, all that jumping around in the timeline. Like the last one, the awful crime thing. Just start at the beginning, for God's sake. Why couldn't people just tell a story straight any longer, from start to finish?

The year before Angela died, Daniel turned up on Carla's door- step one Sunday night around eight. He was upset and agitated, a graze across his cheekbone and a cut on his lip. He had a long and complicated story about an argument with a girlfriend, fol- lowed by a mugging – Carla couldn't quite follow the thread, but he said he had nowhere to go. He didn't want to call the police and he certainly didn't want to go to his mother's. 'She doesn't want me there,' he told Carla. 'She's never wanted me there.' Carla said he could stay. She opened a bottle of wine, which they seemed to drink very quickly, so she opened another. About halfway through that, she knew she had to stop.

She went upstairs, showered, and teetered unsteadily straight from the shower to bed, still wrapped in her towel. She woke with a fright, the way she often did from drink. She lay still, her heart hammering in her chest, and it took a while for her to realize that she'd thrown off the covers, thrown off her towel. It took a while for her eyes to grow accustomed to the darkness and for her to see that she wasn't alone. That he was sitting on the floor next to the door, looking up at her, his sketchbook in his lap.

'Daniel,' she whispered, pulling the covers up sharply, 'you scared me.' In the gloom, she could not make out his expression, only the whiteness of his teeth.

'Couldn't help myself,' he replied.

In the morning, she found him sitting at the counter in her kitchen, drinking coffee.

'Morning!' He greeted her without a trace of embarrassment.

'I was just wondering,' he said, as she busied herself, filling the kettle, putting the glasses from last night into the dishwasher, 'if you could put me up for a few days?'

Carla turned to face him. He was smiling at her, guileless and beautiful. 'I'm sorry, Daniel,' she said. His smile faltered only for a second. 'I would, it's just . . . Theo,' she said. 'He wouldn't . . .' She turned away.

'It's fine,' Daniel said. 'I get it. It's fine.'

When, a month after his mother died, Daniel came to Angela's house to pick up his things, he looked tired and unhappy. He didn't want to come into the house – they almost argued about it.

'You need to see what there is, Daniel. I can't sort through everything for you, I can't choose for you.'

'I just want *my* things – my notebooks, my stuff. I don't want anything of hers.'

When eventually he did enter the house, he walked straight up the stairs and into his bedroom. He picked up the box in which Carla had placed all his notebooks. 'You haven't looked at these, have you? Because . . .' he pulled a face, 'they're not great.'

Carla shook her head. 'No, you've always been clear that they were private.'

He smiled. 'Thanks, Aunt Carla.'

It always tugged at her when he called her that. It reminded her of him as a little boy, those enormous eyes in his pinched face, wary and vulnerable. The poor little savage. She stepped forward to kiss him on the cheek, but he moved his head at the last minute, brushing her lips with his.

'I've rented a boat,' he told her as he turned to go, 'on the canal, just by the Whitmore Bridge. It belongs to a friend of a friend, so I get mate's rates. It's a shithole, but it's all I can afford at the moment. You'll come by and visit, won't you?'

Carla watched him walk out of the room, the box in his arms. She watched him scuff the carpet at the top of the stairs with his trainer.

He turned to her and smiled. 'Be careful, yeah?'

A day or two later, maybe three, Carla was at Angela's, doing a final check of the rooms to make sure everything was clear before the cleaners came in, when she discovered a batch of letters in the bottom of Daniel's wardrobe. Three of them, sent by her sister to Marcus, Daniel's father, the envelopes marked *return to sender*. The letters themselves were well handled, read and re-read – conceivably by Angela, but since she was the person who'd written them, it seemed more likely that the person who had pored over them was Daniel.

And when she thought of him reading them, she imagined little Daniel, she imagined looking down on his neat head, on his bruised neck. It was that Daniel she imagined reading his mother's words, not the strange man he'd become, and the thought of it hurt her heart.

It hurt her heart to think of him reading all the hurtful words his mother had written to the father who'd rejected him. It hurt her heart when she saw how Angela had begged for help with her 'impossible' son, a boy who was never framed as anything but a problem, something about which something needed to be done. *I am going out of my mind*, she wrote. *I cannot stand to be near him. You have to help me, Marcus, I've no one else to ask.*

On her way to the canal, she bought a bottle of wine. She tried not to think about why she didn't want to talk to him without a drink in her hand; she tried not to think about the night of the funeral, tried not to think about him scuffing the carpet, which meant nothing anyway, did it? She made her way down to the canal and, next to the Whitmore Bridge, she saw two canal barges, one a beauty, freshly painted in racing green with a dark red trim, the next one along a shabby, rusting mess in blue and white. She knocked on its windows, climbed up on to the back deck and knocked again on the cabin door, which swung open.

'Daniel?' she called out. 'Are you here, Daniel?'

He wasn't, but she was clearly in the right place – the box of notebooks he'd taken from Angela's house was sitting on the counter, some of its contents decanted on to the bench on the other side of the cabin. The boat itself was awful: the sink and hob were filthy, the main cabin stank of rot, while the tiny sleeping area to the back of the boat reeked of sweat and semen. Daniel had obviously been keeping company, and the thought of it provoked a horrible twist in Carla's stomach, followed by a flush of shame. Daniel was a grown man, he was twenty-three years old, there was no reason why the thought of him being with someone ought to make her feel uncomfortable. It oughtn't to make her feel any way at all.

Retreating from the bedroom, she picked up one of the notebooks on the bench, guiltily flicking quickly through its pages. It was full of pencil sketches: unrecognized faces, disembodied limbs. She replaced it on the bench and picked up a second, this one full of pen-and-ink drawings, more detailed, sophisticated work – a full graphic novel, by the looks of it, with Daniel himself the protagonist. On the first page, she noticed, he'd written a title – *The Origins of Ares* – and her vision was quickly blurred with tears. Warlike Ares, the most hated of all the gods, the one even his own parents couldn't stand.

Oh, Daniel.

She turned the pages, her stomach flipping queasily once more as she recognized herself, drawn young and luscious, more beautiful and certainly more voluptuous than she had ever been in real life. Her skin burning with embarrassment, she closed the book, put it back on the bench and then, almost without thinking, picked it up again. It was still in her hand when she climbed off the back of the boat, when for a second she locked eyes with a woman watching her intently from the back deck of the handsome red and green barge moored a few yards away.

Carla zipped her suitcase shut, carried it downstairs and left it in the hallway. In the living room, she listened to her messages: one from Detective Barker, asking her to call at her earliest convenience, and another from Theo, inviting her for dinner. 'Your favourite, lamb chops. Not sure if you've heard yet, but there's good news, Cee. At last. Good news.'

28

Theo stood at the sink in his kitchen, his left hand under the hot stream, watching the water run red to pink in the bowl. He had sliced a millimetre, perhaps two, from the very tip of his left forefinger and it was bleeding a surprising amount. The culprit – his recently sharpened Santoku knife – lay bloodied on the counter, next to a pink-tinged garlic clove. The Santoku was hardly the right instrument for thinly slicing garlic, but his little chef's knife was missing from the magnetic strip on the wall, lost, no doubt, somewhere in the chaos of the miscellaneous cutlery drawer, never to be found again.

Still, not to worry. There was good news. Good news, at last!

Despite the sudden and bitter cold, Theo had been out for a walk that morning and had, by coincidence, bumped into the young policeman, the one with the shaving rash, standing in the queue for coffee from the café on the towpath. Theo's attempt to slip by unnoticed was unsuccessful; the young man collared him, his face the picture of apprehension.

'Mr Myerson,' he said, sotto voce, 'I was hoping I'd see you. There's good news.'

'Oh?'

The young man nodded. 'It's not official yet, they haven't put

PAULA HAWKINS

out a statement or anything, but I expect you'll be hearing from them soon enough.' He took a deep breath, savouring his moment. 'They've made an arrest.'

Theo gasped extravagantly. 'Oh,' he said, his adrenaline spiking, 'that *is* good news. Who . . . uh, can you tell me who they've arrested?'

'Laura Kilbride,' the police officer said. 'The young woman you saw, the one I mentioned before. The one I said' – he spoke from one side of his mouth – 'had a history of violence.'

'And they've charged her?' Theo managed to ask.

'They will do. It's only a matter of time. They found the knife,' he said.

'They . . . what? You mean the weapon?' Theo's heart was pounding so hard in his chest he thought he might pass out.

The young man grinned, ear to ear. 'They've got her, Mr Myerson, bang to rights.'

On the short walk home, Theo felt as though he'd scaled a mountain peak, his jellified legs could barely support him; he almost fell over twice, trying to take evasive action from joggers. And yet at the same time he felt like dancing! It was over. They had her. It was *over*. And the thing that made his heart soar was that it was not just this particular mess that was over, not just this awful, brutal business with Daniel, but *the whole thing*. Daniel was gone and so was Angela. Carla would suffer, she would grieve, she would feel whatever it was she needed to feel, but after that, she could start to get better, without anyone to drag her back down. The Sutherland mess, all that poison they had injected into his family, into his marriage, it could start to drain away now.

Theo knew they would never go back to what they had been – he wasn't stupid – but he could see a way forward. He could see

220

them building some sort of life for themselves, some sort of peace, and they could do it together, now, with nothing and no one left to divide them.

With the blood finally stopped, Theo bandaged his finger, washed the knife, threw away the sullied garlic clove and returned to his recipe. He left the chops marinating in oil, garlic and mint, put on a coat and took himself outside, on to the back porch to smoke a cigarette. He noticed, as he put the filter to his lips, that he still had blood in his nailbeds. He thought suddenly of the morning he'd seen that girl outside – Laura, the one they'd arrested. After he'd seen her, he'd gone back to an empty bed and fallen asleep. When he woke, Carla was in the shower, and when she emerged, he'd called her over to him, reached out his hand, tried to pull her back to bed, but she'd resisted. He'd kissed her fingertips, the nailbeds scrubbed pink.

Back inside, he was just pouring himself a glass of red when the doorbell rang. Carla must have forgotten her key. He picked up the pile of mail on the mat by the front door, slung it on to the hall console, opened the door with a smile on his face and butterflies in his stomach, like the old days.

'Oh,' he said, disappointed. 'It's you.'

29

Some things were the same, some things were different. Laura sat, bent over, her head resting on top of her folded arms. Last time was late at night, this time was early morning, although really, who could tell? There was no natural light in the room, it could have been any time. It was a different room, but to all intents and purposes it might just as well have been the same. Last time it had been overly warm, this time it was bloody freezing, but there were the same bright lights, the same cheap furniture. A nasty grey carpet like the one in her hallway at home. (*Don't think of home. Don't think of home, or you'll cry.*) Like last time, Egg was there, and Eyebrow too, sitting opposite her, their expressions grave. Graver than last time, she thought. Whenever she caught Egg's eye, he looked away, and that made her scared.

She was exhausted. It seemed like days had passed, even weeks, since she'd received the phone call at Irene's yesterday afternoon. She'd gone to meet the police at her home, as per their request. She'd been cautioned, standing outside in the car park with all the neighbours watching, and they'd escorted her up seven flights to her floor. There were people already there, waiting on the walkway outside, dressed in those white protective suits like you see on TV.

'What's going on?' Laura asked. 'You've already done this, haven't you? You searched here before, why do you have to do it again?' New evidence had come to light, someone said, they were going to have to search more thoroughly. There was a bit of waiting around, and then they brought her here, to the police station. It was late by that time. They put her in a cell and told her to get some rest. She hadn't slept a wink.

'Laura?' Eyebrow placed a cup of water in front of her. 'The duty solicitor's just on his way now, all right? We'll get started in a minute.'

'Yeah, all right,' Laura replied. 'Cheers.'

That was the same – the polite, faux-friendly thing they did. They'd always done it; every run-in with the police she'd ever had, they did it. She'd imagined, though, that this time might be different, because this time *was* different. This wasn't trespass, or disorderly conduct, it wasn't public intoxication or petty theft. This was murder.

Murder! Laura felt a giggle rising up in her chest. She jerked upright, biting her lip, but fight though she might, she couldn't keep it down: a chuckle rose out of her. Egg looked up from his notes, surprised. Laura laughed some more. It wasn't funny, it wasn't fucking funny. She laughed louder, longer, tears coming.

'Are you all right, Laura?' Egg asked her.

She leaned forward, placing her forehead on the desk, chewing the inside of her cheek. *Stop laughing stop laughing stop laughing stop fucking laughing.*

The door opened and Laura stopped laughing. She looked up. A small, slender man with ginger hair and very pale skin held out a limp hand for her to shake. The duty solicitor, different from the one before. He gave her his name, which she immediately forgot, and a quick, nervous smile. Why was *he* nervous? That wasn't a very good sign, was it?

Egg said something, he was introducing them all, for the record. Laura listened to everyone's names and then forgot them (again): Egg, Eyebrow, Nervous Guy. Laura Kilbride. They started asking questions, the same as last time. Where had she met Daniel, when, what time had they got to the boat, what had they done when they got there? All the same stuff they'd been over before, first in the flat and then at the police station.

'Fucking hell, change the record, won't you?' Laura said at last. 'We've done this already, haven't we? We've sung this duet. Quartet?' She looked at Nervous Guy. 'Would this be a quartet? You're not really contributing all that much though, are you? Do you do harmonies?'

Egg pursed his lips, his expression pained.

'Do you think this is funny, Laura?' Eyebrow asked. 'Do you think this is a joke?'

'It *is* a fucking joke, yes! Because I've already told you about Daniel Sutherland, I've already told you, we argued, shoved each other around a bit, and that was it. I did not stab him. We've been over all this and you've got nothing – you've got fuck all, haven't you? It's just that you haven't found anyone else, so now you've got me back in here, and you're harassing me.'

She turned to Nervous Guy. 'They need to put up or shut up, don't they?' He looked down at the notepad in front of him, its pages blank. Fuck's sake, he really wasn't much use, was he? 'You need to charge me or let me go.'

Egg leaned back in his chair and looked her in the eye as he calmly explained that, in addition to a witness who had seen her, bloody and agitated, leaving the scene of the crime around the time of Daniel Sutherland's death, they had her DNA on his body, and his on hers. They also had the fact that she had stolen a watch from him. Moreover, he said, the analysis that had been carried out on her T-shirt showed that, although the majority of the blood present in the fabric belonged to her, a small but significant amount had been detected that belonged to Daniel Sutherland.

'Can you explain that, Laura?' he asked. 'If, as you say, Daniel was still alive and well when you left, how do you explain the presence of *his* blood on *your* clothing?'

'*Turns out*,' Daniel had said, sometime in the early hours, when he'd finished for the second time, '*gimp-fucking isn't really my thing*.' It came out of nowhere, that. She hadn't been ready for the casual cruelty of it. She knew Daniel wasn't exactly a *nice guy*, she wouldn't have gone with him if he had been, she didn't like nice guys, nice guys usually turned out to be the worst, but she hadn't expected *that*. She hadn't expected him to push her away, to laugh when she stumbled and fell; not a forced laugh either, a real one, as though he genuinely thought it was funny. When she got up, she could hardly see for rage. She went for him so fast she caught him off guard, and she saw the look on his face. For a moment, just a fraction of a second, he was afraid.

'Laura?' Eyebrow this time, leaning forward over the table. 'Can you? Can you explain the presence of Sutherland's blood on your T-shirt?'

'I bit him,' Laura said.

'You bit him?' Eyebrow repeated, deadly serious, and hard as Laura tried to mirror Eyebrow's straight face, she just couldn't. She started to laugh again, because how could she not? This was serious, it *was* deadly fucking serious, and she looked across the table at the detectives and she laughed and laughed, and they, for their part, looked unhappy (Egg) and self-satisfied (Eyebrow).

At her side, Nervous Guy twitched. He raised his palms, spread his fingers and looked at her as if to say, *What the fuck*?

'I bit him hard, here' – Laura pointed to a place on her neck, above the clavicle – 'and I drew blood. I had blood in my mouth, on my lips. I wiped it away. I must have got it on my shirt.'

Eyebrow smirked, shaking her head as she did. 'Is that it?' she asked. 'Is that your explanation?'

'It is, yeah. Ask your forensics people,' Laura said. 'Ask them if there was a bite on his neck.'

'Given the position of his stab wounds,' Egg said quietly, 'it's possible that we wouldn't be able to tell.'

'Hah!' Laura barked, leaning back in her chair with a smile, victorious.

'But I don't think it's very likely that a bite would account for the blood that we found, unless the bite was extremely deep. Was it?' Egg asked.

Laura swallowed. 'Well, no. I'm not a fucking vampire, am I? There was a bit of a scuffle. Something broke – maybe a plate, a glass, I don't know. A glass. Was there glass on the floor? Bet there was. He had blood on his . . . on his hand, I think, and he pushed me – yes, he pushed me in the face, because I remember, I had blood on my face when I got home. He pushed me in the face, and maybe again on my chest as he moved past me.'

Beside her, Nervous Guy scribbled furiously on his notepad.

'You didn't mention this before, Laura,' Egg said. 'Why didn't you say any of this before?'

'It didn't matter,' Laura said.

'Of course it *mattered*. It matters when you lie to the police,' Egg said, his voice strained. 'Why wouldn't you just tell us that? Why would you lie about something like this?'

'Why *wouldn't* I lie?' Laura snapped. 'I was already in trouble, I'm always in fucking trouble, I just didn't want to make it worse. I lied, all right?' She was shouting. 'I lied then, but I'm telling the truth now.'

From somewhere, Laura couldn't say where – perhaps she had a bag of tricks beneath the table – Eyebrow pulled out a clear plastic bag which she placed on the table between them. Laura stared at it.

'What can you tell us about this, Laura?' Eyebrow asked.

Laura opened her mouth and then closed it again. 'What can I . . .' She was going to laugh again – she bit down hard on her lower lip. 'What can I tell you about it? It's a knife, by the looks of things. It's a small . . . smallish knife. It has a black handle. Wooden, I suppose. There's something on the blade. I have no idea what it is, but I'm guessing . . .'

'Don't guess,' Nervous Guy interjected sharply.

'Yeah. OK. Good point. What can I tell you about it? I can tell you it looks like a knife that I've never seen before.'

Egg nodded. 'All right. Well, would it surprise you to hear that we found this knife in your flat?'

Laura shook her head. 'No . . . I mean, yes! Yes, of course it would fucking surprise me, I just told you I've never seen it before! It's not mine. It's not.' She got to her feet. 'It's not!'

'Please sit down, Laura,' Egg said gently.

She sat. 'Why would I . . . ?' She started again. 'No, OK, say, for the sake of argument—'

'Ms Kilbride, I—' Nervous Guy had woken up at last.

'No, it's all right, it's all right. Say, for the sake of argument, it was in my flat. Why would I leave it there? Do you think I'm insane? A moron? Why would I just leave it lying around for you to find?'

'You left Daniel's watch lying around,' Eyebrow pointed out.

'Oh, for fuck's sake, you don't kill people with a watch!'

'But you do kill people with knives?'

Laura rolled her eyes. 'You see this?' she said, turning to the solicitor. 'You see? Trying to put words in my mouth, trying to trick me. Typical fucking rozzers. That knife is not mine. I don't know where it came from, it isn't mine.'

'So . . . what?' Eyebrow prompted. 'What are you saying? I don't want to *put words in your mouth*, so tell me what you think happened.'

Laura opened her mouth and closed it again, like a fish. She threw her hands in the air. 'I don't fucking know, do I? Someone put it there. One of your lot, maybe. Trying to stitch me up. Desperate, aren't you, because it's been two weeks since he died and you've got fuck all.'

'Someone put it there,' Eyebrow repeated, very slowly. 'You think someone placed the knife in your flat? Does anyone else have access to your flat, Laura? Anyone else have a key?'

'What, aside from the butler?' Laura snapped. 'Aside from my cleaning lady, and my personal trainer, and— Oh, hang about. *Miriam!*' It came to her, just like that. 'Miriam had my key!' The detectives exchanged a quick glance. 'She must have . . . fucking *hell*. Look, I was joking about the butler, but there's this woman, her name's Miriam, she lives on the . . . Oh, you know her, you've *spoken* to her, she said she found him, didn't she? Well, she had my key.'

Another look passed between the detectives before Eyebrow leaned forward and prompted, 'You're saying Miriam Lewis had your key?'

'I don't know her last name – she's the one on the boat, who said she found him. How many Miriams can there be?'

'Only one, and that is definitely Miriam Lewis,' Egg replied. He looked genuinely, gratifyingly baffled. 'Why would you believe that Miriam Lewis had put this knife in your flat?'

Laura's breath was coming quick and shallow. She was seeing things as she hadn't before, she was seeing a glimmer of light, she was feeling – what was this strange sensation? – *hope*. 'My

key,' she said. 'You remember, I told you I lost it? I hurt my arm?'
Egg nodded. 'Well, it turns out she had it. She said she found it in
his boat, she didn't say why she took it . . . The point is she could
have come into my flat at any time since he died! And the thing
is, you see . . .' It was all becoming clear to her now. 'The
thing is, she has a grudge against the Myersons. Did you know
that? Hates them, thinks they're evil. I'm not entirely sure why,
but she told me, right, she told me that she thought it was Carla –
that's Daniel's aunt, yeah? – she told me that she thought Carla
killed Daniel, which I thought was really weird at the time, but
now I think it was because she was trying to deflect attention
elsewhere. I mean, she says she found him, but how do you even
know that's true? Maybe she found him because she knew he
was there to be found? Don't they often say that it's the person
who found the body that did it? And I know it sounds maybe
kind of far-fetched because she's an old woman . . .'

'She's fifty-three,' Egg said.

'Yeah, exactly, but just because she's old doesn't mean she
couldn't have killed him. She's seriously damaged, you know? I
know – I know what you're thinking, you're looking at me like,
Look who's talking, but sometimes it takes one to know one. Did
you know she says she was abducted by a serial killer once? That
she wrote a book about it? She's . . .' Laura drew little circles in
the air with her forefinger, pointing at her temple, 'she's fucking
nuts.'

The detectives were both leaning back in their chairs, their
arms crossed. For a moment, Laura seemed to have stunned
them into silence. Eyebrow was the first to recover. 'This key you
say she has, she—'

'*Had*, not has. I got it back from her.'

'You got it back from her? Yesterday, is that right? When you
went to her boat, when you attacked her?'

'When I *what*? No, I didn't *attack* her, I didn't—'

'Ms Lewis made a complaint against you, Laura,' Eyebrow said, 'she—'

'Oh, now this is bullshit. This is such bullshit. I did not attack her! She pushed me! Look!' Laura pointed to the bruise on the side of her face. 'She pushed me, I fell, but . . . but that's not even the point, is it?' She turned to Nervous Guy. 'Shouldn't you be doing something? Saying something?' She poked the plastic bag containing the knife with her finger. 'Are my fingerprints on there? They're not, are they?'

'We're still carrying out tests.'

'Tests? For fingerprints?' She spluttered a derisive laugh. 'You've found fuck all, haven't you? Look, are you going to charge me with something or not? Because if you're not . . .'

'We are going to charge you, Laura.'

Hopes dashed.

'But . . . but the key,' Laura said. 'Doesn't that say anything to you?'

'You had motive, means and opportunity,' Eyebrow said firmly, ticking items off on her fingers. 'You lied to us about the seriousness of your altercation with Daniel. His blood was found on your clothing. The murder weapon was found in your possession.'

'It wasn't in my possession.' Laura started to cry. 'The key, it must be . . . *please*.' She looked at Egg, who looked as though he might be about to cry, too. He wouldn't meet her eye, he looked down at the desk and then over at Nervous Guy. 'We'll take her down to hear the formal charge now,' he said.

'No, please,' Laura said again. She held out her hands to Egg, she wanted to beg him, she wanted to fling herself at his feet, to offer herself to him, but there were other people in the room now, people in uniforms, someone helping her out of her chair.

They were gentle enough, but the gentleness made it worse. She started to push them away, started to fight.

'Laura.' She could hear Egg's voice, concerned, reprimanding. 'Laura, come on, don't do this . . .' But she wanted to do this, she wanted to fight, she wanted them to grab her, to throw her to the ground, to knock her out. She wanted oblivion.

30

Carla had changed her outfit twice, she had started and abandoned the letter she was writing to Theo three times, and finally, on the fourth draft, she thought she'd got it right. Instead of just doing a flit, she'd decided that she would go round to his for dinner, after all. She would stay the night, as she usually did, and in the morning she'd slip away, leaving the letter on his desk.

She had a car booked to take her to King's Cross station at eleven thirty the following morning, allowing ample time for her to retrieve from Hayward's Place the things that she had stupidly taken across and left there – the dog's lead, the letters and the notebook – things she could not bear for Theo to find. She didn't want him to have to face reality as she did, he didn't have her constitution. And look, after all, at what it had done to her.

What a pity that Daniel wasn't doing a bit more with his talents! That was what Carla was thinking on the day that she took the notebook from the boat, as she leafed through it, sitting on her sofa at home. He drew so beautifully, rendered facial expression so vividly, he captured movement, he registered nuance; he was empathetic on the page in a way he never seemed to achieve in real life.

She felt guilty for thinking this, guilty for looking at the notebooks at all – Daniel had always been clear that they weren't for other eyes, that he drew for himself. A confidence issue, Carla had assumed, although now she wasn't so sure. She felt distinctly uneasy as she dwelt on the pages on which her own image appeared, because she knew for sure now something that she'd only suspected in the past, that there was something wrong with the way Daniel loved her. Worse, she was afraid that the way she loved him was somehow wrong, too. She felt all these things – guilt and unease and fear – and yet she couldn't stop turning the pages, because what he had drawn was beautiful.

It was idealized, all of it: the house on Lonsdale Square – where she and Angela had grown up and where Daniel had spent his early childhood – was now more castle than Victorian villa, the grounds more park than London garden. Daniel as a young man was broader of shoulder, more heavily muscled, and when she saw Ben, her breath caught in her chest. A dimpled cherub, doe-eyed perfection: Daniel had captured perfectly the generosity of his little smile, the soft curl of his hair at the nape of his neck. It almost stopped her heart.

She put the book down.

When she picked it up again, as she skipped back and forth through the pages, trying to make sense of where on earth this story was going, she realized that not *everything* was idealized. Angela, for example, was cruelly depicted: scrawny and scantily clad, a lush, a fall-down drunk. But Daniel, too, suffered in the telling. As 'Ares', although he was physically beautiful, his character was rotten: he was malicious, he persecuted younger boys at school, occasionally incurring retaliatory beatings; he seduced and discarded young girls, who appeared somewhere on the scale from naive to idiotic; he bullied and humiliated his mother. It was just so bizarre, Carla thought, so unnerving and yet so affecting to see Daniel depicted as monstrous, and to know he had drawn himself this way. What did it mean that instead of making himself the hero of his own story, he had made himself the villain? It cut her to the bone. But, as she turned the pages, that bloody block of pain sitting just beneath her breastbone began to shift, to dissolve, and was replaced by a feeling of dread, a creeping certainty that she should put the book down, that she should close it and not look at it ever again. But then, around halfway through, she came across herself once more, arriving at Lonsdale Square on a sunny afternoon with Ben in her arms, and she knew immediately what day it was, and she could not look away.

In Daniel's version of events, Carla is wearing a dress, her hair is long and wavy, falling over bare shoulders, Ben – gorgeous, golden Ben – is smiling and laughing, perched on her hip. From the balcony, Daniel, his pinched face half in darkness, watches as Carla hands Ben over to Angela. Leaning out over the balcony into the sunlight, Daniel calls and waves to his aunt, but she has already turned away without acknowledging him. His little face falls.

Over the page, night has fallen. Daniel is watching television in the playroom, alone. He gets up and goes upstairs to his mother's bedroom to look for her, to say goodnight, but she is not there. So he goes back down to his own room, where he finds that his little cousin has woken up, has climbed off the mattress on which he was sleeping and is now lying in the middle of the floor. He is drawing, scribbling in a book, surrounded by similar books strewn all around him, their pages covered in his ugly scrawl. The anguish on Daniel's face is vividly drawn: Ben has ruined all of his books, his carefully drawn comic books! Distraught, he calls for his mother, but no one comes. He looks for her, searching room by room until eventually he arrives at the study. The door is shut, but he can hear someone inside, making a noise. Carefully, he pushes the door open, and there she is – straddling a man, some stranger, some person he's never seen before. Her head is thrown back, her red-lipped mouth open wide. She turns, catches sight of her horrified child and starts to laugh.

Daniel flees the room.

The next scene shows Daniel lying in bed, his imagination a cloud above him in which various scenes play out: in one, he imagines himself hitting his mother's lover on the head with a champagne bottle; in another, he slaps his mother's drunken face. Then the cloud of his imagination dissipates. Daniel props himself up on one elbow and gazes across the room at the little boy, now asleep on his side, his long lashes grazing his cheek-bones, his head haloed with curls.

In the morning, Daniel goes upstairs to his mother's room. She is asleep, alone. He leaves her, closing her bedroom door behind him. He returns to the first floor, to his own bedroom, where he gently shakes the little boy awake. The child, delighted to see his big cousin, smiles a huge, goofy smile. Daniel helps him from the bed, he takes his hand, he leads him to the study, opens the door. The pair of them cross the room, hand in hand, picking their way through the evidence of last night's debauchery – clothes strewn around, ashtray overflowing, an empty champagne bottle lying on its side. Daniel leads the child to the balcony, he opens the doors and from behind his back produces a toy – a bright red truck. He offers it to the child, who laughs delightedly, reaching out to grab it, and as he does, Daniel rolls the truck carefully out on to the balcony, towards the broken railing. He watches as the child toddles after it.

In the final panel, Daniel is alone again, sitting on the edge of the balcony with his feet dangling over the edge, a smile on his lips.

31

I rene sat, perched on an uncomfortably hard chair in Theo Myerson's living room. She could tell before she sat down that the chair was not going to be comfortable, but she sat in it anyway, because it was relatively high and she calculated that she'd be able to get out of it without help, which was important. She had no desire to be at Myerson's mercy. With some difficulty, one hand gripping the chair and the other holding her handbag tightly in her lap, she managed to scoot the chair a few inches closer to the wood burner in the fireplace. It was fearfully cold; winter had returned with some vengeance. On the radio that morning they'd talked about snow.

Myerson was in the kitchen, fetching her a sherry. She didn't want one – she'd never been much of a drinker – but when he'd offered, after only grudgingly inviting her in in the first place, she'd thought it best to accept. He was drinking wine. Alone, in the middle of the afternoon.

While he was gone, Irene admired his bookshelves. Say what you like about Theo Myerson, he had beautiful bookshelves. Oak, Irene thought, and custom built, running from floor to ceiling on either side of the fireplace, with one of those nifty rolling ladders to allow you access to the very top shelves. From where she was sitting, she couldn't read the names on the spines, which was frustrating. Irene liked few things more than a good nose through other people's bookshelves, although now was clearly not the time.

'Carla should be along any minute,' Theo said when he came back into the room. He handed her a small crystal glass. 'She's coming for dinner.'

Irene accepted the drink with a nod. 'I didn't know where she lived,' she said, vaguely aware that she'd already explained that to him. 'But I found your address, as I said, on an envelope in a book . . .'

Theo nodded. He sank down into an armchair quite some distance across the room. He took a large gulp of wine and glowered at her. 'You need to speak to her urgently? Can you tell me what it's about?'

'I think it's best we wait for Carla,' Irene said. She sipped her sherry. Theo raised his eyes briefly to the heavens, before glowering at her once more. He was not a subtle man. They sat in silence for a few moments and then, cracking under the pressure, Irene said, 'I just need to speak to her about something I found in Angela's house.' She took another sip of the sherry. 'A notebook I found, one of Daniel's.' She took it from her handbag and held it up briefly, before thinking better of it and slipping it back into the bag.

'And this is urgent, is it?' Myerson said, his voice flat.

'Well, I . . . You haven't seen it before, have you, Mr Myerson?' Theo shook his head, thankfully uninterested. He shifted in his seat, patently irritated; he seemed on the point of asking her to leave. Nervously, she took another sip. 'It's what you'd call a graphic novel, I suppose. There was one on the Booker list, wasn't there, not so long ago? Very odd, I thought. I mean, how on earth do you compare a comic with a real book?' Theo raised his eyebrows. He glugged his wine. He was starting to make her very uncomfortable. 'Well, no accounting for taste, I suppose.' She fell silent a moment. 'I found this in one of your books,' she said, holding up the envelope with his address on. 'The crime one.'

In the long, tense silence that followed, Irene pondered the wisdom of bringing up the manuscript she'd read, the one that Laura had given her. But then, now was perhaps not the best time to accuse Myerson of plagiarism. She wouldn't want to get distracted from the matter at hand. She once more raised her glass to her lips and was surprised to find that there was little more than a drop remaining.

'This notebook,' Theo said eventually, frowning at her, 'you said you found it in Angela's house. What were you doing in Angela's house?'

'Well, you see, the thing is . . .'

Irene tailed off. She did not have a good answer to this question. The short answer was, she'd been nosing around next door. The longer version was that when she'd heard on the radio that Laura had been charged with Daniel's murder, she knew at once that she *must* speak to Carla, because she was certain that a mistake had been made. She didn't have contact details for Carla, but she felt sure that there must be something in Angela's house with a number or an address on it. Only when she got there, she'd been disappointed, because the house was completely empty. She'd walked from room to dingy room, noticing for the first time what a desperate state the place was in, the wallpaper bubbling and peeling off, the damp around the kitchen window, the frames in the bedrooms succumbing to rot. At the bottom of a wardrobe in the back bedroom – pretty much the only remaining piece of furniture in the house – Irene discovered a pile of papers. Three or four letters, all addressed to Angela, and a notebook. Irene took them home with her. She didn't find an address for Carla, but the notebook gave her something else. Not understanding – Irene wasn't sure that was possible – but a glimpse of something else, a glimpse of the place where all this might have started, where the seed of destruction had been sown.

Theo leaned forward. 'Well? What were you doing in Angela's house?' His voice was brittle now, his expression quite menacing. 'As far as I'm aware, you don't have any business there, that's Carla's property.'

'Is it?' Irene asked. 'Does the house belong to Carla?'

Myerson got to his feet abruptly. 'Oh, for God's sake! It's none of your business who owns the house. Carla is having a terrible time at the moment, the last bloody thing she needs is some meddlesome woman bothering her, interfering in her affairs.' He crossed the room towards her, holding out his hand. 'Give the notebook to me,' he demanded, 'and I'll hand it over to Carla. If she wishes to discuss it with you, she'll get in touch. I wouldn't hold my breath.'

Irene drew her handbag closer to her chest. 'I'd like to give it to Carla myself, if you don't mind,' she said, her tightly prim tone disguising her fear of this large man towering over her, fear of what he might do if he saw what Daniel had drawn.

'I do mind,' Theo snapped. 'Give me the book,' he said, his hand held out in front of her face, 'and I'll call you a taxi.'

Irene pressed her lips together firmly, shaking her head. 'I'm asking you not to read it. I don't—'

'Carla can look at it, but I can't?' he asked. 'Why?'

'I'm certain Carla has already seen it,' Irene explained. 'It wouldn't come as a shock to her.'

'A shock?' His hands dropped to his sides. 'Why would it be shocking to me?' He raised his eyes to the ceiling once more.

'Oh, for God's sake. It's about Carla, isn't it? Are there pictures of Carla in it? He was fixated on her, you know, in an unhealthy way. He was quite a disturbed young man, I'm afraid.' Irene said nothing, only looked down at the bag in her lap. 'Is it not that?' Myerson asked. 'Is it something about me? He has a pop at me, does he?'

'The thing is . . .' Irene started to speak, but she was silenced by a sudden act of violence as Theo's hand shot out, as he roughly grabbed her handbag from her lap. 'No!' she cried. 'Wait, please!'

'I've had about enough of this,' Theo snarled, snatching the book from the bag, which he then discarded, tossing it back towards her. It fell to the floor, spilling her possessions – her spare spectacles and her powder compact, her little tweed change purse – on to the carpet.

Taking great care, Irene knelt down to gather her things, while Myerson towered above her. Ignoring Irene, he opened the book and began to read. ' "The Origins of Ares"!' He smirked. 'God, he thought a lot of himself, didn't he? Ares, god of war! That little shit . . .' His eye skimmed the pages as he flicked quickly through the book, until abruptly, and with an audible intake of breath, he stopped. The curl of his lip disappeared and his skin seemed to whiten before Irene's eyes; his fingers began to curl into fists, crumpling the pages of the notebook as they did.

'Mr Myerson,' Irene said, her heart sinking in her chest, 'you shouldn't be looking at it . . .' She pulled herself slowly to her feet. 'You don't want to see what he drew,' she said, although she could tell by the horrified expression on Theo's face that it was too late. 'It's terribly upsetting, I know, I—'

Suddenly Irene's head was swimming, the carpet beneath her feet seeming to tilt and rock like a boat, the wood burner, the beautiful oak shelves, blurring before her. 'Oh . . . I don't feel very well,' she said, and she reached out her hand to where she expected the chair to be, but found that it wasn't. She stumbled, righted herself, squeezing her eyes tightly shut and then opening them again. It was the sherry – the sherry and the heat from the fire. She felt quite odd, and there was Myerson, staring at her, his mouth red and open and his face darkening and his hands clenched to fists. Oh God. She took a step backwards, reaching for something to hold on to and finding nothing. What a fool she'd been, to bring the notebook with her! She thought she was being brave, coming here, but she'd been a fool, an old fool, just as people thought she was.

32

Theo had killed with the stroke of a pen many times. Over the course of a few thousand pages of fiction, he had stabbed, shot and eviscerated people, he had hanged them from makeshift gallows, he had battered them to death with a sharp rock held in the palm of a small hand. And he had contemplated worse (oh, the things he had considered!), as he wondered what we (he, anyone) might be capable of in extremis.

The notebook was gone, fed to the fire. The old woman was back on her feet, but flustered and frightened; she'd not expected him to react so quickly, so strongly as he had. As he watched her, it occurred to him how little it would take: they were so fragile at that age, and she was already unsteady on her feet, she'd drunk that glass of sherry very fast. Now she swayed a little in front of him, her eyes full of tears. She stood on the edge of a rug whose corner had ruched up when she'd been scrabbling around on the floor, almost exactly midway between the sharp-cornered stone hearth and his clean-lined coffee table in glass and bronze.

Were he writing this scene, he'd be spoiled for choice.

The One Who Got Away

He can't see anything except for red.

When he woke that morning, he didn't think he'd be the hero of the story. If he'd thought about it at all, he might have called himself the hunter.

When he woke that morning, he couldn't imagine how it would be, how she would be – different from what he wanted, not the one he wanted at all. He couldn't imagine how she'd lie and trick him.

When he woke that morning, he never thought he'd be the prey.

The unfairness of it, bitter in his mouth, trickles down the back of his throat as he succumbs to her, the one who got away, the girl with the ugly face, red-handed, rock-handed, vengeful. She's all he can see, the last thing he'll see.

The One Who Got Away

She knows, before she sees, that he has found her. She knows, before she sees, that it will be his face behind the wheel. She freezes. For a second she hesitates, and then she leaves the road, takes off, running into a ditch, over a wooden fence, scrambling into the adjacent field. She runs blind, falling, picking herself up, making no sound. What good would screaming do?

When he catches her, he takes handfuls of her hair, pulls her down. She can smell his breath. She knows what he is going to do to her. She knows what is coming, because she has already seen him do it, she saw him do it to her friend, how savagely he pushed her face into the dirt, how he pawed at her.

She saw how hard her friend fought.

She saw how she lost.

So she doesn't fight, she goes limp. She lies there in the dirt, a dead weight. While weakly he paws at her clothes, she keeps her eyes on his face all the time.

This is not what he wants.

Close your eyes, he tells her. Close your eyes.

She will not close her eyes.

He slaps her across the face. She does not react, she makes no sound. Her pale limbs are heavy, so heavy in the dirt, she is sinking into it. She is taking him with her.

This is not what he wants.

He climbs off her body, beats the earth with his fist. He has blood on his face and in his mouth. He is limp, beaten.

This is not what he wants.

He starts to cry.

While he is crying, she picks herself silently up off the ground.

Go, he says to her. Just go. Just run.

But this girl doesn't want to run, she has done her running. She picks up a stone, jagged-edged, its tip pointed like an arrowhead. Nothing too big, just large enough to fit snugly into the palm of her hand.

Her hand cups the warm stone and his eyes widen in surprise as she swings her arm towards him. At the sound of the bone at his temple splitting, joy fizzes up in her and she swings a second time, and again, and again, until she is drenched in sweat and in his blood. She thinks she might have heard him begging her to stop, but she cannot be sure. She might just as well have imagined it.

When the police come, the girl will tell them how she fought for her life, and they will believe her.

33

Miriam sifted through her keepsakes, the objects she'd gathered during the course of brushes with other lives – the lives of others, other lives she might have lived. She noted with some sadness how they were depleted: the key she had taken from the boat was gone, as well as one of Lorraine's earrings, which pained her terribly.

The things she chose to hold on to represented important moments for her, and when she thought about those times – those few moments alone with Daniel on the boat, her escape from the farmhouse – she liked to have associated objects to hold, to help bring her back to how it really was, how she really felt. Now, as she held the little silver cross that her father had given her for her confirmation, her first communion, she closed her eyes tightly and imagined herself at fourteen, before the horrors of the farmhouse, when she was still an innocent.

Miriam was aware that this habit of collecting trinkets to transport her back to important moments was a trait she shared with psychopaths and serial killers, which was something that bothered her, but the truth, she believed, was that we all have our monstrous moments, and these objects helped her stay true to who she really was, to the monster she had made of herself.

Sometimes, when she found herself in a very dark place, she felt overwhelmed by the urge to confess. If she had a confessor, where would she start? Would it be with the most recent transgression, or the very first one? It had to be the latter, she supposed. The first was the defining one, the one that set her on this path.

Start with the night she escaped from the farmhouse, when she stood in front of the broken window and prayed and prayed. When she clambered out of the window, when she ran along the dirt road. When she heard the thunder that wasn't thunder, the sound of the car coming from behind her, coming from the farm. When she realized he was coming for her and started to run again, scrambling over a fence, flinging herself into a ditch, wriggling forward on her stomach until she was concealed, at least in part, by an overhanging tree. There she lay, listening to the car's gears grinding as it slowed, its lights illuminating the branch above her head. The car passed.

For a while after that she lay in the ditch. How long, she couldn't say. She could never say. Miriam remembered so much detail about that day and the night that followed – the smell of the house, the pale, blasted blue of the evening sky, the song in the car and that sound Lorraine made, that awful sound, after he punched her. But she could not for the life of her remember how long she lay in that ditch, frozen and unable to move, only her mind whirring, thinking, *It's not my fault he chose you.*

She could not remember, either, how long she stood in the locked room in the farmhouse, paralysed with terror in front of the broken window, could not remember how long it had taken her to decide that her best chance was not to stay and fight, but to run, to raise the alarm. She could not remember how long she stood there and prayed, prayed that he wouldn't come down the stairs, that he wouldn't come for her. That he would take his time with Lorraine.

Her mind moved on, and it wasn't until she sat at Lorraine's dressing table in her bedroom, pocketing her gold earrings, considering what a bad person she was, that they returned to her, those despicable things she had thought, all the time she had wasted while she was thinking them.

Miriam was tested and found wanting; she discovered then that she lacked some essential goodness, some critical strand of moral fibre.

She was not good then, and has not been good since.

At the bottom of the wooden box, beneath the letter from the lawyer, lay the dog tag.

Miriam didn't like to think about that moment, the moment with the dog. It wasn't something she was proud of, it was a loss of control in a moment of pain. She kept the tag as a reminder to herself that the transfer of hatred from one person to another didn't work. Didn't make sense. She thought about Jeremy, how she'd longed to push a knife into his throat. Sometimes she thought about Myerson, too, about smacking him over the back of the head with a claw hammer, pushing him into the canal, watching him sink beneath the surface of that filthy water.

She thought about it, but she didn't have the courage to act. And then it happened, one day, that there was a rude customer in the shop, and a near collision on the towpath with a cyclist who called her a stupid fat bitch, and, arriving home with her chest tight and her vision blurred, in the early stages of a full-blown panic attack, she found the dog on her back deck, tearing into the food recycling bag she'd put out that morning and forgotten to take to the bins, and almost without thinking she snatched the dog up. She took it down to her cabin, placed it in the sink and quickly, with a sharp knife, cut its throat.

The animal didn't suffer, it was a clean kill. Not literally, of course. Literally it made a terrible mess, blood all over her hands and her clothes and the floor, so much more than you would have thought – it took an age to clear it all up. Sometimes she thought she could still smell it.

Later that night, she put the dog in a bag, carried it along the towpath and tipped it out of the bag into the water behind Theo's house. She thought the little body might be found, but it must have drifted into the tunnel, perhaps snagged on the propeller of someone's boat, so in the end Theo never got to wonder who had done such a terrible thing, he just got to wonder where the dog was, and in some ways Miriam found that more satisfying, the sight of him wandering up and down the towpath and along the roads nearby, calling the animal's name, putting up pitiful little posters.

Miriam slipped the dog tag into her pocket and headed out, walking west towards Myerson's house. If she were to confess anything, it would be to that, the shameful incident with the dog, and if she were to confess it to anyone, then surely it should be to Myerson. He might report her to the police, of course, but something told her he wouldn't. He wouldn't want to admit to them how this thing had started, he wouldn't want to go into detail. It would hurt his pride.

She had convinced herself of all this, reassured herself, certain now that telling him about the dog would be the right thing to do for *her* – it would have the twin benefits of punishing Myerson while at the same time easing her burden. So, fists determinedly clenched at her side, jaw set firm, she marched up the steps from the towpath and around the corner to Noel Road, where she came to an abrupt halt.

There he was, standing outside his front door, looking furtively this way and that, scanning the pavement anxiously. His eyes met hers and widened in sudden astonishment before, flanked by two uniformed police officers, he began to make his way down the path and into a waiting car.

Off they went. Miriam, her heart beating fit to burst, could scarcely believe her eyes. Had she won? Had some justice been done, at last?

She stood there, so astounded for a moment by what she had witnessed that she almost forgot to feel elated. But then that moment passed, and her confusion gave way to happiness, a smile spreading over her face, and she raised both hands to her mouth and started to laugh. She laughed and laughed, a strange sound even to her own ears.

When she recovered, she noticed that someone was watching her, a man across the street, a little further down the road. An older man, in a wheelchair, with a shock of white hair. Then he wheeled himself down off the pavement and looked up and down the road, as though he were about to cross. Miriam thought for a moment that he was going to come over and talk to her, but a car pulled up, one of those large taxis, and the driver got out and helped the man into the back of the car. The taxi swung out into the road, performing a wide U-turn.

As the car drove past, Miriam's eyes met those of the man in the car, and all the hair stood up on the back of her neck.

34

Everything is material. And comedy equals tragedy plus time. Isn't that how it goes? Sitting in a stuffy room faced by two detectives, Theo wondered bitterly just how much time would need to pass before what had happened to him – the death of his child, the subsequent disintegration of his marriage – would become funny. It had been fifteen years since his son died, after all. Shouldn't it be just a little bit funny by now?

Bullshit.

As for everything being material, he was finding it hard to make mental notes of his surroundings, all of his observations turning out to be banal: the room was grey, boxy, it smelled like an office – bad coffee, new furniture. The only sound he could hear was an insidious white-noise hum overlaid with the rather nasal breathing of Detective Chalmers opposite.

In front of him, on the table between him, Chalmers and Detective Barker, was a knife in a clear plastic bag. A small knife, with a black wooden handle and a dark stain on the blade. A small chef's knife. *His* small chef's knife – not lost in the chaos of the cutlery drawer, after all.

When they placed the knife on the table in front of him, Theo's heart sank with the realization that this was not going to be *material*. This wasn't going to be a funny story he told later on. It was going to be a very, very long time indeed before this became comedy.

'Do you recognize this, Mr Myerson?' Detective Chalmers asked him. Theo peered at the knife. Many thoughts came into his head, all of them stupid. He heard himself making a small *hmmm* noise, which was also stupid. No one looked at an object and said, *Hmmm*. They said, *Yes, I recognize that*, or *No, I don't recognize that* – but in this case, the latter course of action was not open to him, because he was well aware that if the police were presenting this knife to him at this moment, they must know he'd recognize it.

Think fast, think fast, think fast, Theo thought, which was irritating, because it stopped him thinking anything other than the word *fast. Think something other than fast, for God's sake.*

The knife was his, and they knew it – they had not connected it to him by accident. So, that was that, wasn't it? This was the end. The end of the world as he knew it. And as the song goes, he felt fine. The odd thing was, he actually *did* feel fine. Well, perhaps *fine* was a stretch, but he didn't feel as bad as he'd expected to feel. Perhaps it was true, what they say, that it's the hope that kills you. Now that there was no longer any hope, he felt better. Something to do with suspense, he supposed. Suspense was the agonizing thing, wasn't it? Hitchcock knew that. Now the suspense was over, now he knew what was going to happen, he felt shocked and sad, but he also felt relieved.

'It's mine,' Theo said quietly, still looking at the knife rather than the detectives. 'It belongs to me.'

'Right,' Barker said. 'And can you tell us when you last saw this knife?'

Theo took a deep breath. For a moment, he saw himself back in his living room with Irene Barnes. He saw the pictures that

Daniel had drawn, the vulgar images of his beautiful wife, the graphic depiction of his little boy's death; he saw himself rending the pages from the book before throwing them into the fire. He exhaled slowly. Here we go. 'Well,' he said, 'it would have been the morning of the tenth.'

'The tenth of March?' Detective Barker gave his colleague the briefest of glances and leaned forward in his chair. 'That would be the morning Daniel Sutherland died?'

Theo rubbed his head with his forefinger. 'That's correct. I threw it away. The knife. Uh . . . I was going to throw it into the canal, but then I . . . I saw someone. I thought I saw someone coming along the towpath and I didn't want to draw attention to myself, so I just threw it into the bushes instead.'

The detectives exchanged another look, longer this time. Detective Barker cocked his head to one side, his lips pressed together. 'You threw the knife into the bushes? On the morning of the tenth? So, you're saying, Mr Myerson . . .'

'That I went to Daniel's boat early that morning, while my wife was still asleep. I . . . stabbed him. There was blood, of course, a great deal of blood . . . I washed it off myself in the boat. Then I left, and I threw the knife into the bushes on the way home. As soon as I got home, I showered. Carla was sleeping. I made coffee for both of us, then I took it to her in bed.'

Detective Barker's mouth fell open for a moment. He closed it. 'OK.' He looked at his colleague again and Theo thought, though it was quite possible he was imagining things at this point, that he saw Chalmers shake her head very slightly. 'Mr Myerson, you said earlier that you did not wish to have legal representation here for this interview, but I'm going to ask you again if you'd like to change your mind? If there is someone you would like us to call, we can do that, or alternatively we can arrange for the duty solicitor here at the station to come in.'

PAULA HAWKINS

Theo shook his head. The last thing he wanted was a lawyer, someone trying to mitigate outcomes, someone overcomplicating what in the end was a simple thing. 'I'm quite all right on my own, thank you.'

Barker read the caution then, pointing out that Theo had come in willingly, that he had refused legal representation, but that, in the light of what he had just said, a formal caution was needed.

'Mr Myerson,' Detective Barker was struggling to keep his tone even, Theo could tell – this must, after all, be an exciting moment for a detective – 'just to clarify, you are confessing to the killing of Daniel Sutherland, is that right?'

'That's correct,' Theo said. 'That is correct.' He took a sip of water, another deep breath. Here we go again. 'My sister-in-law,' Theo said, and then stopped speaking. This was the difficult part, the part he was going to struggle with, the part he didn't want to say out loud.

'Your sister-in-law?' Chalmers prompted, her face an open book now – she was astonished by what she was hearing. 'Angela Sutherland? What about Angela Sutherland?'

'Angela told me before she died that my wife, my . . . Carla . . . and Daniel were having a relationship.'

'A relationship?' Chalmers repeated. Theo nodded, his eyes squeezed tightly shut. 'What sort of relationship?'

'Please don't,' Theo said, and he surprised himself by starting to cry. 'I don't want to say it.'

'You're saying there was a sexual relationship between Carla and Daniel, is that what you're telling us?' Barker asked.

Theo nodded. Tears dripped from the end of his nose on to his jeans. He hadn't cried in years, he thought all of a sudden. He'd not cried when he sat at his son's graveside on what should

have been his eighteenth birthday, and now here he was, in a
police station, crying over *this*.

'Angela Sutherland told you about their relationship?'

Theo nodded. 'I went to see her, about a week before she
passed away.'

'Can you tell us about that, Mr Myerson? Can you tell us what
happened when you went to see her?'

'I think it's best if I show you,' Angela said to him. 'Would you . . .
would you just come upstairs?'

Theo followed her into the hallway. As he watched her
climbing the stairs, he imagined the things that she had up
there, the things she wanted to show him. Daniel's things, presumably. More pictures, perhaps? Notes? The thought turned
his stomach. Theo started up the stairs after her. He imagined
the look on her face when she showed him, pitying, but with a
hint of triumph, a hint of I told you so. *Look at your beautiful
wife. Look at what she does with my son.* A few steps from the
landing, he stopped. Angela was waiting for him, looking
down at him, and she seemed afraid. He remembered how
she'd cowered in front of him, the day that Ben died; he remembered how he'd longed to grab her, to throttle her, to dash her
head against the wall.

He felt none of that now. He turned away from her and
headed back down the stairs. He heard her crying as he opened
the door and closed it behind him, stepping out into the bright
afternoon sunlight, pausing to light a cigarette before he set off
towards home. As he walked along the lane towards St James's
churchyard, he was overcome with longing for a time when he
didn't hate Angela, when actually he had loved her very dearly,
for the time when his heart used to lift when he saw her, for she

was always so much fun, such enjoyable company, she always had so much to say. Such a very long time ago now.

'Can you tell us about that, Mr Myerson? Can you tell us what happened when you went to see her?'

Theo wiped his eyes with the back of his hand. He wasn't going to tell the police about that, about his longing. It wouldn't serve his purposes now, would it, to tell them that he had loved her once, as a sister, as a friend?

'She told me that there was something going on between Daniel and my wife. We argued about it. Not . . . I didn't touch her. I wanted to. I wanted to wring her scrawny neck, but I didn't. I didn't push her down the stairs either. As far as I'm aware, Angela's death was an accident.'

As far as he was aware. And he was not about to admit to the police that for the rest of his days, whenever he thought of Angela, he would think of her as she was that day, crying at the top of the stairs, and he would think of the words he'd spoken to her, when he'd called her lazy and neglectful and a bad mother, and he would wonder whether those were the last words that *anyone* ever spoke to her. He would wonder if, when she teetered at the top of the staircase or lay dying at the bottom of it, his was the eulogy she heard.

'So you argued, you left . . . Did you confront your wife? Did you ask her about what Angela had told you?'

'I did not.' Theo shook his head. 'There are some questions,' he said softly, 'which you don't want answered. Which you *never* want answered. In any case, it wasn't long after that conversation that Angela died, and I was hardly going to bring it up with my wife then, while she was grieving. But I suspected . . . I felt sure that Daniel would use his mother's death to try to get closer to Carla. I couldn't bear that. I just wanted him gone.'

Detective Chalmers paused the recording, got up from the table and said they were going to take a short break. She offered him coffee, which he refused. He asked for a bottle of water instead, fizzy if they had any. Chalmers said she'd do her best.

It was over. The worst was over.

Then it struck him that the worst wasn't over at all. The newspapers! Oh God, the newspapers. The things people would say, on the internet, on social media. Christ Almighty. He hung his head and wept, his shoulders heaving. His books! No one would buy them any longer. The only good thing he'd ever done – apart from Ben, apart from loving Carla – was his work, and it would be tarnished for ever, along with his name. His books would be taken from the shelves, his legacy ruined. Yes, Norman Mailer stabbed his wife with a penknife and William Burroughs fatally shot his, but times were different now, weren't they? Times had changed, people were so intolerant, you couldn't get away with that sort of thing any longer. One step out of line and you were cancelled.

By the time the detectives came back to the room, Chalmers carrying a bottle of Evian, which was, of course, not fizzy, Theo had collected himself. Wiped his eyes, blown his nose, steeled himself. Reminded himself of what was truly important.

The detectives had something else to show him – a photograph this time, of a young woman. 'Have you seen this person before, Mr Myerson?' Detective Barker asked.

Theo nodded. 'She's the one you charged with the murder. Kilbride, yes?' He looked up at them.

'That's the only time you've seen her?'

Theo considered this a moment. 'No, no. I couldn't swear to it in a court of law, but I believe she is the woman I told you I saw, on the towpath, the morning of Daniel's death. I said at the time, I told you that I saw her from my bedroom window. That was not true. In fact, I . . . I think I might have passed her. On the way to the boat, I think. She was . . . she was shuffling along, or limping, perhaps. I thought she was drunk. She had dirt or blood on her clothes. I assumed she had stumbled. I mentioned her when you first questioned me, because I was trying to deflect your attention.'

'Deflect our attention away from you?' Barker said.

'Yes, away from me! Obviously away from me.'

The detectives exchanged another of their inscrutable looks. 'Would it surprise you,' Barker asked, 'to hear that this knife – the knife which you have identified as belonging to you and which, you say, you used to kill Daniel Sutherland, was found in the flat of the young woman in the photograph?'

'I . . .' Surprise didn't begin to cover it. 'In her flat?' A terrible thought passed through Theo's mind, that he had fallen on his sword unnecessarily. 'You found the knife in her flat?' he repeated dumbly. 'She . . . well. She must have picked it up. She must have seen me discarding it . . . Perhaps she was the person I thought I saw later on, perhaps that was when I saw her—'

'You just said that you thought you saw her on your way to the boat,' Chalmers pointed out.

'But it may have been later. It may have been later. My recollection of that morning is not exactly *crystal clear*. It was a stressful time. An emotional time. I was . . . I was obviously very upset.'

'Do you recognize this, Mr Myerson?'

They had something else to show him now – a scarf.

He nodded. 'Oh yes, that's mine. It's Burberry, that one. A good one.' He looked up at them. 'I was wearing it that morning. I think I dropped it.'

'Where do you think you might have dropped it?' Chalmers probed.

'I've really no idea. As I say, my recall of these events is far from perfect. Was it in the boat, perhaps? Or somewhere on the path? I don't know.'

'I assume it would surprise you to hear that this was also found in Laura Kilbride's flat?'

'Was it? Well, if I dropped it at the same time as I threw away the knife, then . . .' Theo sighed, he was exhausted. 'What does it matter? I told you I did it, didn't I? I don't know how the girl got my scarf, I—'

'Ms Kilbride believes that the scarf and the knife were planted in her flat in an attempt to incriminate her,' Barker said.

'Well . . .' Theo was baffled. 'That may well be, but they weren't planted by me, were they? First, I have no idea where she lives, and second, I've just told you that they belong to me. Why would I plant them and then tell you that they're mine? That makes no sense at all, does it?'

Barker shook his head. He looked very unhappy, Theo thought, not like a man who had just cracked a case at all. 'It doesn't make sense, Mr Myerson, it really doesn't. And the thing is,' he said, sitting up straight now, his elbows on the table and his fingers steepled before him, 'the thing is that we found just one fingerprint on the knife, and it is yours. A thumbprint, to be exact. But since this is your knife, finding your fingerprint on it isn't particularly surprising. Especially since the print we found is here,' Barker indicated a point on the side of the handle where it met the blade, 'which isn't really where you'd expect a thumbprint to be if you were wielding a knife to stab someone, although it is where you would expect the thumbprint to be if you were, say, chopping onions.'

Theo shrugged, shaking his head. 'I don't know what you

want me to say. I did it. I killed Daniel Sutherland because of his relationship with my ex-wife, Carla. If you bring me a piece of paper, I'll write it all down. I'll sign a confession now. Aside from that, I don't think I want to say anything more, if that's all right. Is that all right?'

Chalmers pushed her chair abruptly from the table. She looked annoyed. Barker shook his head miserably. Neither of them believed him, Theo thought, and the realization rankled. Why didn't they believe him? Did they not think him capable of such a thing? Did he not look like a man who would kill for love, to protect his family? Who cared whether they believed him, Theo thought, glowing with virtue. He had done the right thing. He had saved her.

35

Carla only wanted to hear him deny it.

That Friday night at Theo's house, a couple of days after she'd read Daniel's notebook, she fell asleep early, dead drunk, only to jerk awake a few hours later, her head aching and her mouth dry. The scenes Daniel had drawn ran like a newsreel across the ragged screen of her mind. Beside her, Theo snored softly. She got up. No point just lying there, she wouldn't sleep again – she dressed quietly, picked up her overnight bag and padded down the stairs. She drank a glass of water standing at the sink, and then another. She'd had more than a bottle of wine the night before, more than she'd drunk in a single sitting in years, and the pain behind her eyes was blinding. She found a box of paracetamol in the downstairs loo and took three.

Back in the kitchen, she looked for a pen and paper to leave a note. *Couldn't sleep, gone home*, something like that. He would be hurt, he wouldn't understand, but she didn't have space for his feelings right now, she didn't have space for anything. Only Daniel.

She couldn't find a pen. It didn't matter, she would call him later. She'd call him in a while. They'd have to talk about it sometime, she'd have to come up with some sort of story for why she'd been feeling the way she had, acting the way she had.

'You look shellshocked, Cee,' he'd said to her when she turned up as usual for Friday-night dinner. 'Are you having trouble sleeping?' She'd told him she was and he'd pressed: when did it start, what was the trigger? She hadn't wanted to talk about it. 'After a drink,' she'd said. She drank two gin and tonics before they started on the wine. Didn't eat a thing. No wonder she felt like this.

No wonder.

She could see, looking through the kitchen doors, that there was frost on the lawn. It was going to be cold out. She put on her gloves and grabbed one of Theo's old scarves from the hallway, which she draped around her shoulders. As she walked back through the kitchen, she noticed that the knife Theo had been using to slice the lemons for her gin and tonic was still there. Just lying there on the chopping board.

She only wanted to hear him deny it.

She let herself out of the kitchen doors, drawing the scarf tighter around her neck as she went. She unlocked the back gate and stepped out on to the deserted towpath, then turned left, towards home.

A gentle mist, silver in the moonlight, rose off the water. The lights of the narrowboats were all out: it must have been four thirty – five, perhaps? Still dark. Carla walked slowly, with her hands dug deep into her pockets and her nose tucked into the scarf. She walked a hundred yards, two hundred; she passed the steps she would usually climb to take her home. She kept going.

Her mind seemed to clear in the cold. She could go to him now. She would hear him deny it, hear him say, *This isn't true, it's not real, it's just . . .* Just *what*? What could it possibly be? A fantasy? A nightmare? What did it mean that at some time over the past few years he'd sat down and drawn those pictures – of him-self, of her. Of her boy. What did it mean that he'd drawn them all like that?

All she wanted was an explanation.

As she approached the boat, she was surprised to hear voices, raised and angry. Instead of stopping and knocking on the win-dow as she'd planned, she quickened her pace, kept walking along the path and headed up the steps to the bridge. She stood there, looking down on the boat, her breath, quick and hot, clouding the air in front of her.

After a moment or two, she saw Daniel climbing out on to the back deck of the boat. Dressed in jeans, he pulled a sweat-shirt down over his naked torso as he stepped on to the towpath. He seemed to be saying something, but his words were snatched by the wind and spirited across the water. Carla watched him rolling his head from side to side, pressing his hand to his neck. He took a few steps towards the bridge and then paused to light a cigarette. She held her breath, willing him to look up at her. He took a few drags on the cigarette and then flicked it away, pull-ing the hood of his sweatshirt up over his head as he passed beneath the arch on which she stood.

A few moments later, a girl emerged from the boat. Young – too young, surely, for Daniel – and dishevelled. She stood for a moment, her back to Carla, looking this way and that, as though not sure which way to go. She glanced momentarily up at the bridge and then she spat on the ground and shuffled away in the opposite direction to the one Daniel had taken, laughing as she went.

It was starting to get light. The first, most committed runners of the day had laced up their trainers and made their way to the water; one or two had already passed beneath Carla's bridge, and soon there would be more. It was cold and she had no desire to wait, she wanted to go back, not home, but back to Theo's warm bed, to coffee and comfort. There would be another day for this confrontation.

And as she thought this, as she thought that very thing, she saw Daniel emerge from beneath the arch of the bridge, his head directly beneath her. She watched him stroll back to the boat, cigarette held delicately between third and fourth finger – in movement he was so much like his mother – and climb on to the back deck, and as he did she felt so sure that he would raise his eyes to hers, that he would see her. Instead, he ducked into the cabin and was gone.

Carla could see no one else on the towpath in either direction. She walked quickly back to the steps, took them two at a time, ran to the boat, stepped up on to the deck and ducked down into the cabin – it must have taken her less than half a minute, and now she was alone with him. His back to her, he was in the process of taking off his sweatshirt as she arrived and he turned, alarmed by the noise or the movement of the boat. He dropped the sweatshirt at his feet. For a moment, his expression was blank, and then he smiled.

'Hello,' he said. 'This is a surprise.'

He spread his arms out wide, stepping towards her, reaching for an embrace.

Carla's hand, which at that moment was thrust deep into her bag, closed around the knife handle. With one movement she pulled it out and thrust it towards him, putting all her strength, all her weight, behind it. She watched his smile falter. There was music on the radio, not very loud, but loud enough to cover the sound he made, not a scream or a shout but a muted cry. She withdrew the knife and stabbed him again, and then again, in the neck this time. She drew the blade across his throat to quieten him.

She asked him, over and over, if he knew why she was doing this, but he was not able to answer her. She never got to hear him deny it.

Afterwards, she closed and locked the cabin doors, undressed, showered, washed her hair and changed into the clothes that were in her overnight bag. The bloodied ones she put into a plastic bag she found on the sink. She placed that, and the knife, which she wrapped in Theo's scarf, into her overnight bag, and then she unlocked the doors and left, leaving the cabin door open, walking at a brisk pace back along the towpath towards Theo's house, a middle-aged white woman out for an early morning walk, attracting no attention whatsoever. She let herself in again through the back gate, into Theo's garden, into the kitchen, where she left her overnight bag. She padded softly up the stairs, slipped through the bedroom, where Theo lay sleeping, and into the bathroom. She took off her clean clothes and showered again, standing beneath the hot jet of water for a long time, exhausted, her hands aching, her jaw clenched tight, the muscles in her legs deadened, as though she'd run a marathon.

If she'd only wanted to hear him deny it, why didn't she give him the chance to do so? Why take the knife? Why go back to Theo's, instead of home, if not to give herself at least the chance of an alibi? She could lie to herself all she liked, but when she lay awake, as she did now, night after night, thinking about what she had done, she saw the truth. She'd known from the first moment she saw that drawing, of Daniel on the balcony, smiling down at her child, exactly what she was going to do to him. Everything else, all the rest, was a lie.

36

When the guard told her there was good news, the first thing Laura thought was that her mother had come to visit, and the second was that she wished her mother was not still the first person she thought of. Of course, it wasn't that. Her mother had not come to visit, nor had she requested a visit. Her father had – he was due the next day, and that was nice, but she couldn't help it, she wanted her mum. Somehow, despite everything, in her darkest moments Laura still wanted her mum.

The guard, who was probably about her mum's age and, if she thought about it, actually had a mumsier demeanour than her own mum, smiled kindly and said, 'It's not a visitor, darling. Better than that.'

'What?' Laura asked. 'What is it?'

The guard wasn't at liberty to say, but she led Laura out of her room and down one corridor, through some doors, and then down another and another, and all the time Laura was asking, 'What? What is it? Oh come on, tell me.'

Turned out it was Nervous Guy.

'Him?' Laura couldn't hide her disappointment. '*Him?*'

The guard just laughed. She indicated that Laura should take a seat, and winked at her as she closed the door.

'Fuck's sake,' Laura muttered, sitting down at the table.

Nervous Guy said a chirpy good morning. 'Good news, Laura!' he announced, taking the seat opposite her.

'Yeah, so everyone keeps telling me.'

And then, would you believe it, it turned out that it was.

Dropping the charges! Laura wanted to dance. She wanted to fling her arms around Nervous Guy, she wanted to kiss him on the mouth, she wanted to rip off all her clothes and run screaming around the remand centre. They're dropping the charges! They're dropping the fucking charges!

She managed to control herself, but she did scramble to her feet, yelping like a puppy, 'I can go? I can just go?'

'Yes!' Nervous Guy looked almost as relieved as she was. 'Well, no. I mean, not right away. There are some forms I'll need you to sign, and . . . Is there anyone you'd like me to call? Someone you'd like to come and pick you up?'

Her mother. No, not her mother. Her father. But that would mean a confrontation with Deidre, which would kill her buzz stone dead. It was pathetic, really, when you thought about it. She'd no one, no one at all.

'Could you call my friend Irene?' she heard herself ask.

'Irene?' He readied his pen. 'She's a family member, is she? Or a friend?'

'She's my best mate,' Laura said.

It was like flying.

No, it wasn't like flying at all, actually, it was like her insides had been knotted up for ages and ages, weeks and months and years, and then all of a sudden someone had come along and unpicked the knots, and everything had been able to unravel, and the hardness in her belly was gone, the fire dampened down, the cramp and ache, the tortured, twisted feeling, it was gone, and finally – finally! – she could stand up straight! She could stand up straight, shoulders back, boobs out, and breathe. She could fill her lungs. She could sing, if she wanted to, a song her mother used to sing.

So there was Laura, singing, *'Well I told you I loved you, now what more can I do?'*

The nice guard told her to go to her room and get her things together, then head up to the canteen and have some lunch, because it would probably be a while before they had all the paperwork sorted and she was bound to be starving and she'd have nothing in when she got home, would she? The knots started to re-tie themselves, but Laura pulled herself up straighter still, she stretched her arms right up over her head, she quickened her pace.

'Told you I loved you, you beat my heart black and blue.'

There was Laura, smiling to herself, head buzzing and skin tingling, skipping along, tripping towards her room, when from the opposite direction came a big girl with a nose ring who, three days ago in the canteen, apropos of nothing, had called her a fucking ugly gimp cunt and told her she was going to cut her face next time she saw her.

'Told you I loved you, now what more can I do?'

The big girl hadn't seen Laura yet, she was talking to her friend, smaller but squat, powerful-looking, not one you'd mess with either.

'Do you want me to lay down and die for you?'

There was Laura, singing, but keeping her head down all the while, chin to chest, *Don't look up, don't catch her eye, whatever you do, don't catch her eye.* The big girl was getting closer, she was laughing at something her squat friend was saying, making a noise like a drain, exactly like a drain, and now there was Laura, laughing too, head still down but laughing, unable to stop herself because it was funny, it was just plain funny, undeniably funny, that drain-like sound coming from the girl's wide ugly mouth.

There was Laura, her head wasn't down any more, it was up, she saw the big girl's smile turn into a snarl, heard her friend say 'What the fuck?' and there was Laura, laughing like a loon, like a bell, like a swarm of flies.

There was Laura, her head smacking the linoleum floor. There was Laura, screaming in agony as a boot slammed down on her hand. There was Laura, struggling for breath as the big girl knelt on her chest.

Here I am here I am here I am.

There she was.

37

Three days it had been since Irene last left the house. Three days, or four? She wasn't sure, she only knew that she felt terribly tired. There was nothing in the fridge, but she couldn't face going out, couldn't face the supermarket, the noise, all those people. What she really wanted to do was sleep, but she didn't even have the energy to rouse herself from her chair and take herself upstairs. So she sat in her chair by the window instead, her fingers working constantly around the edge of the blanket placed over her knees.

She was thinking about William. She'd heard his voice not so long ago. She'd been looking for her cardigan, because the weather was still terrible, still very cold, and she'd walked from the living room to the kitchen to see if she'd left it, as she sometimes did, hanging on the back of the chair, and she heard him, clear as day. *Fancy a cuppa, Reenie?*

Irene had left Theo Myerson's terribly shaken. That was days ago now, but she remained shaken. There had been a moment – brief, but nonetheless terrifying – when she'd really thought he was going to hurt her, advancing towards her with his hands outstretched. She had almost felt them around her neck. She had cowered, terrified, and he had seen her terror, she was sure.

He put his arms around her, gentle as a mother, he lifted her and helped her across to the sofa. He was shaking all the time. He did not speak and he did not look at her, he turned away, and she watched as he knelt before the fireplace, as he viciously tore pages from Daniel's notebook and tossed them one by one into the flames.

A while later, she left in the taxi he had called for her, almost overcome with shame at the damage she'd done. If he had hurt her, she thought, she might just have deserved it.

Terrible as the afternoon had been, that wasn't the worst of it. The worst of it came later. A couple of days after the incident with Myerson, Irene had received a phone call from a solicitor saying that Laura Kilbride was due to be released from remand prison, and asking whether Irene might be able to come out to east London that afternoon and pick her up? Irene was elated – she'd been so excited, so *relieved* – only for there to be another call from the same solicitor, just moments after Irene had finished organizing a taxi to take her there, saying that Laura would not be released after all, that she had been attacked and seriously injured, that they were transferring her to hospital right away. Irene was so upset that she'd taken down neither the solicitor's name nor the name of the hospital, and when she phoned the remand centre for more information they were no help at all. They wouldn't tell her how serious the injuries were or how exactly Laura had come by them or where she was now, because Irene wasn't family.

Since then, Irene had not been able to eat a thing, she'd not slept a wink, she was beside herself. Strange expression that, and yet it seemed apt, because she did feel as though she were hovering outside of herself, living through events that barely seemed real, that felt as though she'd read about them, or watched them unfold on a television screen, at once distant and yet oddly heightened. Irene could feel herself on the edge of something: she recognized this sensation, it was the start of a slide into a different state of consciousness, when the world as it really was faded away and she was left somewhere else, somewhere frightening and confusing and dangerous, but where there was the possibility that she might see William again.

Irene's eyelids were growing heavy, her chin just starting to drop towards her chest, when she felt a shadow pass in front of the window and jerked awake. Carla was outside in the lane, rifling through her handbag, looking for something. Leaning forward, Irene tapped on the window. Carla started, she looked up and saw Irene and nodded, didn't bother to smile. Irene motioned for her to wait a moment, but Carla had already turned away, she'd found whatever she was looking for in her handbag – the key to next door, presumably – and disappeared.

Irene sank back into her chair. There was a part of her that wanted desperately to just *leave it*, to forget the whole thing – after all, Laura was no longer under suspicion for Daniel's murder. The damage to the poor girl was already done. The police had a new suspect for their crime now, they had Theo Myerson. It was all over the papers: he hadn't been charged, so the police hadn't named him, but the secret was out: some sharp-eyed photographer had snapped Myerson exiting a police car at the station, and this, added to the news that 'a 52-year-old Islington man was helping police with their enquiries' and that charges against Laura Kilbride had been dropped, left little room for doubt.

Poor Theo. Irene closed her eyes. She saw for a moment his stricken expression when he had seen the drawings in the notebook and felt a sharp pang of guilt. While her eyes were closed, Irene saw herself, too. She imagined looking in on herself from outside this room, from out in the street, the way Carla Myerson had looked in on her a few moments before. What would Carla have seen? She would have seen a little old woman, bewildered and frightened and alone, staring into space, thinking about the past, if she were thinking about anything at all.

There, in her imagination, was everything Irene feared – seeing herself reduced to a cliché of old age, a person without agency, without hope or future or intention, sitting by herself in a comfortable chair with a blanket over her knees, in the waiting room of death.

Well, *bollocks*, as Laura might say, *to that*.

Irene hauled herself out of her chair and tottered into the kitchen, where she forced herself to drink a glass of water, before consuming two and a half rather stale chocolate digestives. Then she made herself a cup of tea, to which she added two heaped teaspoons of sugar, and drank that, too. She waited a few minutes for the rush of sugar and carbohydrate to take effect, then, thus fortified, she picked up her handbag and the keys to number three, opened her front door, walked a few paces round to the left and knocked, as firmly as her small and arthritic hands would allow, on Angela's front door.

As she'd expected, there was no answer, so she slipped the key into the lock and opened the door.

'Carla?' she called out as she stepped into the hall. 'Carla, it's Irene. I need to speak to you—'

'I'm here.' Carla's voice was loud and alarmingly close, it seemed to come out of the air, out of nowhere. Irene started back in fright, almost tripping over the threshold. 'Up here,' Carla said, and Irene inched forward, raising her eyes towards the source of the voice. Carla sat at the top of the stairs like a child escaped from bed, picking fibres from the carpet. 'When you've said whatever it is you want to say, you can just drop that

273

key off in the kitchen,' she said, without looking up at Irene. 'You've no right to let yourself into this house whenever you feel like it.'

Irene cleared her throat. 'No,' she agreed, 'I suppose I don't.' She approached the staircase and, placing one hand on the bannister, bent down to drop the keys on to the third step. 'There you are,' she said.

'Thank you.' Carla stopped plucking at the carpet for a moment and raised her gaze to meet Irene's. She looked awful, *blighted*, her skin grey and her eyes bloodshot. 'There are journalists outside my house,' she said in a small, peevish voice, 'and Theo's place is being ripped apart by the police. That's why I'm here. I don't have anywhere else to go.'

Irene opened her handbag and peered into it, fumbling about with its contents.

'Do you have something else for me, Irene?' Carla asked. She sounded ragged, raw-throated. 'Because if you don't, I'd really rather—'

Irene pulled from her bag the two little jewellery boxes, the one containing the St Christopher's medal and the one with the ring. 'I thought you'd want these back,' she said quietly, placing them on the third stair next to the key.

'Oh!' Carla's mouth fell open. 'His St Christopher!' She scrambled to her feet, almost tumbling down the stairs to fall upon the little box, picking it up and clutching it to her. 'You found it,' she said, smiling at Irene through tears. 'I can't believe you found it.' She reached for Irene's hand, but Irene stepped smartly away.

'I didn't *find* it,' Irene said in a measured tone. 'It was given to me. By Laura. Laura Kilbride. Does that name mean anything to you?'

But Carla was barely listening, she was sitting again, on the

274

third step now, with the jewellery box open on her lap. She took the little gold token, turned it over in her fingers and pressed it to her lips. Irene watched her, grimly fascinated by the peculiar pantomime of devotion. She wondered if Carla had lost her mind.

'Laura,' Irene said again. 'The girl who was arrested? The medal and the ring, they were in the bag that Laura stole from you. *Carla*? Does any of this mean anything to you?' Still, nothing. 'You left the bag here, right here, in this hallway. The door was open. Laura saw it and she snatched the bag. She felt bad about it, so she returned the things to me, only . . . Oh, for God's sake. Carla!' she snapped, and Carla looked up at her, surprised.

'What?'

'Are you really going to do this? Are you going to sit here and feign oblivion? Are you really going to let him take the blame?'

Carla shook her head, her eyes returning to the gold medal. 'I don't know what you mean,' she said.

'Theo didn't kill that boy,' Irene said. 'You did. You killed Daniel.'

Carla blinked slowly. When she looked back up at Irene, her eyes were glassy and still, her face impassive.

'You killed Daniel, and you were going to let Laura take the fall, weren't you? You were going to let an innocent girl pay for what you did. Did you know,' Irene's voice rose, it trembled, 'did you know that she was hurt while she was on remand? Did you know that she's been so badly injured they had to take her to hospital?'

Carla's chin dropped to her chest. 'That has nothing to do with me,' she said.

'It has *everything* to do with you,' Irene cried, her voice echoing through the empty house. 'You saw what he'd drawn in his notebook. You can deny it, it makes no difference. I saw the pictures. I saw what he drew . . . what he imagined.'

'*Imagined?*' Carla hissed, her eyes narrowing, her face suddenly vicious.

Irene took a step back, away from the stairs and closer to the front door. There, in the middle of the empty hallway, she felt unmoored; she wanted desperately to sit, to rest, to have something to hold on to. Steeling herself, biting her lip and holding her handbag in front of her like a shield, she inched closer to Carla once more. 'I saw what he drew,' she said. 'You saw it, too. So did your husband, before he threw the pages into the fire.'

Carla flinched at this, narrowing her eyes at Irene.

'*Theo* saw?' she said, her brow knitted. 'But the book is here, it's . . . Oh.' She sighed, huffed a sad little laugh as her head dropped to her chest. 'It's not here, is it? You gave it to him. You showed it to him. Why?' she asked. 'Why in God's name would you do that? What a strange, interfering woman you are, what an *utter* pain in the arse. Do you realize what you've done?'

'What have I done?' Irene demanded. 'Come on, Carla, tell me!'

Carla closed her eyes and shook her head like a truculent child.

'*No?* Well, in that case why don't I tell you what *you* have done? You saw those pictures that Daniel had drawn and you decided that he was guilty of killing your child, and so you took his life. The knife you used was in the bag that Laura stole, which is how it ended up in her flat. And then your husband – your ex-husband, who loves you more than life itself, for some reason I haven't yet worked out – he stepped in and he took everything upon himself. And you! You just sit there and say it has nothing to do with you. Do you not feel anything? Are you not ashamed?'

Carla, hunched over her medal, her shoulders bowed,

muttered, 'Do I not *feel* anything? For God's sake, Irene. Do you not think I've suffered enough?'

And there, Irene thought, was the crux of it. After what Carla had endured, how could anything else matter? 'I know that you've suffered terribly,' she said, but Carla wouldn't have it.

'You know nothing,' she hissed. 'You couldn't possibly conceive—'

'Of your pain? Perhaps I can't, Carla, but do you honestly think that because you lost your son in that terrible, tragic way, that gives you the right?' Before her, Carla crouched as though ready to spring at her, trembling now with grief or fury. But Irene would not be cowed, she went on. 'Because you suffered that terrible loss, do you think that gives you the right to lay waste to everything, to do as you please?'

'As I *please*?' With one hand on the bannister, Carla pulled herself to her feet; standing on the third stair, she towered over Irene. 'My child is dead,' she spat. 'My sister, too, and she died unforgiven. The man I love is going to prison. You think there is some pleasure for me in all of this?'

Irene took a small step backwards. 'Theo doesn't have to go to prison,' she said. 'You could change that.'

'What good would it do?' Carla asked. 'What . . . Oh.' She turned her face away in disgust. 'There's no point trying to explain to you. How on earth could you possibly understand what it is to love a child?'

That again. What it always came down to. You couldn't understand, you're not a mother. You've never experienced love, not really. You don't have it inside you, whatever it is, the capacity for limitless, unconditional love. The capacity for unbounded hatred, neither.

Irene clenched and unclenched her hands at her side. 'Perhaps I don't understand love like that,' she said. 'Perhaps you're right. But sending Theo to prison? Where does love come into that?'

Carla pursed her lips. 'He understands,' she said, chastened. 'If Theo did see Daniel's notebook, like you said he did, then of course he would understand why I had to do what I did. And you, standing there, outraged, consumed with self-righteousness, you should understand, too, because I didn't just do this for Ben, I did it for Angela.'

Irene shook her head in disbelief. 'For Angela? You're really going to stand there and say that you killed Daniel for *Angela*?'

Carla reached out and, surprisingly gently, placed her hand on Irene's wrist. She closed her fingers around it, drawing Irene closer to her. 'When was it,' she whispered, her expression suddenly earnest, almost hopeful, 'when was it, do you think, that she knew?'

'Knew?'

'About *him*. What he'd done. What he *was*.'

Irene pulled her hand away, shaking her head as she did. No, Angela could not have known. It was too horrible to contemplate, the idea that she'd lived with that. No. In any case, there was nothing to know, was there? 'It was a story,' she said. 'He wrote a story, perhaps to try to process something he lived through when he was a little boy, and for some reason, he cast himself as the villain. Perhaps he felt guilty, perhaps he felt he should have been watching Ben, or perhaps it was an accident . . . it might have been a mistake.' She was aware that in part she was trying to convince herself. 'It might have been a childish mistake. He was so little, he couldn't possibly have understood the consequences.'

Carla nodded her head, listening to her. 'I considered that. I considered all those things, Irene. I did. But think about this: he was a child – yes, *then*, he was a child. But what about later? Say you are right, say it was a childish mistake, or an accident, that doesn't explain how he behaved later on. He knew that I blamed Angela for what happened, and he let me blame her. He allowed me to punish her, he allowed Theo to reject her, he watched her slowly become crushed by the weight of her guilt, and he did nothing. In fact,' Carla gave a quick shake of the head, 'that's not true. He didn't do nothing. He did something – he made things worse. He told his psychologist that Ben's death was Angela's fault, he allowed me to believe that Angela was mistreating him. All of it, it was all . . . God, I don't even know what it was. A game, perhaps? He was playing a game with us, with all of us, manipulating us, for his enjoyment, I suppose. To give himself a sense of power . . .'

It was monstrous, unthinkable. What impossibly twisted sort of mind could think that way? Irene caught herself suspecting that perhaps it was *Carla's* mind that was monstrously twisted; wasn't her interpretation of events every bit as disturbing as the images in Daniel's notebook? And yet, when she thought back to Angela, railing against her son, wishing him out of existence, Carla's version of events rang horribly true. Irene remembered the missed Christmas dinner, when Angela spoke of envying Irene her childlessness, she thought of her apology the next day. *You'd see the world burn*, she'd said, *to see them happy.*

Carla had turned away from Irene, and now she walked slowly up the stairs, swivelling to face her once she reached the top step. 'So, you see, *it was* in part for her. It sounds so awful, doesn't it, when you say it out loud? I killed her son for her. But it's true, in a way. I did it for me, for my son, for Theo, but I did it for her, too. For the ruin he made of Angela's life.'

As Irene let herself back into her own home next door, she reflected on how, while it could be trying at times, it was sometimes fortunate that people like Carla looked at little old ladies like her and dismissed them as dim, distracted, forgetful and foolish. It was, today at least, lucky that Carla saw her as waiting for death, not quite of this world, not up to speed with all its complicated ways, its technological developments, its gadgets, its smart phones, its voice-recording apps.

38

The weather had turned again, the freezing air of the past week suddenly banished by a blessed breath of warmth blowing up from the Mediterranean. Two days ago, Miriam had been huddling in front of her log burner with a coat and scarf on; now it was warm enough for her to sit out on her back deck, drinking her morning coffee and reading the newspaper.

What was in the newspaper might well have been the stuff of fiction: Theo Myerson had been released from police custody, although he still faced charges for wasting police time and for perverting the course of justice, while his wife was the one now facing murder charges after the police had been furnished (by an unnamed source) with a dramatic recorded confession.

So, after all that, it turned out that the person Miriam had been trying to frame for the murder of Daniel Sutherland actually was the person who had murdered Daniel Sutherland. How about that? Didn't say much for Miriam's framing skills.

The stuff of fiction! Miriam couldn't help but laugh. Would Myerson try to wrangle a novel out of this mess? Perhaps *she* should try to wrangle a novel out of it. How would that be for a worm turning? For Miriam to take *his* life story and use it as material, to twist it any way she liked, to rob him of his agency, his words, his power.

Then again, there was perhaps an easier – and almost certainly more lucrative – way forward: what about a quick phone call to the *Daily Mail*? How much would they pay for the inside scoop on Theo Myerson? Quite a bit, she imagined, Myerson being precisely the sort of person – rich, clever, sophisticated, leftish, metropolitan-elite-made-decadent-flesh – that the *Daily Mail* loathed.

She finished her coffee and pottered down to her kitchen table, where she opened her laptop and had just begun to type 'how to sell a story to the newspapers' into Google when there came a knock at the window. She looked up and very nearly fell off her stool. Myerson! Bent over on the towpath, peering through her cabin porthole.

Warily, she made her way out on to the back deck. Theo stood a few yards away, hands thrust into his pockets, expression glum. He'd aged since last she saw him, being led away by the police. Then he was still his portly, red-faced self; now he looked thinner, wrung out, hangdog. Miserable. Her heart twitched in her chest. She ought to be jumping for joy – wasn't this what she wanted? To see him brought low, to see him suffering. Why on earth did she find herself feeling sorry for him?

'Look,' he said. 'Enough's enough. All right? I just . . . I'm sure you realize that I'm going through something . . .' He shrugged. 'I can't even put into words what I'm going through. Yes, I see the irony. In any case, the point is, I don't want to get the police involved. I've had quite enough of them over the past month. Enough to last me a lifetime. However, if you continue to harass me, you really will leave me no choice.'

'I beg your pardon? *Harass* you? I haven't come anywhere near you.'

Theo sighed, an exhausted sound. He pulled from his inside jacket pocket a piece of paper, which, slowly and with great deliberation, he unfolded. He began to read from it in a flat voice, devoid of intonation. ' "*The problem with people like you is they think they're above everyone. That story wasn't yours to tell, it was mine. You had no right to use it in the way you did. You should have to pay people for using their stories. You should have to ask permission. Who do you think you are to use my story . . .*" Et cetera, et cetera. There are half a dozen of them like that. Well, not quite like that, they started off as polite expressions of interest in my work, clearly designed to bait me into saying something about my inspiration for the story, but they quickly deteriorated. You get the gist. You know the gist. You *wrote* the gist. They're postmarked Islington, Miriam, for God's sake. I can see that you've tried to disguise who you are, but—'

Miriam gawped at him, mystified. 'That is *not* from me. Perhaps you stole someone else's story? Perhaps you do it all the time.'

'Oh, for God's sake!'

'It's not from me!'

Theo took a step back, exhaling in one long, shuddering breath. 'Is it money you want?' he asked her. 'I mean, you say here, "*You should have to pay people*", so is that it? How much would it take? How much would it take for you to just leave me . . .' – his voice cracked and Miriam was horrified to feel tears spring to her eyes – 'to just leave me alone?'

Miriam quickly wiped her face with her sleeve and climbed down off the boat. She held out her hand. 'Could I see those, please?' she asked. Theo handed the pages over without question.

The paper was thin, of poor quality, the handwriting careful but childlike.

Myerson,

Why won't you answer my letters? The problem with people like you is they think their above everyone. That story wasn't yours to tell, it was mine. You had no right to use it in the way you did!!! You should have to pay people for using their stories. You should have to ask permission. Who do you think you are to use my story without asking. You didn't even do a good job. The killer in the story is weak. How would a weak man do what he did? What would you know about it anyway. You didn't show respect.

She was shaking her head. 'This isn't from me,' she said, turning the page over in her hand. 'You can't possibly think this is from me – this person is barely literate.'

She started on the next one.

The police took you away so maybe your not so much better than everyone else after all? Maybe I should talk to the police about you taking my story. There should be a fee at least but the thing that's really bugging me is how you knew about Black River.

Miriam's breath caught in her chest.

I will leave you alone and wont' write anymore if you tell me how you knew about Black River.

Beneath her feet, the earth shifted.

She read the line out loud. ' "*Tell me how you knew about Black River.*" '

'It's a song,' Theo said. 'It's not a reference to the place, it's—'

'I know what it is,' Miriam said. The world was turning black, the darkness closing in too fast for her to push it back. She opened her mouth, but she could draw no air into her lungs; her muscles weren't working, not her diaphragm nor the muscles in her legs or her arms, she was trembling violently, her vision gone almost altogether. The last thing she saw before she collapsed was Theo Myerson's startled face.

'It was on in the car, on the radio. The song. I remember him fiddling with the tuner, he was trying to change the station, but Lorraine asked him not to. She was singing. She was singing, and she said, "Don't you like this one? 'Black River'."'

Myerson set a glass of water down on her bedside table and then stood, awkwardly, looking down at her. It should have been embarrassing: Theo Myerson helping her up from where she'd collapsed – *swooned*, like a ridiculous Victorian damsel on a warm day – on the towpath, the two of them shuffling like an old couple back to the boat, where he put her to bed, like a child. Like an invalid. Miriam would have been mortified if she'd been capable of feeling mortification, if she'd been capable of feeling anything other than a sort of bewildered terror. She lay on her back, her eyes trained on the wooden slats of the ceiling, trying to concentrate on her breathing, in and out, trying to concentrate on the here, on the now. But she couldn't, not with him there.

'Who else did you show it to?' he asked. 'Your . . . uh, your *manuscript*. Who else read it?'

'I never showed it to anyone else,' Miriam said. 'Except for Laura Kilbride, but that was only very recently, and according to the newspapers she's not in a fit state to write anyone any letters. I never showed it to anyone else.'

'That can't be true. You showed it to a lawyer, didn't you?' Theo said, towering over her, rubbing his big balding head. 'You must have done! You showed it to *my* lawyer, certainly, when you made your, uh, your complaint.' He shifted from one foot to another. 'Your claim.'

Miriam closed her eyes. 'I didn't send anyone the whole manuscript. I selected a number of pages, I pointed to various similarities. I never mentioned the singing, even though it was . . . even though it was perhaps the clearest evidence of your *theft*.' Theo grimaced. He looked as though he wanted to say something, but thought better of it. 'I didn't want to mention her singing, I didn't even want to think about it, about the last time I heard her voice like that, the last time I heard her happy, carefree. The last time I heard her unafraid.'

'Jesus.' Theo exhaled slowly. 'Do you mind?' He indicated the bed, and for a startling moment Miriam wasn't sure what he was asking. He sat, perching his large bottom on the corner of the bunk, an inch or two from Miriam's feet. 'It can't be, Miriam. He's dead. Jeremy is dead. You said so, the police said so . . .'

'I wished him so, and the police made an assumption. People said they saw him, in all sorts of places – Essex, Scotland, Morocco. The police followed it up, or at least they said they did, I don't know how seriously they took any of it . . . But you know all this, don't you? It was in the book.'

Theo winced. 'There was something about a foot?' he ventured, his face flushing.

Miriam nodded. 'Some kids playing on a beach near Hastings found a human foot a few weeks after Jeremy went missing. It was the right size and the right colour, it had the right blood type. This was all pre-DNA, so there was no way of checking for sure, but it was assumed that it was him. They thought maybe he'd been dashed against the rocks somewhere, or caught up in a boat propeller. That was the end of it, in any case. They stopped looking.'

'But . . .' Theo was shaking his head. 'Think about it. If some-how he'd got away, faked his own death, changed his identity, there would have been others, wouldn't there? Other girls, I mean, other women. A man like that, a man capable of doing what he did to you, to your friend, he doesn't just do it once and then stop, does he?'

'Maybe he does,' Miriam said. 'Where is it written that they *all* get a taste for it? Maybe he tried it and he didn't really like it. Maybe it frightened him. Maybe it didn't satisfy him in the way he thought it would. Or maybe' – the boat rocked in some other vehicle's wake, and Miriam opened her eyes to focus on the ceil-ing once more – 'maybe he *didn't* do it just once. Maybe he did it again and again, and people just didn't make the connections. It was easier back then, wasn't it, for men like him to just keep going, to move around, to exist on the margins, to drift, to carry on for years? He could have gone abroad, he could have changed his name, he could be . . .' her voice faltered, '*anywhere.*'

Myerson shuffled along the bed so that he was no longer sit-ting next to her feet but at her side. He reached over and – she could scarcely believe this – took her hand. 'I have his email address,' he said. 'The police will be able to trace him using that. I can give them the letters, I can explain . . . *we* can explain – we can explain everything.' His eyes met hers. 'Everything.'

Miriam withdrew her hand. *Everything?* Myerson was offer-ing, she understood, an apology. An acknowledgement. If they went to the police with these letters, they would have to explain how it was that Theo came to be their recipient, how it was that the two of them had deduced that only one man on earth could know about that song, about its significance. And in doing so, Theo would have to unmask himself, he would have to acknow-ledge Miriam as the inspiration for his story. She would get everything she wanted.

She blinked slowly, shaking her head. 'No,' she said. 'No, that won't do.' She wiped her face with the back of her hand and propped herself up on her elbows. 'You won't contact the police, you'll contact him. Respond to his questions. Some of his questions, in any case.' She paused for a moment to think things through. 'Yes, you will get in touch with him, apologize to him for neglecting his letters. Arrange a meeting.'

Theo nodded, his lips pursed, rubbing his head. 'I could do that. I could ask him to meet me to talk about his questions. And when he comes, the police will be there, they'll be waiting.'

'No,' Miriam said firmly. 'No, the police won't be waiting.'

For a long moment, Theo held her gaze. Then he turned away. 'All right,' he said.

39

There she was, in the back bedroom of Irene's house, looking at the neatly made single bed, a bright yellow towel folded at its foot. There was a wardrobe and a bookcase and a bedside table, on which Laura had placed the defaced photograph of herself with her parents. She looked at it a moment before turning their faces to the wall.

From downstairs, she could hear Irene's surprisingly girlish laughter. She was listening to something on the radio, a programme where people had to talk for as long as they could without repeating themselves or hesitating. Laura found it mystifying but it cracked Irene up, which was in itself hilarious.

Once Laura had finally finished unpacking her things – she didn't own much, but she was doing everything one-handed – she sat down on the bed, propping herself up against the wall. Picking idly at the cast around her wrist, the edge of which was starting to fray, she listened to people moving about on the other side of the wall, their voices a low murmur. The house – Angela's house – was up for sale, and there was a constant stream of viewers, none of whom had yet made an offer. Or so the agent had told her. 'Rubberneckers,' he'd complained when she'd met him outside in the lane, smoking furiously, 'collecting material for their poxy true-crime podcasts.'

A few of them had knocked on Irene's door, but Laura had seen them off. They'd had real reporters coming, too, but Irene wasn't talking to anyone. She'd done her talking, to the police. She'd done the listening, too, and the recording – Laura was insanely, stupidly proud of her, she felt prouder of her than she'd ever have felt of a member of her own family. Laura had started calling her Miss Marple, although Irene had put a quick and surprisingly irritable stop to that.

Now, in between listening to things on the radio and reading her books and helping Laura deal with all the legal stuff she had to do, her personal injury compensation claim and her forthcoming court appearance and all that, she talked about the two of them taking a trip. She'd always wanted to go to a place called Positano, apparently, which is where they set that film about Hannibal Lecter. Or something like that.

Laura said she couldn't afford to go on holiday, or not until she got her compensation money anyway, but Irene said it wasn't a problem. 'We had savings, William and I,' she said, and when Laura said they couldn't spend that, Irene just tutted.

'Why ever not? You can't take it with you.'

Laura had felt quite light-headed. Low blood sugar, maybe, or perhaps it was the dizzying effect of watching her horizons, narrowed for so long, expanding once again.

They weren't going anywhere just yet. Laura was still recovering from concussion and a cracked rib and a seriously mashed-up left hand. That girl, the big one with the nose ring, she'd stuck her great big size eight foot on it and stamped hard. 'There are twenty-seven bones in the hand,' her doctor had told her, pointing to the image on the screen to show her the extent of the damage, 'and you've broken fifteen. You're very lucky—'

'I certainly feel lucky,' Laura said.

The doctor smiled at her indulgently. 'You're lucky that the breaks were clean. With the right physical therapy, you should get back your full range of motion.'

Back in physical therapy. Just like old times.

'It feels like we've come full circle,' Laura's mother said. She'd been weeping histrionically at Laura's bedside for what was probably just a few minutes but felt like days. 'I can't believe we're back here again – you gravely hurt, in hospital . . .'

'Still, at least this time it's not because your bit on the side ran me over with his car and drove off, is it?'

Her mother didn't stay long. Her father didn't either, because Deidre was in the car outside, parked on a double red line. 'With any luck, they'll tow her away!' he said with a nervous laugh, glancing over his shoulder as though worried she might over-hear. He squeezed Laura's good hand and kissed her on the forehead, promising to visit again soon.

'Perhaps, when you're better,' he said as he paused in the doorway on his way out, 'we could spend a bit more time together. We might even get a place together, what about that, chicken?'

Laura shook her head. 'Dad, I can't, we tried that. Me and Deidre, it's never going to work . . .'

'Oh, I know,' he said, nodding vigorously. 'I know that. I know you couldn't live with her again. I was thinking a bit fur-ther down the road, you know. After I've left her.'

Laura smiled at him reassuringly. She wasn't going to hold her breath.

*

Egg had come to see her, too. Detective Barker, his name was, she'd finally got it into her head, though in her heart he would always be Egg. He came to say how sorry he was that she'd been hurt, and also to say that Miriam from the canal had withdrawn her complaint about Laura. 'She admitted having your key,' he told her. 'We've had to talk to her about a number of statements she made during the investigation which turned out to be not quite accurate.'

'I'm shocked,' Laura said, smiling at him. 'Truly shocked.'

He raised an eyebrow. 'She had quite the story. She claimed to be trying to help you, whom she believed to be guilty, while also trying to incriminate Carla Myerson, whom she believed to be innocent but who was, in fact, guilty.'

'You really couldn't make this shit up,' Laura said.

He smiled at her then. 'You'll be hearing from us, Laura,' he said on his way out. 'There's still the matter of this stolen bag, with the knife and the jewellery.'

'Don't forget the thing with the fork,' Laura reminded him.

'Yes, of course. The fork.'

At night, lying in her single bed, threadbare sheets tucked tight around her body, Laura lay with her good palm pressed against the wall, on the other side of which was Daniel's room. There was something uncannily circular about all this, how it started out with her in Daniel's bed and finished with her separated from his bedroom by just a few inches of Victorian brick.

She returned often, in her mind, to the night on his boat, to the morning dawning – and the strange thing was that what tormented her was not him, not the sudden change in his behaviour, the flick of a switch from charm to cruelty; it wasn't the look on his face when she lunged at him, teeth bared.

No, the thing that she could not get out of her head was the moment she left the boat, the moment she stepped from the back deck to dry land and glanced up to her right. The moment she saw, in that grey dawn half-light, a woman up on the bridge, looking down at her. The thing that tormented her now was that she could not if her life depended on it conjure up that woman's expression. She could not say whether she looked sad or angry, broken or resolute.

Epilogue

A man has been found dead on a houseboat on the canal. *Stop me if you think you've heard this one before.*

Carla heard the rumours, the silly jokes from the other women, at lunchtime. *He another one of yours, Cazza? Been a busy girl, incha?* She went to the library that afternoon; she wasn't permitted to read news stories about crimes on the internet, but she persuaded one of the guards (a 'Myerson mega-fan!') to print the story off for her at home and bring it in.

SUSPECTED KILLER FOUND MURDERED

The badly decomposed body of 58-year-old Jeremy O'Brien, who was also known as Henry Carter and James Henry Bryant, has been found on a partially submerged boat on the Regent's Canal. O'Brien, who was wanted in connection with the 1983 murder of teenager Lorraine Reid, had previously been assumed to have taken his own life after he disappeared within days of the Reid killing.

Police say it appears that O'Brien had been living with his stepbrother in Spain since the 1980s, where he went by the name James Henry Bryant. He was badly injured in a car accident in 1988 where he suffered spinal damage; he used a wheelchair. Police say they believe he returned to England last year after the death of his stepbrother and has been living in sheltered accommodation in north London under the name Henry Carter.

Despite some similarities between the O'Brien murder and that of Daniel Sutherland, 23, six months ago – both bodies were discovered in boats on the canal and both died as a result of stab wounds to the chest and neck – police say they are not connecting the killings, pointing out that the woman convicted of murdering Daniel Sutherland – Carla Myerson, who has been imprisoned at HMP Bronzefield since July – pleaded guilty to the crime and made a full confession.

Carla stopped reading. She folded up the piece of paper and handed it back to the guard. 'Thank you,' she said. 'Theo's said he'll put a signed copy of his latest book in the post.'

A few days later, Carla received a letter from a criminologist, asking if she might visit her to talk about her case. Carla had no particular desire to talk to anyone about her case, but she did crave conversation with someone educated. She said yes.

The criminologist, a bright-eyed, freshly scrubbed, impossibly young woman, turned out to be a student with hopes of getting a first (and possibly even a book deal!) on the back of her thesis, of which she was hoping to make Carla the focus. There had already been one false confession in this case, was it possible that there had been two? Could Carla be a (self-harming) victim of a miscarriage of justice? Was there a serial killer targeting men living on or near the Regent's Canal? Was there a serial killer targeting other killers?

The poor thing was so painfully earnest, Carla felt quite bad about bursting her speculative bubble. There was no miscarriage of justice, she told the young woman calmly, there is no serial killer operating on the canal. The one case has nothing to do with the other.

'But your husband, he thought—'

'Oh.' Carla smiled at her apologetically. 'You've been talking to Theo. You need to take him with more than a pinch of salt, I'm afraid. He's a dreamer, he lives in his own world.'

'So it was definitely . . . you definitely did it?' the young woman prompted, disappointment written all over her pretty face.

Carla nodded. 'I did, yes.'

'Well . . . *why*? Could we talk about why?'

Carla shook her head. 'I did say in my email that I wasn't prepared to talk about the background in detail. I'm sorry.'

'Oh, really? But you're so *atypical* – you're middle class, you're educated, you're unmarried . . .'

'What does that have to do with anything?' Carla asked. 'My marital status, I mean.'

'Oh, well, female killers tend to conform to traditional gender roles – they're usually married with kids, that sort of thing. You don't really fit the mould.'

'I was married with a child once,' Carla said sadly.

'Yes, but . . . OK.' She was stumped. She looked unhappily but hopefully about the room, like someone stuck with a bore at a party casting about for someone more interesting to speak to. 'Well,' she said at last, 'could you at least tell me this: do you regret it?'

When Carla had made her confession to Irene – not the one she made to the police, which wasn't anywhere near full, it was barely a half-confession; they got the bare bones, she refused to elaborate on the meat – she had dismissed the idea that what

Daniel had done had been a childish mistake. She'd talked of torture and manipulation, and she had meant it.

Now, though, when she allowed her mind to wander – and it had little else to do – it went to places she'd really rather it wouldn't.

It wondered whether perhaps what she had read, in that first flush of fury, as manipulation might in fact have been something else. What if Daniel's flirtatiousness wasn't calculated, what if that was just the way he loved? What if he didn't know any better? Maybe the story she'd told herself was no truer than the myth Daniel had made for himself.

It was a dark road to start down, and became darker still as she realized that it was a one-way route: once started along, there was no exit, and no way back.

These days, when Carla thought about what she'd done, she saw her actions in a different light. No longer anaesthetized by fear, by exhilaration (and yes, it had been exhilarating, in the feverish moment), now she saw what she'd done. Blood, so much of it! The noise he made, the sickening gurgle in his throat, the wild whiteness of his eyes, the smell of iron, the smell of urine, the scent of his agony, his terror.

She must have been mad. Could she tell herself that story? Could she convince herself that she'd been delirious with pain, with grief, that she'd acted unthinkingly?

Sitting in the visitors' room of the largest women's prison in Europe, sharing space with the bewildered, the sad and the deprived, as well, of course, as the very worst that British womanhood had to offer, she asked herself: did she belong?

What, after all, might she have done differently, had she not been mad? Had she been sane, could she have let it be? Could she have chosen to go on living her life, have taken the knowledge of what Daniel had done and chosen to lock it away somewhere? Only, how could she possibly have *sanely* chosen that? How could she have chosen to live in a world in which Daniel was still alive, in which she might see him, breathe the same air that he breathed? A world in which there existed the possibility that she might still feel something for him – some tenderness, something like love.

That possibility she had to kill.

'Mrs Myerson? Do you regret it?'

Author's Note

The locations for this book are inspired by the streets and houses on and near the section of Regent's Canal that cuts through Islington and Clerkenwell in London. Neither the houses nor the streets are entirely faithfully depicted throughout; I have taken artistic licence where I saw fit.

Acknowledgements

Thank you to Sarah Adams and Sarah McGrath for their incisive edits and apparently limitless patience.

Thanks to Lizzy Kremer and Simon Lipskar, the best agents on both sides of the Atlantic, for their brilliant advice and unfailing support.

Thank you to Caroline MacFarlane, winner of the CLIC Sargent charity auction, for the use of her name.

Thanks to early readers Petina Gappah, Frankie Gray and Alison Fairbrother.

And thank you to Simon Davis, because God knows the past three years can't have been easy.

Credits

PAULA HAWKINS worked as a journalist for fifteen years before turning her hand to fiction. Born and brought up in Zimbabwe, Paula moved to London in 1989 and has lived there ever since. Her first thriller, *The Girl on the Train*, has been a global phenom-enon, selling 23 million copies worldwide. Published in over forty languages, it has been a No.1 bestseller around the world and was a No.1 box office hit film starring Emily Blunt.

Into the Water, her second stand-alone thriller, has also been a global No.1 bestseller, spending twenty weeks in the *Sunday Times* hardback fiction Top 10 bestseller list, and six weeks at No.1.